£6-50

The son of a prosperous Dublin solicitor, J... was educated at Rugby School and Ballio... theological college, he became a writer. Hi... George Bernard Shaw – was published to wic... success, he spent the pre-war years living in ...hanged in 1940 when he became a farm labourer wor... ...he land in Dorset and Sussex. These experiences were published as the classic *The Worm Forgives the Plough*.

In 1947, Collis' talents were officially recognised when he won the Heinemann Foundation Award for Literature.

He wrote biographies of Christopher Columbus, Havelock Ellis and Leo Tolstoy and is also celebrated for his works on natural phenomena in which he took a scientific subject and described it from the layperson's point of view. Full of curiosity for the things most of us take for granted, these are the works of which Collis was most proud.

Bound Upon a Course

An Autobiography

JOHN STEWART COLLIS

HOUSE OF
STRATUS

This edition published in 2001 by House of Stratus, an imprint of Stratus Holdings plc, 24c Old Burlington Street, London, W1X 1RL, UK. Also at: Suite 210, 1270 Avenue of the Americas, New York, NY 10020, USA.

www.houseofstratus.com

Typeset, printed and bound by House of Stratus.

A catalogue record for this book is available from the British Library and The Library of Congress.

ISBN 1-84232-634-1

CONTENTS

FIRST MOVEMENT…

... ARRIVING

To be born. Nothing very original about that, it is often done. Yet, to make an appearance without having previously existed is astonishing enough. When a mother shows me her baby and I gaze upon it with wonder as I always do with absolute sincerity, she displays no surprise at my interest before the phenomenon. Millions and millions of years passed before this bit of consciousness came into the world to keep watch for a brief period and then go, launched upon a course as surely as any ship, bound for tempest, and certain of sinking in the end. It is not surprising that everyone is an important person at least twice, commanding as much attention as any celebrity – on first appearance and final departure. To arrive from nowhere is a strictly unthinkable event, but it does happen, and it happened to me. If I had not existed it would have been unnecessary to invent me, but I have been invented, and I want to unravel some of the main threads and the chief quest of my life.

I was born in Ireland in 1900 of Irish parents at Killiney which is where County Dublin borders upon County Wicklow. It has no lakes like Killarney, but it has the Irish Sea, and travellers are fond of comparing the beauty of Killiney Bay with the Bay of Naples; certainly if it had a Mediterranean climate it would be as famous. From Killiney Hill you get a view of sea and mountains good enough to satisfy anyone. When Bernard Shaw was asked whether he had ever known real happiness he replied, 'Yes, when my mother told me that we were going to live at Torca Cottage at Dalkey' – which commands one of the best views of the bay and the Wicklow Mountains. A special feature of the locality is the railway tunnel from Dalkey to Killiney. The journey from Dun Laoghaire to Dalkey is very dull and enclosed. Then comes the tunnel, and you emerge from it into a new world with the sea directly below and the Wicklow Mountains in the distance. The delight of this experience never fails throughout the years. In the days before air travel when we always returned to Ireland from Euston via Holyhead this emergence from the tunnel into the New world always came as a fresh revelation, never ordinary; it would never pall if one did it a thousand times. The reverse journey – that is, *from* Killiney *to* England – was less happy. In fact it was a somewhat traumatic experience entering the tunnel then: the sun shone upon the glittering bay, the waves beat upon the rocks, the Wicklow Mountains, the Big Sugar Loaf and the Little Sugar Loaf and Bray Head, such old friends, so firmly there – all suddenly withdrawn, a total blackout of the scene, and now visions of the climax of one's journey – the Euston Station taxi driver.

Our house, Kilmore, was on a hill which sloped directly down to the Station Road which ran beside the beach. The area round about was then chiefly occupied by large houses with large gardens. A long high wall separated us from a big garden and house owned by a retired Judge called Bramley. Two fields below was Court-na-Farraga where the Smythe family lived, the grandfather a retired Captain from the Indian Army. The beauty of the grandmother, the mother, and the two daughters, Bay and Erica, was outstanding: even as a child I realized the soft beauty of the grandmother. As for the youngest, Erica, I still think she was the prettiest girl I have ever known, her voice, eye, and grace of movement an enchantment. I would run down and look for her on the beach: if she were not in sight, what a desolation the place was! If I saw her there, all Shakespeare could not outline the thrill. I tried to keep myself from falling asleep at night to hold the luxury of thinking of her.

The house directly above us changed hands from time to time, eventually being taken by Mrs O'Sullivan, the mother of the film star Maureen O'Sullivan and grandmother of Mia Farrow. It is a strange thought, to me, that Mia Farrow, during the time when she gave him the best year of her life, may have mentioned Killiney to Frank Sinatra, for the idea of that curious gentleman having anything to do with Ireland, let alone Killiney, is strange indeed.

A little further off was a house inhabited by the Starkie family, distinguished since in literature and scholarship. There may have been the conditions here for a cheerful community of happy families. But this was not noticeable. There was no particular unity, nor any degree of cosiness, nor a sweet-stay-at-home atmosphere. Killiney may be snug or smug now, but then there seemed to be a pressure driving people outwards, my brother Maurice to Burma, Maureen O'Sullivan to Hollywood, Enid Starkie to Oxford, Walter Starkie to Spain, myself to London, Erica Smythe to India, and my brother Dr Robert Collis to many places during his great career which reached a climax in Nigeria.

Kilmore is quite a large house (not passing from our hands till 1946) with great bay windows and balconies facing east and south. Along the avenue on one side there was a row of an unusually high growth of rhododendron trees (not bushes) which had deep red flowers in great abundance – which became famous. The vegetable garden which lay below the fruit garden and the greenhouses led to a white garden gate which I mention because it always squeaked when swung open, and acted as a kind of bell from afar off. It was never oiled. As the years passed it became important to us that it never should be oiled. It had squeaked when we were children, it squeaked when we went to school, when we were grown up still it squeaked, when we went into far countries and returned it squeaked still. We dreaded the day when someone might be unIrish enough to oil it. Even after Kilmore had been sold we would sometimes stealthily test it when over in Ireland. But I foolishly tried it again this year (1969) and I grieve to say that the tradition had been disregarded, it had been repainted a yellowish brown and had been oiled, and thus falling silent ceased to echo its messages and memories.

On one side of the house two lawns had been cut out, one of which made a good croquet and grass tennis court. On the other side were the stables which housed my father's hunters before the place was turned into a garage. That is to say, that though a modern man living in the modern world with its cars and aeroplanes and almost time-machines, I have also known the pre-motor car period. That was worth knowing since there will never be a post-motor car period. The vehicle in which I went out for drives as an infant with brother, sister, and governess was a donkey-trap. I do not know whether we exceeded five miles an hour, it was often very much less. I was not thrilled by it, and it could be fairly described as boring. Had I been told that quite soon some people would be travelling at 20,000 miles an hour and that I could stand at my window looking up at the moon while two men on the moon spoke to me and simultaneously showed me a picture of themselves walking on the moon, I would not have listened attentively, for I never much cared for fairy-tales.

We had a resident donkey, and I was fond of him, often seeking him out in the grass part of the garden, putting an arm round his neck, pulling his ear, and saying, 'We understand each other, do we not, Neddy dear?' There were many donkeys in Ireland at that time: the term 'beasts of burden' very much applied to them for so often one would see them carting huge loads along the country roads, forced on by the stick. 'Whenever you are tempted to lift your hand agen the donkey, or to stamp your foot on the little grasshopper, remember that the donkey is Pether Keegan's friend, and the grasshopper is Pether Keegan's brother,' were almost the first words that I heard from the plays of the gentle-souled Bernard Shaw, and I responded eagerly. I have few memories of anything at all before the age of nine, but a scene concerning a donkey is still very present to me. We used to spend terrible summer holidays at Ballycastle and Bundoran. The cold beastly beaches, the windy desolate sandhills appeared so vile to me that the thought of them still fills me with horror. A hired donkey trap took us to the beach. One bleak afternoon when we were 'at play' on the strand I saw some 200 yards away that the donkey was kneeling upon the donkey-man. It was an alarming sight. The donkey-man, who had evidently ill-treated the animal, must have gone too far, for the donkey had suddenly turned upon him and somehow got him down on the ground, and was kneeling upon him and biting him savagely. It was frightening to see the man (I remember his blue serge clothes) thus captive and prostrate at the mercy of the mauling of the furious donkey.

I suppose Killiney could be described as suburban, for though we were out of the town we were not properly in the country. But I never heard the term used until I came to England just as I never heard the term Middle Class. There were the Gentry and the rest – the gentry often being referred to by a word which would startle a modern reader, 'the quality.' But this term was often used by poor people whose own quality was extremely high. Your true gentleman in Ireland is so often found among the poor that one inevitably thinks of quality distinction rather than class distinction. One of the reasons why it is difficult to think of Killiney as suburban is because the Wicklow Mountains are so near, and I think that the nine-hole Killiney golf course with its view of the hills is one of the most delightful in the world. I spent much of my boyhood cycling over the Wicklow Mountains. I am surprised now at the length of such rides. To go from Killiney to a little place called Enniskerry, then up a very long hill (past a brutally desolate Reformatory) to Lough Bray, then over the Sally-Gap to Lough Taye and down to Calary Common and round to the Big Sugar Loaf and then down to Bray, makes quite a long car journey; to have done it by bicycle strikes me now as excessive. When I was with others I used to go downhill with such recklessness that when I reached the bottom I would find myself alone for a long time, and fearing that something must have happened to the others I would often have to walk back up the hill to find out! I think that all of us were much relieved when we were on the way home approaching Bray, for these mountains are terribly oppressive, the melancholy being mightier than the beauty.

There has been astonishingly little change in these hill districts since I was a child. Indeed I find today when visiting my old haunts that apart from the superficial changes wrought by excellent forestry, everything everywhere is exactly as it has always been. The same sparseness of inhabitants; the same air of desolation; the same wide expanse of empty acres browned or purpled by heather, and the darker spaces that keep moving because they are not made of heather but of cloud shadows; the high haycocked field on a green hill far away, upon which alone the sun is shining; the all-pervading silence emphasized by the bleating of one sad sheep out of sight; here and there great boulders perched on the top of eminences, and granite rocks sinking ever lower into the heather; the abandoned bogs; the recurrent rainbows seldom complete in their archways, and more often as pillars not in the sky but set against a verdured hill or mountain crest; the silken greens in the evening sky; the translucent light after rain, the very light that never shone on land or sea; the white cottage discerned at the foot of the dark mountain, Image of Loneliness; the lake down below, black as ink seen from above, the colour of Guinness Stout when seen closer, and upon the water no sign of a rowing-boat, no sail, and on the golden strand no person; the white road winding away through the hills and losing itself at the foot of distant mountains whose green has turned to blue. The atmosphere of *remoteness* is very strong, and the mournfulness. It is hard to think of the daily realities up there. Bernard, Shaw, who seldom went in for natural description, put exactitude into the mouth of Larry Doyle. '... Your wits can't thicken in that soft moist air, on those white springy roads, in those misty rushes and brown bogs, on those hillsides of granite rocks and magenta heather. You've no such colors in the sky, no such lure in the distances, no such sadness in the evenings. Oh, the dreaming, the dreaming, the dreaming!...' That is really what is meant by the Celtic Twilight which is a perfectly definite thing to be experienced at any time. But few do experience it, for they keep away from it. When I'm up there politics seem very unreal, I never want to know who is killing whom or which theological clown is destroying religion. The fact is these mountains, unlike the Alps, are very old indeed and have been nearly washed away by Time. And it may be that human life will never be very possible here, and that it is not only Ireland's history, but something deeper which makes for the atmosphere of mournfulness and even hopelessness which spreads out also into the cities, especially Dublin in spite of its modern superficies.

Thus it has always surprised me that the idea of 'the funny Irishman' should be so widespread in England. But I think the idea of 'funniness' per se being especially characteristic of the Irish is due to the fact that the

7

language is humorous. An English person will say, 'Mrs Jones passed away last night', which in the Irish vernacular would be, 'Mrs O'Brien is after dying on me last night', – not meant to be particularly humorous. Perhaps the Irish genius is best displayed in throwing the harsh light of comedy upon squalid characters and sordid scenes, supported by poetic phraseology and Catholic imagery. We can get plenty of laughs out of the great dramatic poet, John Synge, but it is all a by-product. Incidentally, there is a tendency to suppose that the fine phrases in his plays are all taken from what he had heard. He said that he took some, so it is assumed that he took all. A great many must have been his own invention. One of the Irish Players once told me that when Synge was dying, an atrocious organ-grinder would persist in playing just outside his window. He got up and shouted down to the man, 'May you be followed by the curse of the living and drowned in the sweat of the damned!' His dialogue is really an elaborate stylism built on a solid foundation. 'Aid me for to win Pegeen. It's herself only that I'm seeking now,' cries Christy to the Widow Quinn. 'Aid me for to win her, and I'll be asking God to stretch a hand to you in the hour of death, and lead you short cuts through the Meadows of Ease, and up the floor of Heaven to the Footstool of the Virgin's Son.' An ordinary peasant would never be capable of such elaboration in imagery and rhythm, and most of Synge is rather like that. But he had a solid foundation of speech to build upon, speech which seeks to raise the situation, whatever it may be, and make even the insupportable supportable by a touch of poetry or humour. A room in a wretched Wicklow cottage was so damp that a man said to my brother, Bob, 'its drench runs down the walls like white waves of foam.' He sought instinctively to bring the thing into the realm of art and thus soften the harsh reality of the scene. A beggar on the public way once called out to me in a very fine voice for a contribution, and added 'May the Holy Virgin reward you, for you're a fine boy I'm thinkin', and the woman who bore you was a fine woman!' for he was not prepared to accept something for nothing, and repaid the sixpence with more than sixpence-worth of fine words. What is most evident is the habit of thinking and speaking in pictures. After a country funeral I overheard two men, both slightly the better for drink, discussing the dubious merits of the departed. They wished to be fair regarding the prospects of his final destination. 'He's ayther up above or down below,' said one of them, pointing first up and then down. 'That's right,' said the other, 'he's ayther up above or down below, in one of them two places.' It was a simple geographical statement, strangely complete and comforting.

No doubt these Wicklow Mountains had a good deal of effect upon me at this time, for later in life I was always longing to get a glimpse of them again, to be among them if only for a day. But in my boyhood I was unaware of any particular love of nature. My sense of beauty was undeveloped. There was nothing Wordsworthian in my reaction, the 'sounding cataract' did not haunt me like a passion. The mountains were simply in our vicinity and we took rides through them, and I was depressed rather than elated by the solitude, and frightened by that terrible Reformatory on the mountain-side near Lough Bray. But we did love Powerscourt's Domain (not now so accessible) with its river and waterfall and forest. We loved to see the deer flashing through the bracken between the trees, and it was always a great moment when we saw a fine antlered stag suddenly revealed before us, alert, ears posed, utterly still.

By 'we' I mean myself and my brother Bob[1] who was my twin – though we are by no means 'identical' twins. We grew up together and went to the same schools, but there was a shadow between us and we were not emotionally free. My brother Maurice[2] was eleven years older, and I saw little of him till some thirty years later, after his early retirement from the Indian Civil Service in Burma, when with matchless industry and single-mindedness he addressed himself to the production of those books for which he has become celebrated. My sister Mary was ten years older and died in 1941. She sometimes went bicycling with us, for she was very active, but she preferred horse riding. She was very good with animals and would speak to them continually. Her speech was low and swift and not always easy to hear or to follow, but the animals understood and loved her... As a matter of fact all our family without a single exception had a respect for animals. I cannot recall an occasion of unkindness shown to any of them. The idea of shooting birds for fun and calling the dead animals 'game' seemed to us rather unattractive, nor did fishing for pleasure appeal, nor the idea of going out with a net, capturing and then killing butterflies so as to display the slaughtered creatures as 'specimens.' I think this attitude of ours was more or less unconscious, I never heard it discussed. Not very long ago I was being driven by my brother Bob along a Wicklow mountain road when he ran over a hare. He got out and bent over it to see if he could assist it at all, but it was far gone. 'Sorry, hare,' said my brother in a low voice. The hare seemed to sense the sincere tone of the apology, and looked up as if to say, 'Please don't mention it.' But the words were so unaffected that the scene has always remained with me, and the words 'Sorry hare' really sum up our family attitude towards animals. I have no absolute rules in this or any other matter, but my rule of thumb here is never to injure any creature, even the most minute, unless it is about to sting or bite, and I regard it as a sort of mad necessity to escort into the open any of the minutiae who have been misguided enough to crawl across my table or over the paper I am using. I give it no big term such as 'reverence for life', only regarding it as an outrage to kill without cause…

My sister Mary was a powerful personality and a complicated character, and she met with the indulgence usually accorded to those who are 'a law unto themselves'. I was not close to her, for I was never at ease in her presence. After her children had grown up she painted watercolours of considerable appeal, and I have one which is most striking in its power to represent winter wind bending lonely trees on a mountain side. She married Pat Hone. I remember her standing one day in the drawing room looking down at him on the tennis court and referring to him as 'the poet'. It was the right word to use though he did not actually write poetry, for if there is such a thing as the poetry of personality, he had and has it to an extraordinary degree. At one time he captained 'The Gentlemen of Ireland' in cricket, and later he wrote one of the three most readable books on cricket – in the course of which he tells us that when Oscar Wilde was at Trinity he objected to the game on the ground that 'the postures were indecent'. The literary man of the Hone family was his brother Joseph Hone, best known for his biography of Yeats. He was a very tall man with an unusually high brow and cavernous features set in an expression of noble abstract melancholy. He was famous for his silences. If he went out to tea he would take a seat and say *nothing* – perhaps secretly as a bid to balance the garrulity of a Gogarty. I sometimes walked beside him the length of the station road, and even if communication had been possible in spite of his great height, no word ever fell from his lips. My sister became engaged during the rehearsals held at Kilmore when private theatricals were given of Lady Gregory's plays, Pat Hone taking the lead in *The Rising of the Moon* – my first, and perhaps most pleasurable, experience of drama.

My sister Joyce was four years older. She had more sense of humour, I think, than any of the family, but her health pulled her down, and she was so lacking in confidence that she failed to make, as far as I could see, any assault whatsoever in the field of men, and died in 1951. Unable to cope with the family atmosphere she had the sense and the courage to join the Catholic Church. This demanded courage for she was surrounded by Protestants of a particularly revolting narrowness, sublimely unaware that the Catholics were superior to them in religious feeling, lack of sanctimoniousness, and broad humanity. When a relation dies one is generally filled with remorse about the things that one did not do and could have done. I realized afterwards (because of her response to one letter) that she would have welcomed and enjoyed long letters from me when grown up and in England. But I did nothing of the sort. This was not due to callousness. It was simply because I was not close to her as a friend, and I had so little an opinion of myself that it never occurred to me that she would appreciate my letters or the fact that I wrote to her. People are often hurt by the neglect of others without suspecting the reason. They suspect indifference or haughtiness when the cause is really humility, for it may make us unkind; and it is our past failures in kindness which cause greater remorse than our more sensational sins.

My father was a solicitor in Dublin – the firm of Collis & Ward in Clare Street. He had a very strong constitution (he had been a great Rugger international in his day) which he handed down to his sons. He was not adventurous in mind, there was no touch of the radical in him, and in this he was a good example of the typical Victorian who, when money was coming in well, felt the more convinced that he would end up in the workhouse. And there was a workhouse nearby, at Loughlinstown, for us all to see. Near the end of his life he had a motor accident in the vicinity and was carried into the place. 'I knew I would come here at last,' he said. He was physically fearless, ready to take on any number of roughs who chose to attack him, and during the First World War gave his intense bottled up desire for adventure a chance by joining a motor ambulance unit to Italy. He was both good and kind, and while giving his sons every chance to get on, he put no pressure upon any of us to enter his business, and let us go our own way without interference; but he was never intimate with any of us, and we did not make much attempt to understand him or give him help or comfort. He lived into his eighties, preserving his health till his last year in 1947 when, losing full consciousness, a male nurse was obliged to watch over him. One day he was heard to utter the words, 'Before I got lost,' and at last he said 'I will die today,' and he did die.

I must say a word regarding my father's approach to sex instruction, for I feel rather strongly that any views held about the present day are the more helpful if the commentator has seen and *felt* the previous era. My father was never a bully or a hypocrite, not a particularly stern person in the Victorian manner, but he was a complete victim of the Victorian mores. He was not an ordinary man but his mind moved in the ordinary way prescribed by the times, and his attitude to sex was absolutely *fatal*. One day when my twin brother and I were walking with him to Church – a long walk – he began to speak to us in a hushed tone suggestive of fearful import. He told us that one of the Commandments in the Bible (he named its number) was 'though shalt not commit adultery.' His tone impressed and alarmed me a good deal, but I hadn't a notion of what he was talking about, and it was not in my character

11

to blurt out that I didn't know what he was getting at. It was a truly extraordinary way of introducing the facts of life. Needless to say I do not blame him in the least for being baulked by this, since it is only today that sex instruction is being regarded as a first necessity of education, to be taught to children while they are young and matter-of-fact – well *before* they have reached the sniggering stage. In this respect my father was merely negative, but on the subject of auto-eroticism he was positive and appalling, introducing not only mental ideals of abominable guilt and sin but fearful warnings of ruined health, teeth dropping out, and the rest of it. The result of this in my case was that I fought against the practice with frightened fervour and when I 'fell' became riddled with feelings of guilt and shame and sin, and physically pale and washed out. Only one word can properly describe the attitude towards sexuality in my youth: *unhealthy*, and there are few more damaging words in the language. Today there is much criticism regarding the 'permissive' society, but it is not unhealthy, and I feel that only someone like myself who has seen both extremes can appreciate how healthy the atmosphere is today in comparison with the past. People say that on account of the extremities of permissiveness now reached there will be a swing back to Puritanism. I do not think there will be a swing back to unhealthiness. I do not even believe that there will be a full-scale reaction from extreme licence, though I expect and hope that there will be some retreat. I hear people say that the exposure of sex at present in the theatre and on TV is 'boring', for people love to use that word to advertize their superiority. It is very far from boring, but it is embarrassing because it is so often vulgar and unseemly. That is my personal complaint – that it is unseemly. What strikes me most forcibly about the public in general today is the extraordinary lack of aesthetic taste. It just doesn't seem to exist. Consider for example the Olympic Games. There you have young men and young women who represent the world's most athletic figures. Beautifully shaped limbs and superbly healthy skins. How are they clad? The men wear preposterous singlets which are downright ugly, hopelessly detracting from the beauty of the arms and torso. Is it not fantastic that we have endless TV bedroom scenes in which undressed persons, often spotty and repulsive, appear to be engaged in eating one another, while the Olympic runners have their beautiful bodies covered in the most absurd manner? (You think they need singlets so that a huge Number may be written thereon? I deny the necessity. Who can distinguish the numbers on the jerseys of jockeys, yet we get all the information we need from the excellent commentators.) Exactly the same applies to the girls whose bodies are cut to pieces by an unnecessary costume. Think of the pleasure it would give aesthetically (and sexually I hope) if the men wore nothing but the briefest of shorts (not loose and flapping, for that spoils the line from foot to waist) and the girls the briefest of bikinis. But this isn't done for there is no public demand for physical beauty, and yet a surprising acceptance of the distasteful and unseemly. We see this all the time. Take the Beauty Queen contests. They really *are* boring. People complain about the puppet-like manner of walking and smiling: but the most obvious objection is their hideous one-piece swimsuits, and their ludicrous shoes which are not only incongruous with those swimsuits but conceal the condition and shape of their feet which are as important a feature as any other. These girls by the very nature of the contest are all outstanding examples of the female form. It would be entirely proper and seemly if they wore just bikinis, and nothing on their feet. But no thought, and no sense, is brought to bear on these matters. It is as if there was no such think as aesthetic taste, and only lasciviousness should be encouraged. Still, this muddled state of affairs is likely to clear up, while the terrible unhealthiness of the previous age will not return.

I mentioned above that little attempt was made by us to give our father understanding or comfort. He needed comfort, for ours was not a united family or a happy household. Something akin to neurosis informed our group, for we were all eccentric. To this day, when I am with ordinary families where there may be occasional temper and scenes but no permanent tension, I tend to lean back and bask in a kind of relaxed wonder. Beautiful as were the garden and surroundings of Kilmore, there was no peace or happiness to be observed of felt. My father did not get on with my mother and I do not recall a single pleasant hour they spent together in my life time. I do not know if separation or divorce was ever contemplated. Probably not; for just as poor married couples are held together by poverty, so well-to-do couples are held together by property. My father was much attached to Kilmore and he could never contemplate exiling himself from it. I do not know the cause of their disharmony, not its history. I never had any intimate talk with my father about it. I gave him no comfort. I thought only of myself. So I was not close to him either.

And now I must explain why I have been obliged to use the words 'not close to' so often. Nowadays, not only do I think of other people's problems, but I even tend to consider them before my own – perhaps to make up for the years when my centre was always myself. This brings me to my mother, whom unfortunately I must now mention. If one is to write autobiographical impressions and comments, it is necessary, I am told, to give the date of one's birth and the *mise en scène* of one's childhood. I do not wish to linger a moment longer than necessary over my childhood, nor to give character sketches of my brothers and sisters, which in any case I would regard as an impertinence. I remember nothing before the age of nine, and I am astonished when people record what they did at the age of three, while there is one very eminent author who tells us what he did at the age of one (does it matter much?). The cause of my memory block before the age of nine was unhappiness so penetrating that details have been 'censored' according to the best traditions of natural psychology. And the reason for this was my mother. From the hour of my birth she hated me. There was no let up for forty years. The earliest years were so difficult to take that I have suffered virtual loss of memory. Not very long ago I came upon a photograph of myself at about the age of two. I was utterly amazed to see quite a normal-looking child, extremely 'bonnie' as they say, and with lovely curls. God knows what I expected to see, as far as I knew I had never *been* a baby, certainly not a normal one, looking like that. Here was a child that must have run across a room, fallen over, burst into tears, run to its Mummy, and been comforted in the ordinary way. But that never happened to me; I was never taken up in my mother's arms and kissed. Here was a child that must have gurgled and prattled and laughed and shouted at intervals. Yet I find it impossible to envisage myself doing any of those things if my mother was anywhere near.

How do I know this if I remember nothing? Partly by her treatment of me during the thirty years that followed roughly from the age of nine, and partly from what I gathered from others – for it had become a byword. Certainly I have no recollection of anything save shrinking from her and her shrinking from me, no word of endearment or act of kindness. But she was without malice. She could not help herself. Not that I realized this at the time. When she said goodnight to my twin brother and then passed by my room without a word, or offered him a second helping at meals but not me, or hurriedly got up from sitting in her chair on the steps and went indoors when she saw me approaching from the avenue, and a great many things of that sort all the time, I could not be expected to know that it was beyond her control, let alone reflect upon the far greater cruelties visited by other mothers upon other children. I never questioned her about this behaviour, never pleaded with her, shed no tears, created no scenes, for I somehow sense that it would be as useless to do this as to plead with a 'wicked' horse. Thus I was not close to any of the family, for a film of pain and bewilderment separated me from them. They did not take sides and seek to console me, for they also were bewildered and no doubt saw that I shrank from pitying consolation, and indeed I was horrified when relations or visitors came to the house and were privy to my predicament, and I could not bear it when the cook or maids sought to comfort me and surreptitiously brought me hot buttered scones. I had no character. I had not the smallest self-respect. I was unaware of any gifts. Having no self-knowledge my mother easily caused me to think that her behaviour to me was *my fault*. Her face was very sensitive and mobile, and if I did happen to demur to something, her features assumed a *wronged* expression of unexampled outrage and such a powerful tragedy-queen aspect, that I was instantly subdued. It never occurred to me to say to her in front of the family, perhaps at mealtime, 'Why can you not speak to me like a normal mother?' Everyone would have been amazed – and delighted. But that amount of spirit or good sense was quite beyond me. However, one day I was helped from an unexpected quarter. It was when I was about nineteen and was at an Officers' Training Crops in England, somewhere in Sussex. All the details are lost to me now save the central thing. Some relations invited me to visit them, and I went. I was told that an aunt who was upstairs in bed – I think it was my Aunt May – wished to speak to me. I was shown into her bedroom, and remember only a white hawk face. Perhaps she was dying; at any rate she was eager to speak to me, to give me a message before it was too late. She spoke with vigour and authority. 'It sometimes happens', she said, and these were her exact words, 'it sometimes happens that when a mother has two sons at the same time, she will *adore* one of them, and *hate* the other. I thought it might relieve and comfort you to know this.' It not only comforted me, it came as a startling revelation, and I experienced a sense of relief. I do not know whether this truly good woman ever knew how great was the relief or constant the comfort which she had given me, for I'm sure that I failed to express my gratitude, not did I ever write to thank her.

I have said that I made no scenes, nor called her in question. It would be simpler to say that I did not stand up for myself. But I recall two occasions which qualify that assertion. The hall door was made chiefly of glass. One day, after something unbearable had been done or said to me, I banged the door in front of her, shattering the glass to splinters. I left the house and spent all day some distance from Killiney. At length I returned, expecting a row from my father. I had misjudged him. No word was spoken. Not a single word of reproach or reprimand regarding the shattering of the glass, and no explanations demanded or offered.

The second occasion is more amusing, and was very much later, in fact on one of my visits to Kilmore from England. I was having lunch with my mother and my sister Joyce. My mother had a habit of systematically contradicting anything I said, and once again she came out strong in this respect. Suddenly I rebelled. 'Why do you contradict me, mother?' I asked. 'Why do you always contradict every single thing I say? Isn't it time you gave it up? There isn't a word of sense in what you say. It is deplorably...' and I worked myself up. The effect of this was somewhat expected. She could not take it. She could not take it sitting down. So she got up. She walked to the sideboard with the utmost degree of tragedy, and sighing deeply she removed some articles from one place to another place, then replaced them; took a toastrack and put it opposite a decanter; put a silver salt cellar to the other side of a silver eggcup and then back again, the while uttering no word but breathing heavily between sighs. She was entirely unable to cope. My sister looked on with ill-concealed enjoyment, for she didn't think that 'Jack had it in him' to mount an offensive of this kind. But actually I never found in myself any particular desire to hurt her feelings, nor assumed that she was without them – she was tender towards animals to a degree I have never seen exceeded. I did not seek revenge. When some years later still, my daughters, Elizabeth and Gabrielle, came over to Kilmore for a holiday, she took an immense fancy to Elizabeth and entirely ignored Gabrielle. Elizabeth took no notice of her and was most unforthcoming to her attentions. I could see how deeply this pained my mother. 'She is a little shy of me, but will soon get over it', she said pathetically. I did not like to see her pain at Elizabeth's indifference, and really wanted my daughter to be nice to her.

The incident which I have just referred to when I rebelled took place in the dining room of course. Years later when both my parents were dead and Kilmore had passed into other hands, I called one day and the new owners, Mr and Mrs Joseph McMenamin, received me with great courtesy. I was invited into that dining room for some refreshment. There was a very harmonious atmosphere. A priest was present and when the maid came in with something he spoke to her in a delightful manner. I sat down at a place opposite the window which overlooked the back garden with the gooseberry and blackcurrant bushes, the old wall, and the greenhouses. I do not remember any of the conversation. I sat there almost speechless, for I was scarcely able to utter a word, and I know that I did not lift my glass for my hand was shaking. I told my brother Maurice about this later, and he made a searching observation. 'You must remember,' he said, 'that you were sitting in *the room of greatest tension*.' True indeed. Here was played out much of the tragic queenery, and most of the terrors of inharmony between husband and wife, and all the awfulness of mealtime non-conversation; and here the embarrassment of hearing servants improperly addressed was most evident. Here my mother's invalid act found its best theatre. If the window was open she would shiver, if it was closed she would sigh deeply, sighs which were almost gasps, and would say, 'abreathofairdear, abreathofairdear' to someone between gasps and sighs, and the window would be opened. There would be a fire-going-out tragedy, an egg tragedy, or a toast tragedy, and she would ring the bell in a manner calculated, I should have thought, to ensure that no one answered it. A great unease would spread into the dining room and indeed throughout the house when she was telephoning for groceries or the like. In those days you had to wind a little handle in order to connect with the Exchange, and making contact was often a slow process. When my mother telephoned it became the occasion for an extremity of histrionics: for having wound the little handle and had no immediate reply she conceived herself as shamefully affronted or grossly neglected, and would shout into the mouthpiece with unbridled truculence and then wind the wheel round and round with an energy that would have done for cranking a motor car... Thus, when I took my seat in the dining room that day in the harmonious and relaxed atmosphere, it was not unnatural that I was somewhat shaken.

My mother used an enormous variety of medicines, to be seen in the cabinet in her bedroom, but she did not take much harm from them, and, advancing into her eighties, outlived my father by two years. But near the end, her health did deteriorate so disastrously that she was obliged to spend her last years in a nursing home in Dublin (run by Catholics who extended greater charity towards her than the Protestants did). I was able to visit her there from time to time. She had now greatly changed in appearance, and had a wild and legendary old Irish country look. Her attitude towards me also changed. She seemed glad to see me, evidently liking me to sit with her, and even let fall a term of endearment. I was glad to sit with her, for it was a relief to be able to do so without tension and without pain. She had never looked straight into my face before, not had I looked directly at her, and it was pleasant to exchange a glance. Only one thing was I resolved upon – I did not favour a deathbed reconciliation. When I had grown up and become strong and free, I never (except on that occasion in the dining room) sought to hurt her by action or word; but I was not prepared to have a soft scene for her benefit. It was too late for that. Moreover, I am so easily mollified that I feared falsity on my own part. But I could see it coming. And sure enough one day I found her preparing to try for this. 'There is something I want to say to you,' she began. I looked alarmed: 'Here goes,' I said to myself. 'There is something I must say to you,' she began again. But I would not yield. I would not soften. I would not depart from my resolve. I did not let her continue, but bending over the bed, lightly and swiftly stroked her cheek, and said, 'It doesn't matter, mother, say nothing.' She did not try again, and I think she was relieved... I am persuaded that I was right and used good sense on this occasion. It was quite beyond her to have employed words to

17

deal with this matter without deception, and beyond me to have listened seriously and responded sincerely. If, in a vague way, before passing from the face of the earth, she sought forgiveness, I thought it best that it should be done without words, and in fact I believe that she saw in my action all that she needed without the necessity of either of us uttering a single sentence.

Shortly after this she died. I came over to Dublin and went to the nursing home in Leeson Street. My brothers were there and told me in which room she lay. I said I would go in alone and see her. I went in and saw her lying there, the first dead person I had ever seen, and there she was, looking like an old doll, or an idol, or a thing of wax – the *not breathing* so fearful and strange. There were a lot of flowers on her bed. They got between me and her, a film which I did not want. I took each bunch and carefully placed it on the floor. Then I sat down on the bed and gazed upon her for some time – indeed, it must have been a long time, for the length of my absence was commented upon later. Then with the same care I methodically replaced the flowers on the bed, and left her.

This mother-son relationship, thus briefly outlined, was somewhat of a strain on the nervous system, and had certain bad effects, but I cannot be specific, and am unwilling to provide a psychiatrist's holiday, being persuaded that in this particular field they are largely wise after the event and inclined to display one of the seven clever ways of being stupid and one of the four learned ways of being ignorant. Had I developed a sour attitude towards life or a bitter attitude towards people or a failure to see the beauty of the world, how easy to 'explain' it by reference to my mother – and how annoying if I do not conform! In any case I am not sure that I would have had it otherwise, for it caused in me certain tensions which have made it possible for me to play certain tunes – and I would not lightly allow myself to be deprived of this for the sake of happiness. My twin brother, Bob, in facing the reverse side of the coin had also a stiff time and also came out of it not without scars. In the end it was far more difficult for him than for me to cope – because long after I was free he continued to be bound; when there was no call upon me to bother, his filial offices, his medical attentions, his assumed tendernesses were in perpetual demand for years and years till the very end. Perhaps it is better to be over-adored than hated without apparent cause, but in the extremity of our cases it is almost an open question.

1 Dr W R F Collis, named after William Robert Fitzgerald Collis who was Deputy Master of the Rolls at the time of Grattan, and in the famous engraving of Grattan's Parliament he appears in the centre leaving the Chamber with Lord Edward Fitzgerald.

2 Named after Maurice Henry Collis, surgeon at Meath Hospital 1851-69. He died at the age of forty-five from septicaemia acquired by cutting his finger while operating. His patient lived but he died. It was the first time this operation had been performed successfully in Ireland. His coffin was followed across Dublin by four miles of cabs.

SECOND MOVEMENT...

… GROWING

1

I recall things from the age of nine because that is when I first went to school. It was called Aravon and my brother and I caught the train every morning to Bray – caught is right, for we were generally late and had to catch it by running along the platform and jumping in as it moved out. It went close by the sea all the way and on rough days the waves struck the walled embankment and came right over the train and into the carriage if we opened the window. This was such fun that I longed for high tide with heavy seas, and I doubt whether any boys have ever had so thrilling a way to school. We had sixpence a week pocket money and for a penny could buy a packet of acid drops, the taste of which today would be a mouthful of memory.

And so I was set to Organized Education. It was many a long year before I extricated myself from this curious affair. I was a prime sample for classroom fodder: unawakened, unoriginal, unprecocious. It never crossed my mind to question the pumping system. A man, called a schoolmaster, got hold of a pump, fixed it to my head, and pumped into Floor II all sorts of facts which were left to rot there. There is a Floor I, of course, into which we put things we need and they remain organic with us. But I was an easy victim, and though there were questions I would have liked to ask, when I found instead that I was required to *answer* questions in which I was not interested, I simply accepted the system as slavishly as the social frame work. My mind remained dormant, for there was no Tolstoy around to awaken it – when Tolstoy read in a comedy how a mother had asked, with regard to geography lessons for her son, 'Why teach him all the countries? The coachman will drive him where he may have to go,' he declared that 'nothing more to the point has ever been said against geography, and all the learned men in the world cannot rebut such an irrefutable argument. I am speaking quite seriously. What need was there for me to know where the river and town of Barcelona are situated, when for twenty-three years I have not once had occasion to use the knowledge?' Tolstoy was a schoolmaster for a period, and was as great in that field as he was a novelist, and he did succeed in addressing himself entirely to Floor I, and did succeed in awakening his children who thereafter blessed and loved him.

I realize that this is only a way of saying that there is no solution to the problem of education since the genius schoolmaster who is passionately dedicated to his task is so rare as not to count, and that the farcical pumping must inevitably go on for many years to come. We cannot be romantic and expect the impossible. But what does strike me as extraordinary and inexcusable is that masters and headmasters permit unreadable textbooks to be used in their school. Can they claim to be serious and responsible men, I ask myself, if they permit this? The purpose of a Primer should be to prize open a subject and thus reveal a whole new field of knowledge to a person entirely ignorant of it. Primers should be the most exciting and delightful books in the whole range of literature. Admittedly it requires a genius to do this: that it can be done was clearly proved by William Cobbett in his magnificent Grammars. I am persuaded that any field is subject to a clear and even a highly literary statement, including nuclear physics, as I myself proved when I eventually escaped into self-education.[1] But there is no *demand* from schoolmasters for such works, although there is a thoughtless acceptance of textbooks which are plainly harmful.

Take Algebra for example. Here *par excellence* is a subject which needs to be prized open with a really competent literary lever. The following extract, from page one of an Elementary Algebra, was presented for my consideration at Aravon:

'Algebra treats of quantities as in Arithmetic, but with greater generality; for while the quantities used in arithmetical processes are denoted by *figures* which have one single definite value, algebraical quantities are denoted by *symbols* which may have any value we choose to assign to them. The symbols employed are letters...thus when we say "Let a=1" we do not mean that a must have the value 1 always, but only in the particular example we are considering.'

A willing person like myself, after struggling a little with the cumbersome phraseology, would have been prepared to go along with this and channel the thing into Floor I, if I could then have been immediately told what was the object of this symbolism and why we should ever want a to equal 1; for in that case a new thing, Algebra, would find a place in a general vision of knowledge. But instead of proceeding to do this the author drowns me with divisional nomenclature: an *algebraical expression* is so and so; *Expressions* are either *simple* or *compound*; compound expressions are further distinguished into *binomial*, *trinomial*, and *multinomial* aspects; when two or more quantities are multiplied the result is called the *product*; and each quantity is called a *factor*; when one of the factors of an expression is a numerical quantity it is called the *coefficient* of the remaining factors; if a quantity be multiplied by itself any number of items the product is called a *power*; the number which expresses the power of any quantity is called its *index*.

Now if a person is born with a gift for maths, all this will be obvious, though foolish, and will present no difficulty, just as grammar was always obvious to me (though when later I came upon a passage from a book of mine used for analysis in a Foundation Course in English, I was mystified by the names given to obvious practices). But here was I standing before the closed book of Algebra, ready to open it, but not given a clue as to the point of the thing. Instead, I am immediately told to be careful to distinguish between *coefficient* and *index*; for if we have $a = 4$, then $3a = 3 \times a = 3 \times 4 = 12$, which is the *coefficient*; but $a^3 = a \times a \times a = 4 \times 4 \times 4 = 64$, which is the *index*. Then I am asked, or rather told, to clear a matter up. If $a = 7$, $b = 2$, $c = 1$, $X = 5$, $Y = 3$, find the value of (1) $14X$; (2) X^3; (3) $3\ ax$.

One can puzzle this out like any other puzzle, in a strictly senseless manner, but it is a terribly frivolous approach to any subject. Supposing golf were to be taught in this manner, how long would the teacher or his book be tolerated? He would have you on the first green without explaining why the green all around is never referred to as such, and he would tell you to sink your ball before informing you that there is a hole or telling you why anyone should ever wish to see the ball disappear in this way.

When we failed to understand this or that question in the classroom, the headmaster, Mr Bookie, had a simple remedy; he addressed himself not to our heads but to our hands. We were made to hold out our hands palms upward, which he then struck a number of times with his cane – extremely painful and scarcely an aid to the educational matter in view.

Even more extraordinary was his teaching of history. 'Name the six wives of Henry VIII, Collis,' I remember him saying to me sternly. If he had said, 'I want you to train your memory, so learn by heart the six wives of Henry VIII,' although ridiculous it would have made some sense – though not much, since memory could be trained in a better way than that. But he didn't say this, he called it 'history', and as I couldn't name the six wives of Henry VIII – I 'knew' only one of them – he became very angry and told me to hold out my hand. I did not for one moment question his method of teaching or demur to his philosophy of history, but merely thought what a stupid boy I was 'at history' and wished I were clever.

Dim as I was, I would sit up and take notice if a whiff of spirit blew in. This sometimes happened when a lecturer came from outside and made a good speech. I remember one occasion in particular when I woke up and *took in* and listened with such pleasure that a few of the words remain with me to this day. I have no idea of the lecturer's name or his subject, but he spoke with some art. '... Youth, accomplishment, and beauty used to perambulate through those halls,' he declared, 'and now it is but a thieves' kitchen!' And he ended on a passage with the refrain at the end of each sentence – 'It was the fault, it was the fault of the Motherland!' The words were spoken with such a powerful drive and so appealed to my imagination that I got a lift foreign to anything I received in any classroom. But I do not think that it should be left only to outsiders to give a lift to the growing boy.

My brother and I possessed just sufficient capacity to churn out answers 'satisfactory' enough to get us into the lowest form at Rugby School. When it was announced in front of a class at Aravon that we had passed, we were clapped! Our journeys to school now became quarterly and involved the Irish Sea. In the autumn it was often very rough, and as I have always loved storms I used to hope that we would be caught up in the equinoctial gales, and we frequently were.

Hardly had we started at Rugby when we went through the gate which was then closed behind all our generation: the quiet, orderly pre-1914 era passed away and massive world-engulfing wars brought in the disorder which apparently is to be the norm until further notice. So the Rugby OTC now came into its own and I was steadily drilled and shouted at for years to come.

We had endless field days, dressed in the khaki and awful (and absurd) puttees of the day, when one 'army' would engage another 'army'; and having advanced in columns of fours and split up into sections we would move by 'short rushes' to capture an area or hill, shooting off our blank cartridges. I was never able to achieve even the status of a lance corporal because I could never grasp what was supposed to be happening. I could not have given an order which seemed sensible in the circumstances, not did I understand the kind of orders that were given to me (especially a snapped out 'message' to be conveyed to somebody). When the field day was over we were told which army had won. I wondered how they knew, for to me it had all been a mix up of people rushing about. I put this down to my non-military mind and general stupidity, but years later when reading Tolstoy I found him saying that all battles were a chaos and that no one at all had any idea of what was happening. I imagine that this was true during much of the 1914-18 war – so often after a battle had been fought, involving the loss of perhaps 5,000 men, it was discovered that an advance of only a hundred yards had been achieved.

Meanwhile as the terms passed the senior boys got commissioned, went out to the Front, and were killed. We began to have a school Scroll of Honour, and a special volume or series of volumes were published in which there was a photograph of each dead boy with an obituary on the opposite page. In these obituaries each boys was described as very special and as having been 'much loved' by his school fellows. I knew that some of these boys had not been liked, some even disliked, and finally I returned to Over's Bookshop the volumes I had subscribed for. I very much wish now that I had kept them.

As schoolboys we have more physical life than our elders, but few of us are then more than half alive mentally. The chief aspect of intelligence is imagination, the power to sense reality. This seldom develops much before the age of twenty-five. I gave no thought to what war, killing, or dying actually meant. All I wanted was to get done with the everlasting drill, go to the Front, and become a hero. I was in a dream, we were dreamers – the very stuff for cannon food. Death was not a reality to me. To die did not mean that I would disappear completely from the face of the earth and have no further interest in the scene. Somehow one died without becoming quite unconscious; somehow one enjoyed being a hero even when dead.

If I was lost in thoughtlessness in those days I have made up for it since by much brooking upon that war. Indeed, I feel the mystery of it so much that I cannot even bear satire on the subject, and 'Oh What A Lovely War!' not only completely fails to move me but makes me feel terribly cast down by the misplaced ingenuity; and I wonder why so little notice was taken of that remarkable producer, Tony Essex, whose documented epic, 'The Great War' (backed by quiet and marvellously congruous music), held me spellbound by its power to evoke the mystery as well as the horror. Yet still one broods upon the strangeness of the thing. Not one person really feels that he himself is a puppet; but what was this but puppetry on an enormous scale? Here were men given arms, thousands and thousands of men given arms; this nation and that nation whose men had arms *given* to them, put into their very hands, and then told to go out and – *shoot each other*. Instead of instantly turning their rifles upon the people who made this ludicrous

27

demand, they actually did exactly what they were told, this lot here scuttling about and shooting against that lot there, scuttling about in precisely the same way. How could they do it? How could they be prevailed upon to do it? How could they stop at Christmas-time and then start again as if they had never regained their sanity? One broods without success upon the meaning of this.

It happened that some twenty years after my schooldays I drove through part of Europe, coming back through France. The last lap of the journey was through Flanders. Every few miles we came upon a series of enormous graveyards, with line after line of gravestones looking like regiments turned to stone – as indeed they were. I stopped at one cemetery entirely devoted to British soldiers, and walked among the graves. At the foot of each was a bed of flowering red roses. On each stone was engraved the name of the fallen, save when these words were written, 'Unknown Soldier' at the top, and at the base, 'Known Unto God'. Oh, mercy! Heavens! Here, now, at my feet, lay the schoolfellows I had forgotten for twenty years. This was the reality of that 'going out to the Front' which we had sought: it was to come to this place and lie down for evermore. I had had another twenty years. The sun was warm but I shivered with cold, and chokingly stole away from this scene of unlived lives. We came to the Monument at Vimy Ridge. I had vaguely seen it on paper. I had no idea of its power. Standing on a ridge the Monument is outlined against the sky. There it would stand for centuries. The names of the fallen were carved endlessly upon the pedestal; and never have I seen such sadness as on the countenance of the Figures erected on the steps. We proceeded through Arras, Bapaume, Armentières. As we entered Belgium and approached Ypres the number of military cemeteries increased most drastically. I had no expectation of such a thing. At Ypres stands the Menin Gate. It is a big Memorial Porch bestriding the public way. The inside is carved with long lists of names above which is the superscription – 'Here are recorded the names of officers and men who fell in Ypres Salient but to whom the fortune of war denied the honoured burial given to their comrades in death.' Every evening, since the Armistice, at nine o'clock, two buglers played the Last Post. Our journey was strangely well timed by our happening to arrive just before nine. We stood there, with the few others passing by chance, while in the silence of that summer evening two soldiers stepped out, and standing within the Gate sounded the Last Post – the long and plaintive farewell whose mournful notes reverberated against the names carved upon that stone.

Is this still done? Should it not be done for a hundred years?

* * *

Back now to Rugby of 1914-18 where I was exposed, not only to the drilling, but also to the learning game. It would be pleasant to say that at Rugby it was better than at my prep-school. But it was worse, the pumping system even more rigorous and idiotic. I'm speaking autobiographically, of course, as things were for me then, and no doubt they are better now. For instance, I am sure that today no boy leaves the school (no matter what he may have specialized in near the end) without being able to speak two foreign languages. For could anything be more ridiculous than to be 'educated' between fourteen and eighteen, and to come out from that unable to speak *some* languages! In my time it was only in the lowest form of all (called The Shell) that French was *spoken* to us and that we had to speak in return. Later, it became a matter of learning German irregular verbs and so forth by heart. As for history, words fail me, and since they do fail me, I will say nothing and save space. When in later years I was no longer an unquestioning victim of school knowledge but a passionate pursuer of true knowledge, I used to fancy a Conference of School Masters being held from time to time to discuss 'How Best to Destroy the Desire for Knowledge'. I would imagine the history man saying, 'If we start them with dates and kings or just The Wars of the Roses, we can hope to squash interest almost at once'; the science man saying, 'Give them the idea that it's all a question of test tubes and labs, and most of them will lay off pretty soon'; the languages man saying, 'Insist upon the learning of irregular verbs'; the literature man saying, 'It is not easy in all cases, but we could start with Shakespeare and demand four reasons for Hamlet's delay'; and so on until a really brilliant anti-knowledge man, a botanist, would say, 'It's quite simple in my case. I can destroy love of plants with very little trouble, for from the start I cover them with Latin nomenclature; I have always found that if I do my work well I can delay interest in plants forming in any young person for some twenty years.'

Of course, no harm can actually be done to any boy with an incipient talent or genius in a given direction. He can even gain. Indeed, a boy with genuine scientific talent has the means by which he can advance much more rapidly than on his own. That rare person, the boy who can eventually use history for the purposes of art or to reach into the progressions of mankind, can gainfully use his time in spite of the pump. In my own case, I was not deflected from literature. I have often heard people say, 'I can't read Shakespeare because I was put off him by the way he was taught at school'. I think they flatter themselves. Anyone who can be put off Shakespeare by school treatment should never attempt him. For myself, I ignored all prosaic analyses and simply revelled in the words. 'Now let us rejoice beyond a common joy', cries Gonzalo in *The Tempest*, 'and set it down in gold on

29

lasting pillars'. I had no idea why he was rejoicing like that (and I'm still not sure, though I soak myself in Shakespeare and cannot conceive life without him). All I wanted then was word-music, and it wasn't before many years had passed that I began to acquire the additional joy of words making sense.

Since literature cannot be 'done' without the words themselves, the set books cannot be textbooks, and consequently I count it as one of the blessings of my life that I had Tennyson's *The Coming and Passing of Arthur* as compulsory reading, and I still possess the red school edition in which a rivulet of genuine text flows freely through a meadow of explanatory marginalia. It was more than a blessing, it was a key moment for me when I was given Macaulay's *Essays* as a set book. For I discerned (what no master dreamt of pointing out to me) that Macaulay had a definite technique, a literary scheme. I saw that he cast his material into rhetorical frameworks. I saw that by means of one verb repeated throughout a passage he could bring together into one paragraph (which I then observed was the real unit of literature) in a smooth flow everything bearing upon one aspect of his theme or one group of facts. I saw the particular use he made of commas, semicolons, colons, dashes, the full stop, and the parenthesis. I saw how the long sentence supported by a governing verb and the telegraph poles of semicolons could run swiftly without a hitch, for two pages if necessary,[2] while the short sentence could then be used with great effect. Slow as I was in other ways, I could see these things at a glance, and have ever since been very grateful to my schoolmaster, Macaulay, and grateful also to Rugby School for calling my attention to the existence of such books. Perhaps, from a creative point of view, that is as much as we have a right to ask from any school.

The other chief gains, which personally I would rate highly, are such things as debating, games, friendships, discipline, manners, attitudes, and relief for those who are sick of home, who have, in very fact, contracted home*sickness*. I mention debating, for while I would admit that this is the best way of concealing the truth of the matter, the real object is the exercize of skill with the spoken word. Even when I was very young I warmed above all things to the *spoken word*, and I never even had to look up in a dictionary the word rhetoric, for I knew instinctively what it meant. At Rugby, I derived great incidental stimulus from certain sermons in Chapel. There was a notable master, called Costley-White, who came out with astonishing periods and stupendous effects; and another, Brigstock, whose austere and ascetic countenance and unwordy eloquence fascinated me. But the visitors were the chief attraction. To this day I recall a great preacher called Scott-Holland who ended a sermon by quoting the last stanza of Browning's

'The Lost Leader' with an histrionic ability I have not heard surpassed. Yet none of them compared in my view with the famous Studdart Kennedy who came to preach more than once. He was a rare orator. He appeared to be speaking extempore, and made a great impression not only by his oratory but by his unconventional line of talk. He was an Irishman with a swarthy face, glowing dark eyes, black hair, and vibrant voice. When I knew that he was coming to preach on a given Sunday I looked forward to it with intense excitement, and when the day arrived I took my seat in Chapel with an eagerness of anticipation such as I never experienced later in life.

I became eager to speak myself. During my first term I had attended a meeting of the Debating Society, and was much attracted by it. Unfortunately the Society collapsed that very term. At length I decided to revive it. This called for a solid effort of organization, gathering recruits from various Houses, arranging the time and place of meeting, appointing four speakers, and imposing on them a subject. I carried this out with a determination which, I now realize, no obstacles could have withstood. I chose for subject 'This House Approves the Impeachment of Warren Hastings'. I took my line and my facts entirely from Macaulay's famous essay, and I insisted upon this subject. I imposed my will upon everyone, even getting the much revered master, Brigstock, to oppose the Motion. In the end we had the necessary four speakers (myself introducing the Motion) and a full house. The debate went well. At least it was not a flop. Having prepared my speech with immense care and memorized it perfectly I naturally made some impression and was clapped, though not, I think, with undue enthusiasm. I do not remember whether this revived the Society or not, for I have no recollection of subsequent meetings, only of my determination and successful mobilization of the affair. In any case I do not suppose that I minded much about the revival. My aim was entirely egocentric. I wanted to do this and I did it, calling forth the necessary exertion and will-power for the occasion. I had an aim. Most people are aimless but will follow a lead. So I led.

The Headmaster at this time was Dr David, a tall handsome man with a beautiful voice, great charm, and a compelling manner. In the Speech Room he was unsurpassed, especially when speaking to us on a subject of misdemeanour. At the end of one term he found reason to expel a considerable number of boys for homosexual practices. This purge was a fearful affair causing heaven knows what mental suffering and humiliation in the expelled boys and their parents. Today they would have been helped in these problems, unloaded of their guilt, and cleansed of their anxieties. Such mental clarification of the physical would be considered as one of the aims of a school. I was not one of the purged boys from Rugby at that time for I

31

was ignorant of shared sexual practices (healthier than private ones). I fell in love with other boys, which caused in me an ecstasy as powerful as any I have known, but though to touch the friend was a rapture, I did not understand the sexual element. One boy did have a go with me, but seeing that I did not grasp what he was aiming at he swiftly dropped the experiment. After the purge Dr David addressed the whole school in the Speech Room. A terrible hush fell upon us. The Doctor was very strong on the guilt-loading process. We were transfixed by his unprecedented tone of solemnity and sorrow. One phrase rang in my mind, never to be forgotten. 'If you do it,' he said, 'do it alone – *in silence and in shame*.' Such a phrase, delivered in such a way by such a personality, must have caused a trauma in many an otherwise healthy boy.

Dr David was not so impressive in the pulpit, for he had nothing interesting to say. I enjoyed the compulsory attendances in Chapel. This was partly because of those sermons and partly because of the ritual togetherness of it all. Even the chapel-before-breakfast had an austere attraction about it. A G Bradby, one of the masters, who was famous for a very amusing book called *The Lanchester Tradition* (its scene is Rugby), said once that the first thing anyone should do when revisiting his old school was to go and sit at the seat once allotted to him in the chapel. A good observation. Schools are corporate bodies for people who have not yet joined Corporations, and all that we have enjoyed or suffered in unison while there would flow back into the mind when taking a seat in the old place in Chapel. But some years after I had left Rugby, Dr David introduced voluntary chapel attendance. It would be hard to think of a more misguided innovation. It rested upon the assumption that boys are either religious or irreligious, and that the religious boys would turn up, while it was pointless to force the others to attend. But boys are not religious: they are either pious or pagan. The time for religion is when we grow up and possess the appropriate faculty. The result of Dr David's innovation was that instead of a full house which gave something to everyone whether consciously or not, the depleted voluntary house was not good even for the pious boys.

Besides the excellent ritual of Chapel attendance there were other aspects in the religious sphere of more dubious value, and Dr David may have made improvements there. In my time we were all compelled to go through a miserable process called Confirmation. What I was confirming or being confirmed in had no more connection with my mind than the divinity lessons which were part of the curriculum, and I found the prayerful solemnity of the occasion depressing to a degree. Yet I gained by it. The master who took part in the pious abracadabra frequently helped boys also in a realistic way of great importance. He allowed them to confess their sexual anxieties, chief of which of course was auto-eroticism. When he told me that he had been through it all himself and that I was not the only person in the world thus plagued, I was hugely relieved. So, after all, a truly religious aim was accomplished: freedom from conviction of sin.

My brother and I crawled up from the bottom form and ended as prefects – at Rugby it was called Sixth Power. In the course of events we had been fags and had been beaten, though not much. Such beatings were painful and unnecessary but I would not waste a moment considering whether they did harm, though when I was in a position to beat I did not indulge, having no taste for it. On the whole I enjoyed my time at Rugby in spite of the fact that keeping up with the lessons was a constant nervous strain for me because I did not possess school-cleverness and had no idea how to pad in exams, for I either knew a thing or didn't know it. Games were not a problem or nuisance for me. It was proper that, at Rugby, rugger should be an important item, and I was lucky in taking to it. My brother became Captain of the Fifteen, and though he led the forwards both then and later as an International player for Ireland, he ran with the ball as often as any three-quarter. He did not run particularly fast, but he used a 'hand off' with such extraordinary effect that it was nearly impossible for a single person to tackle and bring him down. I got my Cap (given to me by my brother, but I think I deserved it), and could have got my Fifteen had it not been for a boil under my armpit during the testing matches, a pain so acute that I remember it still! The war-time food (very scarce) was probably responsible for this, but on the whole it did not seem to affect us much. Long-distance running was held in high esteem at that time, one run called The Crick being ten miles, and though I was far from winning it, I believe my own time on one occasion was equal to that of a former winner. Perhaps as a result of this I have always been plagued with extreme physical restlessness, and still run – finding it easier and less exhausting than walking (especially up a mountain) – for an hour or more if I can find a place where I can do it without clothes (or most of them); I find also that a good deal of mental clarity often follows such exertion. Not that I would advocate violent exercize as an aid to fitness. Given the basis of a good constitution, there are, I think, two ways of keeping fit (if I may venture to complete my thoughts on this subject here in case it is of more than personal interest). The first is the constant practice of those simple yoga movements that exercize *all* one's joints and muscles (in contrast to golf or tennis, which I love). Moreover, since so few of us have the will to breathe deeply, we at least are forced to do so while performing the exercizes. It is notable that most successful actors and actresses live to a great age in good condition, and one reason for this is that the nature of their profession obliges them to breathe properly so as to retain and improve the power and the timbre of their voices, and this lung-stretching has a great effect on their health. The second way is, of course, diet. Not 'dieting' but eating less than what is considered ordinary. Most people tend to get fat. Violent exercize has no effect in reducing weight. It is entirely a question of not assaulting the stomach in the astonishing manner which is regarded as normal and is more lethal, I think, than drinking or smoking.

I have not sung the praises of Rugby School for I am prejudiced against heterogeneous information masquerading as knowledge; but schools are natural growths, not really thought up or thought out, and serve many purposes. At the present time, controversy rages as to whether or not schools should be 'comprehensive'. I note that most people who advance angry views on this or that side have an axe to grind. It affects them personally. As it does not affect me at all I have no views worth mentioning. Only a question. One of the main things about the public schools is that good manners are inculcated (not taught in class). Good manners work out into good psychology. 'The trouble with him is that he is so ignorant', I have heard farm workers say of such and such a boss or foreman. They did not mean that the man lacked learning but that he lacked manners and did not know how to treat people; and good manners work out into good morals. For an (unconscious) grounding in this cultivation it would be worth going to any school. Why should not *all* schools promote this? What is the obstacle? If all schools did so, and also promoted cultivated speech, it would cease to matter much to which school any parent sent any boy.

2

The year 1918 came round but the war was not yet over. Most boys went straight to an OCB (Officer Cadet Battalion). This was an entirely class arrangement. You did a certain number of months at an OCB, achieved the status of 2nd Lieutenant, and actually went out to the Front as senior even to a Regimental Sergeant Major! For some reason which I cannot now fathom, and need not pursue, my name had been put down for admission into the Enniskillen Dragoons – the cavalry. Well abreast of the Crimean War, the military authorities supposed that there was still a place for the cavalry charge. Anyway, that summer I found myself quartered at Tidworth on Salisbury Plain as a trooper.

I had the sense at the age of eighteen to realize quite coolly that it was a good thing for me to be forced to rough it. I saw that it would give me a measuring rod in future to set against discomforts silly to complain about. I certainly roughed it here. We rose at 4.00 a.m., cleaned the stables, groomed the horses, harnessed them, and then rode out onto the Plain. While on parade, if one did something wrong, the sergeant major, a very violent man, struck the rider on his back with his whip and the horse on its head. As a stimulus to instruction this may have worked, for in the end we were taught how to jump without stirrups, without reins, and with a sword in one hand. This may sound difficult, and it was not easy, but the horses were on the whole so docile that it was possible. What I did not find possible for more than a few seconds was one part of sword drill when the sword had to be held out parallel with the ground – not as in 'present arms' when two hands are used and the rifle is perpendicular. The routine at this place was so exacting and exhausting that after the dinner-break when we had a quarter of an hour before the next parade, I lay down dressed in full equipment and fell asleep for exactly that length of time. Memories of those days are vivid and satisfactory to me; but far more so are the rides across Salisbury Plain in the early summer morning sunshine. I was on a horse, and a great prairie lay before me like the fabled West, and it was not only morning but the morning of the world.

When it soon became clear to the General Staff that no charge of a Light Brigade would win the war, I found myself transferred to the Inns of Court OTC at Berkhamsted in Hertfordshire, a Corps celebrated for its discipline.

I am inclined to think that one's experiences of truth, beauty, goodness, and that sort of thing, come to us in circumstances least designed to promote them. In this respect I have found nothing better than the musketry drill at the Inns of Court OTC. The whole approach was so completely unpoetical and unreligious that one was forced to think of those things. Thus, I am happy to remember the musketry drill under the furious and theatrical Instructor whose best declarations of faith were displayed in 'The Naming of Parts' and whose best gift to me was the command: 'Range, five hundred yards; *definite object*; six rounds rapid fire!' The definite object was a particularly beautiful beech tree which stood some 500 yards from the musketry grounds. There was a purity about that simple command which struck me more forcibly than would any sermon or lecture on aesthetics designed for my improvement. Here was the military approach to life summed up with masterly style in two words: a tree was simply a 'definite object' to be fired at. I think that my love of trees, resulting in a certain amount of knowledge concerning what a tree *is*, was born in me then.

I would go further. At no other period of my life have I experienced moments of quite such intense nature-love. During certain field days when we were 'advancing by short rushes' through the fields, when the whole purpose of every single thing we did was against life and against beauty and against the peace of the countryside, *then* the recognition of that beauty and especially of that peace became painfully strong in me. The assumption on all sides and inherent in every task that only bullets and bayonets composed the real and serious things of life, had the effect of making me sense a transcendent meaning in bees and butterflies.

I cannot say that bayonet drill itself, as it were, brought me much closer to God. It was not real enough. It was unreal to me in the same way as a butcher's shop is unreal unless I use my imagination, which I am careful not to do. The drill was intended to make me vicious, but it was so ugly and silly that it did not even make me virtuous.

I was vague enough in all conscience at this time, but I was sufficiently awake to note a certain irony concerning one essential point. You joined the army or you were conscripted into the army. That is to say you declared: here I am, ready to give up my life for the country – no less. Often enough, that gift of your life was taken and you were effaced from the surface of the earth for ever. But the moment you presented yourself for this purpose you were instantly regarded not only as a fool but as a particularly low kind of fool at whom it was proper to hurl every species of outraged abuse. As for pay, it was almost nothing, for it was considered that you should be content with the prospect of the wages of death.

It was the special task of certain men to abuse you and to look at you with such reproach in their eyes that you felt appalled by your defective character. These were the sergeants, the sergeant majors, and regimental sergeant majors. Much has been written about these men, and they have generally entered the field of literature or drama as comics. Anyone who has had experience of them – and I had a great deal – must acknowledge that they compose an interesting race, not entirely comic. At their best they are men truly born to command, and, by the spell of their superior characters and personalities, support and pillar a regiment (well represented, without exaggeration, in Tony Richardson's film, *Zulu*). Often enough they are born simply with the desire to *give orders*. I recall not long ago a man speaking frankly of himself in this respect. He declared that it was a heady joy for him, as sergeant, to be able to order a man to do something and make him 'jump to it'. It did not matter, he said, what the order was, or whether there was any sense in it, indeed he preferred it to be senseless. He particularly liked sending a soldier with a message: 'Here, Private X, take this note to the Quartermaster. Hurry up man! Jump to it! You haven't got all day!' The pleasure of being in a position to do this was irresistible, he admitted.

36

I had plenty of sergeant experience. What amazed, and subdued me, was their *anger* – I did not stop to reflect then, whether it was assumed or theatrical or hysterical or pathological. The expression of sudden horror they could display (when passing men lined up for inspection) on coming upon an imperfectly polished button or something, was taken for real, since the performance was so finished. I cannot conceive any actor doing better, just as I cannot think of any comic surpassing their swift patter – *they* needed no scriptwriter. Some, less gifted, sought no more than attention and were content to call a platoon to 'Attention!' as often as possible and then instantly shout 'As You Were!' There was one sergeant especially, a man chiefly composed of larynx and with no discernible features, who never varied his command, but always in one breath shouted furiously – 'SHUNASYOU-WERE!' and for a minute or so the platoon would be springing to attention then to at ease in obedience to a steady flow of shunasyouweres.

One man at Berkhamsted stood out from all the others, and was really a genius in this mode. He was the Regimental Sergeant Major. He was quite small, very dark, with a look in his black eyes that was not quite sane; his voice carried with it extraordinary vibrations and could be heard in distant counties. He walked in the midst of all like a king whose mood is sensed apprehensively by shuddering sycophants. When he appeared on Company Parade everyone from private to lieutenant became terrified. For it was certain that his presence would cause nervous mistakes, and then his rage and scorn would be petrifying. To this hour I recall the terrible moment when in a panic a Second Lieutenant made a false step. The RSM glared down at him affecting to be utterly astonished and pained beyond description at so monstrous a folly, and bawled out in his almost magical timbre: 'ARE YEW... BALMY TEW...!'

At Tidworth a great deal of exertion had been demanded, but it was at Berkhamsted that the full degree of my eighteen-year-old endurance was really called for – and the strength of your eighteen-year-old is something to marvel at later on. We were eight to a tent, and that truly was a test. I was surprised to find that there was virtually only one subject of conversation. It was not till *then* that someone explained the facts of life to me. It took me some years to get over the shock. (And I had been 'educated', surrounded by all sorts of elders teaching me things.)

Occasionally we took a route march and then struck tents for the night in some sequestered field. In those days there were few cars to speak of, few aeroplanes. When it was my turn to act as sentry, the hush, the silence that fell around me made a strong spiritual impact. The chirping of grasshoppers, the rumble of a distant train, added to the peace. On sentry duty, alone, after the notes of the Last Post had died away, amidst the stealthy listening earth, I was filled with 'unutterable thoughts', completely woolly, completely real, a ferment of intimation. Never since have I experienced quite such a surging of emotion as under the spell of that tranquillity.

I had one further move in my military training before the Armistice. This was from Berkhamsted to an Officer Cadet Battalion at Bushey in Hertfordshire. I expected the experience to be still more difficult and oppressive, but it was much less so, and the drilling was very mild in comparison with what I had been through. There it was easier to make lasting friends. One of them was a fair-haired man with high forehead and pronounced rear-head, a very English-gentleman face, voice, and manner, with a first-rate smile. We got talking and discovered a certain kinship in our approach to life. His name was Stephen Potter. We saw a good deal of each other in after years, but our happiest time was at Bushey. I say happy time, for in the common room in the evenings we sat together and – laughed. I do not understand why we laughed so much, but it went on for weeks and the muscles in my face ached painfully. We played a word-game involving atrocious juxtaposition of adjectives and nouns, and I remembered Potter saying, when I expressed the fear that we might run out of material, that by the time we had said 'mashed kodaks' many years would have passed. Amongst other things, we used a system of 'marking' each other's audacities or successes. But in saying that we laughed a great deal it may be thought by those aware of Stephen Potter's later reputation that he was a 'funny man', a humorist, even a comedian. Of course he was no more a funny man than myself or anyone else, even supposing that any man is 'a humorist' more than about twice a year.

The Bushey Golf Course was used for parades and military operations. When off duty we could go to the Club House and play billiards, a game I have always liked, for I used to play with my father at Kilmore. Past games make much of the stuff of memory for some of us, and those were memorable hours indeed; and it grieved me when years later, Potter, a good man fallen among the billiard-room habitués of the Savile Club, abandoned that noble game for snooker. After the war Bushey was again opened as a golf club and we went there to play when we could – which was not often. One afternoon, having made an arrangement to play I put it off, wanting to get on with my work. I never played there again. The course was sold and 'developed'. I didn't advance my work one inch that afternoon, and ever since have regretted not going with a keenness I seldom feel for a good thing or worthy deed not done. Stephen could always beat me at golf, and could talk about the golf championships with facility; but I had no difficulty in dealing with him at tennis; and I was, and still am, such a specialist concerning anything to do with Wimbledon, that he is obliged to refer to me for the anecdotes of the tennis world.

We have never lost touch though there can be long periods between meetings. We still at intervals give each other 'marks', and if either of us loses, say, a wallet with money in it, or a few quids' worth of National Insurance stamps, the other will instantly replace it. In this sort of thing we have never wavered, though our mutual affection has never really needed this kind of test.[3]

The cadets at the OCB varied so much in age that Gerald du Maurier was one of them. He had either volunteered or been conscripted into the Army, and it was a great thing for us when this man, the most celebrated actor of the day, took part in a sing-song and recited a poem. His immense charm was felt by everyone, including the sergeants and officers who showed him favour. This favouritism of du Maurier caused us annoyance. We, who had accomplished nothing in the world, who were complete nonentities, contrived to feel aggrieved because Gerald du Maurier received a little special consideration.

We were all obliged to take turns in commanding a platoon at drill. I used to dread this on a windy day, for my voice did not carry well in the open air. You must give orders while standing still, at attention, while the platoon marches about according to your words of command. If they don't hear you, you cannot run after them and say: 'Excuse me, would you mind about-turning.' On one windy day I shouted in vain the command to ABOUT TURN. They did not hear me, and disappeared over a rise out of sight... Still, at musketry I was a good shot; I was good at not losing my head or temper or getting in a panic, which helped a little. However, there was soon no occasion for me to be put to further tests, for the war came to an end and I was discharged as an Hon. Lieutenant of the Irish Guards.

I was still at Bushey on the Armistice Day, and I obtained leave to go up to London. So it happened that I witnessed an extraordinary scene. In the afternoon I came up from the Underground at Trafalgar Square. It was like coming up into some mad fair in progress. Peace had not been signed, only an armistice, but everyone seemed to sense without official confirmation that the war was over. All restraint was abandoned.

The Lions in the Square had practically disappeared: all but their heads had sunk beneath the crowd. Every person was shouting and waving. A thin lane in the roadway left room for some traffic which slowly moved along. The people were not in any of the vehicles, they were *on* them. The taxis had no one inside, but four or five men and women sat on bonnet and roof, and on the upper decks of the buses, which in those days were open, more people stood cheering and waving. Everyone seemed to have got hold of a flag.

The same thing could be witnessed in all the main streets, and not only did it go on all that day but for several subsequent days, and it was nearly a week before there was any real abatement of this frenzied and unfenced emotion. Any foreigner in London at the time must have been bewildered at so un-English a spectacle. Yet we know that it was not un-English. The English are not stolid, they are restrained, all passion unspent. But if the strain is too much then the restraint is likely to break down completely, as it did on this occasion.

It was natural that out of this first Armistice Day the idea of a Two Minutes' Silence on 11 November should emerge. Natural, that is, in England, and perhaps only possible in England; for in the staging of this kind of drama, and more elaborately at the Death or Coronation or Abdication of Kings, the English are unrivalled. Everything goes without a hitch since the people are to be counted on to obey the rules and observe the frame as in a theatre.

Since that first day I have witnessed many November Elevenths. I have made a point of spending them in London if possible, and have tried to be at Westminster Bridge or Trafalgar Square. Standing again in the Square I have seen the crowd, this time silent, this time still. Big Ben strikes eleven o'clock. Every vehicle stops, every noise ceases. In the extraordinary suspension a thousand pigeons that have been perching in wreaths round the Pillar or like leaves on the trees, take alarm and fly outward wheeling round and round, theirs the only movement, and the flapping of their wings the only sound over the phalanx of rooted men. I have always regarded these Minutes not only as theatre, but also as religion. For two minutes a great multitude is reverent. For two minutes all men aspire towards the best that is in them. For two minutes we are brothers. For two minutes we commit no evil. For two minutes there is perfect peace.

I have written this in the present tense. Yet it is past. It has been abandoned. It is no longer held on 11 November but on the relevant Sunday. Thus it has been destroyed. For some reason it 'has been thought best' to hold it on a Sunday. This supremely English action, has been ruled out without mandate from the people by anonymous authorities, who invariably thing the worst on all simple issues.

I have not the least doubt that plausible reasons have been advanced in support of their ruling – utilitarian or economic or simply convenience reasons. But no such grounds carry the smallest weight. The whole point of the thing was that these two great minutes during which *nothing* was done, outweighed in their value almost anything that could be done. The whole point was that at eleven o'clock (except when the day did happen to fall on a Sunday), when the work of the world was going full tilt, and the traffic roaring along, we had the will and the power and the religious sense to halt it all, to pause, to reflect, to be silent, to be utterly still, in the name of remembrance, in the hope of peace, and for the forgiveness of sin.

Every year now in November a ridiculous debate arises as to whether we should go on celebrating Armistice Day. Only people who have lost all sense of the unreality of the present situation could conduct such a futile controversy. For Armistice Day has already ceased to be celebrated, it has been far worse than totally abandoned. Instead of, on 11 November, two minutes' dramatic silence in the working day and roaring streets, held simply as a prayer for peace and a decent salute to the dead, there is held, on the adjacent Sunday, a *two hours* 'Service' in the Albert Hall, not one minute of which serves any person or any purpose.

3

It was now possible for my brother and me to go to a university. We took the Entrance Examination to Trinity College Dublin, and passed it. Then my father decided that he could send us to Oxford and Cambridge. I went for Oxford, and got into Balliol. I was able to achieve this for two reasons: one was due to the fact that I had passed into Trinity, and the other that the Entrance Examination to Balliol at that time was easier than normal on account of certain concessions granted to students who had been involved in the 1914-18 war, and I counted as one of these. Evidently I dealt adequately with certain papers, while weakness in Latin was not fatal at that time.

I remember Neville Talbot[4], the padre of Balliol when I was there, once saying in Chapel that in some far flung part of the Empire, flung so far that I did not know of it, someone in the region on being asked if he had heard of Oxford replied, No, he had not heard of Oxford, but he had heard of Balliol. Those people who are pained at the fact that certain famous schools are more sought after than others, must find it hard to tolerate the thought of Oxford and Cambridge where even some of the colleges like Magdalen, Christ Church (so grand that you just called it the House), and Balliol are as well known as the University itself. But perhaps they forgive their existence as they are obliged to forgive other growths of the earth for being more beautiful or enduring than those around them. I do not suppose that more is to be gained by undergraduates in a general way at the ancient universities than at the others, but the beauty of buildings and gardens, the aura of memory and tradition that belong to Oxford and Cambridge, will always confer an unfair advantage and privilege upon those who go there.

Balliol is primarily a scholar's paradise where men take Firsts in Greats and are subsequently found at the Treasury and such like. Swinburne, whose portrait hangs in Hall, looks out of place among the elaborately robed worthies beside him. But there was Hilaire Belloc, as great a lyric poet as he was a scholar, and my rooms, overlooking the Martyr's Memorial, had once been inhabited by him – a stimulating if daunting thought. I was daunted too by the scholarship around me but not excessively so, for while I cherish a respect amounting to veneration for the genuine scholar, the man whose art is scholarship, the best example in my time being Gilbert Murray, I was not even then much overawed by the others with their brand of 'learning'. On a certain occasion the members of the College were asked to enter a literary competition and write an essay on Pathos. Many learned papers were sent in; the derivation from the Greek was pointed out; it was divided into different kinds and placed under certain heads, and so on. That sort of approach was beyond me, so I addressed myself to simple particulars and gave instances suggesting the true nature of Pathos, such as in the upheaval of a great revolution, a child found crying because in the haste to get away she had *lost her doll*. This earned me the prize, and I enjoyed a momentary feeling of self-satisfaction. But though I could do this I could not do Latin and I was truly overawed by the ease with which my fellow undergraduates dealt with it; and there was a solid practical reason which made my inadequacy disastrous.

Before being allowed to take an Honours Course and finally sit for a Degree it was necessary to pass an elaborate preliminary examination called History Previous. This included a study of economics through textbooks presenting the thing like a kind of geometry and as far removed from reality or true leaning as was the hateful History of the Papacy with which I was also required to stuff myself. Still, I felt I could deal with this through sheer hard grind. But the requirements of History Previous were such that even if you passed the papers in history and economics, you did not get through unless you also passed in *Latin Unseen*. And if you did not pass the exam you could not carry on into the Honours Course of your choice.

This presented me with a very serious problem. What was I to do? My brother and I had been grounded in Latin in such a way at our prep-school, Aravon, that we never rose from the ground. Neither of us ever recovered from this bad start. What could I do now before being presented with an advanced paper in Latin Unseen? It was clear to me that I could do nothing whatsoever. And I did nothing. I never allowed my tutor to realize my predicament, and when it was necessary to submit specimens of Latin Unseen to him I got someone else to do them for me and then handed them in as my own.

This did nothing to solve the fearful problem which would arise when I went into the examination hall. I was fairly worn out by the time the crucial days arrived. The first day was devoted to history and the second to economics, and I did my best to parrot-out senseless questions on the history of the Papacy, and still more senseless ones on textbook economics. On the first day I carefully noted who was sitting at the desk in front of me, on each side, and behind. I knew three of them slightly. There was nothing for it but to ask one of them to drop his Latin Unseen paper on the floor so that I might pick it up, rib from it, and then drop it on the floor again. The first man that I asked turned down the idea with moral indignation. I tried the next who refused on the ground that it might get him into trouble. So passed the first day. After the exam on history I tried the third man and was turned down again. I tried in vain to find the fourth man who was at Oriel, I think, and whose name I did not know. So passed the second day. This was becoming serious. A great deal was at stake, for if I failed in History Previous I would not be able to go on and work for my Degree, and would have wasted my father's money. As we entered the Hall on this last day I saw the fourth man whose desk was in front of mine. 'Could you possibly let me see your Latin Unseen paper?' I asked. 'Righto,' he said without batting an eyelid. In due course he dropped it on the floor. We were in the middle of the room – not too near the Don sitting on the dais. I let it lie there for a bit, feverishly hoping that none of the others around saw him drop it. At last I stooped and picked it up. At that moment the Don looked straight in my direction. But he did not realize that I was picking up someone else's sheet. I took down the sense, altered the words sufficiently, and then replaced his paper on the floor, which presently was casually picked up by its owner. All was well. I passed the examination. I have always regarded this act of a complete stranger as the kindest ever done me, and my own action as the most sensible.

I was now free to take the Honours Course. I chose English Language and Literature and attended the Lectures (from which strictly *nothing* was gained). The course opened the geography of the subject well, giving one a clear continuity of knowledge of the literature from Chaucer onwards, but an honest attitude was not encouraged, and one was supposed, for example, to admire the Elizabethan dramatists. But the really extraordinary thing was

43

that the syllabus required the study of philology and early texts in Old English and Middle English. No one except rare persons born with a talent for philology and the translation of such texts could gain anything from this. It was a maddening and monstrous imposition, for had the time and energy wasted upon this been given to a sound working knowledge of at least the highlights of European Literature, the gain would have been enormous.

It is sometimes held that the best value to be derived from a University is the discussions between groups of friends going on into the small hours. For myself I did not find this to be so, especially when the discussion turned upon the Arts; for even at that early age I could not help feeling that to talk about and hold 'strong views' on Art without practising Art was simply hot air, and I could not bear it. I favoured the hot air of the Union Society where at least one could practise public speaking. That was the chief gain I derived from Oxford.

The Oxford Union is a delightful institution for those involved. It provides the best audience conceivable, the easiest that any speaker could ever face. Everyone is young, and the high spirits prevail belonging to people not yet weighed down by responsibilities or debts; everyone is ready to applaud a joke or an epigram; in fact everyone is alive. The supporters of the Motion sit to one side of the Treasury Box, the opposition on the other side, the undecided forming the body of the hall. The audience has come to be entertained or excited and will give a rousing reception to a good speaker – an atmosphere in emphatic contrast with what the same speakers find when faced with audiences after they have gone down from the university.

It is not very easy to get your foot in as a recognized speaker and eventually qualify for election to the four official posts, Secretary, Jun. Librarian, Jun. Treasurer, and President. The first thing is to 'catch the President's eye' when you wish to speak after the definite speakers 'on the paper' have finished. When those speakers have done there is a general exodus, members voting for or against the Motion as they leave. A sprinkling of the audience remains, chiefly composed of those who hope to catch the President's eye and speak. At this stage when you have caught his eye, your audience is not very attentive, but that is what you must work with if you wish to get on. I was ready to wait my chance until at last I would be called upon. This was very wearisome, and I prepared many little speeches which had to be thrown away before at last I was given my chance. Leslie Hore-Belisha was President, and he took a poor view of my effort, reporting in *The Isis* that 'in opposing the Motion, Mr J S Collis performed a small act on the floor of the House.' This did not do me much good, and I think it was not for some time that a President put me 'on the paper' to debate as one of the four official speakers. The subject was 'Imperial Preference'. I did not know what Imperial Preference meant, but I spoke on it. It was not a good effort, and the Balliol scholar, F R Althaus, told me afterwards that I used my hands 'as if catching invisible balls', a remark which was made with such good nature that I benefited by it. More time elapsed before I got on the paper again, through the aid of Beverley Nichols.

The level of the best speakers at this time was very high. Being just after the First World War many undergraduates were well into their twenties in 1920. Hore-Belisha was one of these. He was the best undergraduate speaker I have heard. He possessed that touch of magic that belongs to the true orator. A small dark man with rather thick lips set in the perpetual likeness of a smile, he possessed a beautiful voice, and was in command of a phraseology which insured complete attention whenever he spoke. When he went down from Oxford and into politics I thought that if he played his cards right he must some day become Prime Minister. He did become Minister of Transport, erecting the Belisha beacons which still memorialize his name, and subsequently Minister of War in 1939. Then suddenly he made errors and crashed, his career fell in ruins before him, and he passed completely from the stage.

Beverley Nichols also became President, and in my view was only second to Hore-Belisha in ability to command and delight the Union. A slight, neat figure with a somewhat round face, his speech flowed without a hitch from beginning to end in perfectly governed sentences containing a touch of wit and a substance of good sense. There was nothing weighty or especially arresting but the whole performance – the result of hard work in preparation – was graceful to a degree unlikely to be surpassed at the Union. He was not a rich man's son amusing himself, and it was vital to him to succeed and make use of his success. The guest whom he chose to have for his term of office was Horatio Bottomley, financial and press tycoon, with a reputation for oratory, shadiness, mendacity, and unexampled hypocrisy. There was an unusually crowded house, but at the sight of Bottomley coming into the hall with the President and the three other Officers (for that was the procedure), the poet Robert Nichols, who was sitting next to me, cried out to those around him – 'Bumley! good God – Bumley! I couldn't listen to Bumley beefing!', and striking an attitude he strode from the chamber. The speech was in no way distinguished, and he appeared to be nervous of his undergraduate audience. Next morning Beverley Nichols accompanied him to the station with a group of undergraduates whom he persuaded to be photographed waving Bottomley goodbye.

Though most of the debates were political it was often possible for non-political animals to become President on style alone. The President who succeeded Hore-Belisha was T W Earp who won his popularity by a single remark in a debate on the Peace Conference. Earp, who later on became famous as an art critic and was the subject of one of Augustus John's finest portraits, was then a frail figure with a great flop of hair over one eye, a receding chin, an engaging lisp, a soft voice, and a delivery totally unfitted for political argument. He had published a small volume of poems called, I think, *Dressing-gowns and Glue*. At this Debate he was dealing with the angry walkout of the Italian delegate, Signor Orlando, who had hoped to produce a crisis. 'The situation at the Conference', said Earp, 'at this stage may best be described in the words of my fellow bard, Shakespeare: "Alarums without. Exit Orlando, bloody."' This little thing was so well produced that it brought him office at the Union.

The best example of Oxford Unionism at its most sophisticated was Philip Guedalla whom I once heard when he came as a Guest. My brother Maurice had known him at Rugby, a small white-faced boy, who had coolly decided that he could overcome his enemies by the careful preparation of witty remarks at their expense; and in the end was widely admired and feared for the devastating hits by which he brought down philistines and bullies. When he came to the Union it was easy for him to bring down the House. He was a dark electric man who leant over the Treasury Box; his style of delivery was staccato, his elocution sharp as a knife, his jaw thrust forward menacingly when about to utter *le mot juste* or *injuste*. Even when he simply referred to 'the sinister reflections of the Honourable Gentleman from Christ Church' his articulation of the word 'sinister' made it sound like an epigram.

Indeed, the Union always gave a great chance to literary men who knew how to use it. G K Chesterton came to speak on an occasion when the Motion was on the subject of Marriage and Divorce. Chesterton was tall as well as stout, and solid rather than fat; there was nothing flabby about his body any more than his mind. It used to be the fashion to say that he wrote paradoxically for fun, but it is obvious that paradoxes came to him as naturally as leaves to a tree; he had but to look at things with his great clear mind to see that most things are upside-down. He was not a good speaker for his voice was poor and he did not bring to the spoken word the dazzling virtuosity he attained on paper. However, on the occasion of his visit to the Union a perfect Chestertonism naturally presented itself. He looked towards the future: 'I now come to that institution which is still considered the inseparable preliminary to divorce – I mean marriage. Soon it will be part of everyone's education to have been married and divorced. Another Registry

Office and Divorce Court will be built side by side, so that you can go from one to the other under cover. And degrees will be awarded, BA and MA – standing for Bachelor Again, and for Married Again.' As the main purpose of the Union was to provide opportunities to be clever or behold cleverness in others, this perfect epigram, perfectly approached and timed, met with a roar of delight, and was as certain to do so, as at a general audience outside the University it would have been certain to fail.

There was little overlapping between the Union and the Oxford University Dramatic Society, for as a rule actors are not at ease on their own. When in my childhood I first heard a man say 'I have always wanted to act' I vaguely wondered in what direction his activity would take him, whether as an engine driver or adventurer or soldier. Later of course I realized that he did not wish to pursue any of these professions but to imitate persons in professions; he wanted, not to be the Duke of Wellington but to pretend to be the Duke of Wellington, and actually called this work The Profession – as an indication that it stood above all others. I hasten to add that there is some sense in this claim, for the genuine actor becomes one, in the first place because he is so interested in other people, tries to understand them by putting himself in their place, and is prepared to surrender his own self to illuminate the selves of others – and this is great work for humanity. One OUDS man did come across to the Union in my time, Ramage, who played opposite the guest, Kathleen Nesbitt, in *Romeo and Juliet*, and eventually married her. He had a fine figure, and stood very erect at the Treasury Box, delivering his lines loud and clear. He had nothing to say, but I remember so well how once having started his speech with some irrelevancies he simply said, '*That is my preamble.*' It was so well done that they made him President. Charles Morgan was President of the OUDS but also spoke at the Union. He would pour out torrents of words with great earnestness, but with little skill and no wit – surprising, perhaps, in the novelist who was to produce at least one classic novel, *The Fountain*. The one actor of rare quality at this time did not come to the Union, namely, Maurice Colbourne. He was my ideal of a really beautiful young man. He took the part of Nelson in *The Dynasts*, and I am persuaded that this production is likely to remain the best ever staged, and Colbourne's performance not easy to surpass. The death scene was unforgettable by virtue of the cadence with which he uttered the words: '*Bear me along good comrades, for I am only one of many darkened here today.*'

I persevered at the Union and at last began to make progress. I advanced matters by calling upon Beverley Nichols, then living in Beaumont Street, who was President to ask if I might speak on an Irish Question debate. He said he would arrange for this if the occasion arose. It did arise, and he kept

47

his word, and I have always been grateful to him for this. I had been improving rapidly at this time, and now began to enter upon a series of triumphs. I had once heard it said by a celebrated man that in relation to any speech no matter what the occasion, that to make even a *small effect* one requires to make a *great effort*. I understand this, and I was absolutely determined to excel. I prepared my speeches for a fortnight and was always word perfect on the night, though I was careful to have a few notes in hand. I did not write my speeches beforehand – but I wrote them afterwards! I have generally thrown away anything in the nature of early literary efforts. Yet these speeches, which were never thought of as literary efforts or with the faintest idea of publication, I wrote down after the event, and kept. I have just looked at them for the first time after forty-eight years. I evidently wrote them down out of exhilaration, and I included in the text brackets for (laughter) or (laughter and applause) or (shouts). They were written – seven of them – between 1920-22. It appears that in 1927 I wrote a sort of Preface which I attached to the little bundle. It is curious to me coming upon it now, with its very immature handwriting, and I will quote a few sentences since some of the facts are sufficiently surprising.

'Here are seven speeches which I chose to keep a record of out of the many that I made. It is curious turning to these relics now in 1927. My career was certainly a great one. I started not knowing how to speak, and was for a long time unable to catch the President's eye. But I stuck to my guns through any amount of waiting and boredom and disappointment and incalculable irritation, till finally I got "on the paper". Then I made a bad speech, made worse by a series of futile and ugly gestures. That put me back a lot and it was with difficulty that I got on the paper again, but eventually managed it through Beverley Nichols sticking to his word. That gave me my first speech on the Irish Situation – a good one and a great success. Then another followed, with W B Yeats, and was another great success. Later I spoke again on Ireland, this time with Sir John Simon who was so impressed that he invited me to his house at Cadogan Square and urged me to join the Liberal Party. I was elected to the office of Junior Treasurer with a big majority. My speeches on Ireland were in fact so sensational that *The Morning Post* (which sometimes reported the Union) declared that I was the best speaker ever heard at the Union. There followed more successes including a visit to the Cambridge Union, and a debate against a team from America – which led to an invitation to be one of the Oxford representatives in a tour of American universities, though unfortunately I was unable to go. But it seems that I then made some poor speeches and suffered a loss of popularity. I stood for President against a man called Carson who had caught the fancy of the House, though I could only see in him an agreeable mediocrity. At committee we arranged that the Motion should be "That in the Opinion of this House the Principles of the Conservative Party are of Paramount Importance to the Welfare of the Country". With great difficulty and determination I stuck to my guns to speak second and oppose the Motion. I decided to pull myself together and wipe my boots on Carson that night. I made a very great effort and completely succeeded. His speech failed to go down well. By real guts I took hold of the House as never before. It was the hour of my life. I gloated over my peroration afterwards for weeks. A crack of applause at every fresh sentence, louder and louder as my accusations climbed. A bell had to be rung at length to stop the applause when I had sat down. A thrill runs down my neck when I now recall that night. Friends and enemies alike piled congratulations on me. The old servants said they had never witnessed an evening like that before. Lord Middleton, who was our Guest Speaker, said he had heard nothing better since Curzon and Gladstone. It was a triumph far greater than I had ever hoped to achieve at Oxford or anywhere, and I had completely floored my opponent, Carson. But I was not elected President: he was. I found, and find, it difficult to explain this. I can only suppose that people considered that though entertaining I was too immoderate to be voted for as a safe President. While standing in front of the board upon which the result of the poll was pinned, I found the Don, Dr A J Carlyle (whose rugged features bore a striking resemblance to Thomas Carlyle), who often frequented the debates, standing beside me. "The donkeys! The donkeys!" he exclaimed. And I drew a good deal of comfort from that spontaneous exclamation.'

Such was my view in 1927. Looking into the speeches now I find them terribly irritating in their shallowness, general undergraduateness, and what I can only call insincere sincerity. But I see that I had style which though imitative and often florid was on a high level of phraseology when not intolerable. Moreover I was able to weave into the speeches quite effectively references to things said by the speaker who had preceded me, and if interrupted could deal with the interruption at once. Thus if someone from the floor of the House shouted Question! I would instantly pause in my elaborate period, turn towards the interrupter and say something like,

'The Honourable Gentleman cries Question. It would be more appropriate if he had called Shame! But I am unwilling to insult the Hon. Gentleman by suggesting that he is acquainted with the facts.' There would be laughter and applause at this, not because what I had said was good but because instead of ignoring the heckler and going on I had at once stopped and made a quick reply – and in a manner which made it appear to be witty. And it was not long before I had learnt to pull off a thing simply by good timing. My friend, Alan Collingridge, seems to have remembered three such things even after nearly fifty years, and recently he reminded me of them. The first ran like this: 'But supposing the troops were withdrawn, what would happen in Ireland? Mr President, I know that the Irish are fools.' (Laughter. A pause.) 'But, Sir, if I may use a colloquialism, they are not damned fools.' (Louder laughter, and applause, the audience supposing this to be the climax. Another pause.) Then 'like the English.' (Explosion of laughter and applause.) Of course so slight a thing would not go down outside the Union, but the Society was, or is, like that. Again, on another occasion I said: 'we are often told that power corrupts men, and that absolute power corrupts them absolutely.' (Pause.) 'But Sir, a *very little* power', (a longer pause), 'absolutely corrupts – women.' I got a big hand for this. It had an element of truth in it not offensive to the young. Outside the Union it would have been received with silence. Thirdly, remembered by Collingridge but quite forgotten by me, a member had called out from the floor of the House: 'Sir, is the Union to become a Colliseum!?' Now, it was important that I should answer this and get in some sort of a crack in return. I paused and looked across. 'No,' I said, 'it is only an unfortunate Collision.' This was received well.

As to that remarkable peroration referred to in that 'Preface' of mine, I have been able to find it. Apparently what I did was to say that I would now accuse the Conservative Party of seven things. After I had come up with four the House began to enter into the spirit of the thing, wondering what was coming next. My last three Accusations were of Anarchy, then of Fanaticism, and finally of Bolshevism – this achieved a sensation. It strikes me that I certainly must have shaped my speech with a good deal of skill and thoroughly secured the attention of the House to have been able to get away with so histrionic a climax.

It was while I was Junior Treasurer that W B Yeats came to speak at the Union. At this time he was living at Oxford with rooms in the Broad across the road from the Master of Balliol's house. As Jun. Treasurer I called on him to ask if he would speak at a debate on Ireland. I had never seen him before, and I knocked at the door nervously. He greeted me with a raised right arm not unlike the Heil Hitler salute. His vastly poetical appearance and grand manner so alarmed me that I feared I would fail in my mission, but he accepted my invitation to speak, and the debate was held.

It was a memorable evening. Poets are seldom even tolerable speakers. John Masefield was an exception. So was Yeats: he could dominate an audience. He had the mobile nostrils of the dramatic orator, and the famous handsome face and noble carriage. The Motion was 'That this House would welcome complete Self-Government in Ireland and condemns Reprisals.' I propose the Motion. After it had been opposed Yeats rose to second the proposal. Now, it is the custom of the Union, modelled on the House of Commons, for the speaker to stand beside the Treasury Box and remain there until he resumes his seat. Yeats did not conform. Breaking into passionate invective the moment he rose to his feet, he left the Treasury Box and roamed up and down the aisle shaking his fist at the audience. It was a strange scene, long remembered in the annals of the Union. There were roars and counter-roars from each side of the House and the debate became almost out of hand, Yeats raising his voice above the clamour in an ever-increasing passion of denunciation as he walked up and down. It was exciting, but some people thought that Yeats was not very convincing, for while it was a rousing occasion it was far from clear exactly what the poet was saying.

Sir John Simon who also came and spoke on Ireland was very effective. Later in his career he fell into disrepute as Foreign Secretary. But it was easy to fall under his spell in those days, for he was so handsome and had so much style and charm, while no man was ever more expert at the phrase 'I am free to say' – whatever he had chosen to say. His great legal abilities may have told against his popularity. In the Courts his smooth and compelling manner of saying to a defendant, 'Now, Mr — tell the gentlemen of the jury…' was wonderful to hear, simple as the words are on paper. I think I spoke with him twice on the Irish question. When touring the country in the cause of Ireland – the cause was close to his heart, for his wife was Irish – I heard to my amazement through her that he used chunks of my speech *verbatim*. If this was true I am encouraged to think that even I helped a fraction in the introduction of the Treaty which at last brought the strife between England and Ireland to an end.

In those days we had guests only once a term, and this rarity of their appearance (there being neither Radio nor TV) enhanced our interest and attention. Asquith came, a solid figure, remarkably composed, his time implying a veracity denied to others, and speaking with weight and authority without flights in that strange old-time Parliamentary Manner which tends to remove the subject from the realm of everyday reality without bringing it into the realm of art. But he did not much enjoy this particular visit. A speaker called Wharton, a dusky, dynamic young man with a decided touch of magic about him, who was 'on the paper' did not say the usual polite things about the Guest of the evening but made some trenchant criticisms before an astonished House. I was at a party given by Gilbert Murray on Boar's Hill the next day, and discovered that Asquith was a human being, as liable to be upset as anyone else. Hitherto I had regarded these Figures as huge political animals roaming at large through their political jungle with magnificent gait and posture, impervious to anything an undergraduate might say. I was introduced to Asquith at this party, and he said to me to my great surprise, 'That young man, Wharton, has all the qualifications for getting on – ignorance and impudence.' Always willing to fall in with the mood of a man with a grievance, I expect, and I hope, that I said in reply something derogatory of Wharton.

Churchill, Lloyd George, and Lord Birkenhead also visited the Union at this time. It was to be twenty years before Churchill would come into his own and be so confident of his touch that after a London air raid he could refer to 'that bad man over there' with as sure an aim at the hearts of the people as a folk singer. I remember him then chiefly as the politician beating up against the times. But I was very struck by the fact that though so colossally the politician he could put it by for a little while and become the poet: one evening he spoke to a group of undergraduates on the Sahara Desert, picturing how the time could come when by virtue of tree planting 'the scorched earth and barren skies would all be changed, the trees as fountains spraying the heavens that in reply would call forth clouds to pour their riches down and make the waste a garden.'

As we know, Churchill made a literary assault as a speaker, with imperishable success. Lloyd George had little literary power, but he could in his day give the lyric lift which goes with real oratory, and which is so rare, and was seldom, if ever, achieved by Churchill. Lloyd George could make a passage pertain to the condition of song. There is an aria of his which runs something like this: 'There is a bird called Hylyth.' (A Welsh word which I can neither spell nor pronounce.) 'It sings in the morning and it sings in the night; it sings in joy, it sings in sorrow; it sings in the sunshine, it sings in the storm; it sings in the summer, it sings in winter; it sings in peace, shall it not sing in war?' The delivery of this was unashamedly musical and the stress laid upon certain words brought the performance into the region of opera.

Yet of all who came to speak at the union (or at some Club dinner) it is Lord Birkenhead who shines out the most brightly in my mind – his black hair, his swarthy countenance, his great brown eyes, his fruity liquid voice.

He had a facility for extempore speech which may have been surpassed by others but can scarcely ever have been combined with a personality so burdened with talent. It was *how* he said things which made the effect. Referring to some Peer who had spoken about the East End he said, 'I do not know where the Noble Lord is accustomed to perambulate in the evenings...', words which would have been ineffective if spoken by another sounded from him sinister, humorous, and deflating. No one could pronounce the words The Noble Lord with more devastating derogation, and the ease with which he could be rude in this polite mode was one of the delights of his audience, while none who heard it will ever forget his deplorable attack on Lord Carson in relation to the Irish Question 'the solution proposed by the Noble Lord would sound immature on the lips of an hysterical schoolgirl.'

Times change. Today the Union seems to be much the same, but the publicity given to it by TV has some bad effects, and we see speakers *reading* their speeches, which is a really fatal tendency. But there are pleasant changes. Young men do not tend to be feminists, and it was not till some time in the Sixties that Oxford undergraduates allowed women into the Union to attend debates and speak, and not until 1967 that one became President. This is a real step forward. It would be ideal if we could have as many women in public life as men. For that is where the intelligent woman really shines. I would say that the two main characteristics of women are that they are more human than men, and more sensible – good qualities, even if that humanness has its virulent side, and if that sensibleness makes them tend to despise man's sacred sense of humour (too often displayed in senseless guffaws). Anyway, I would rather appear in Court before a woman magistrate (such as Barbara Wooton, say) than a man, and rather listen to an intelligent woman on politics than a man – I repeat intelligent for I am not here concerned with the few millions of hen-brains whose stupidity is more trying than the male variety. But it would be without question a gain if we could get more women into all departments of public life. Thus a great deal more talent would be drawn upon. In saying this I do not wish to add to the current illusion that the enfranchisement of women will mean the appearance of women geniuses in all directions. The hoary old argument is always produced when this question comes up that women have not been able to develop genius on account of being held back and chained down by house and children. But when genius in women is present it succeeds or fails exactly as genius in men succeeds or fails, no matter what the obstacles, even thriving on resistance and difficulties. There are two great arts, though not creatively so exacting as the others, in which women are as plentiful and

53

shine quite as brightly as men – the art of acting and the art of singing. Nothing has held them back there, and the initial difficulties of getting on are more severe, not less, than writing, painting, or composing music. If there is never to be a woman Shakespeare, a woman Leonardo da Vinci, a woman Beethoven, or a woman Newton, it will be because the psycho-physical energy required is not present in the female engine: it is not really sense to expect a counterpart of a Bernard Shaw or a Charles Dickens in female form. In future there will be far more women of talent to be seen in every direction; talent not genius. We need never bother about genius finding a way, but talent needs help and can be impeded by resistance. When the female source is fully drawn upon it will be interesting to see the results. Certainly a woman President of the Union is an encouraging sign of the times.

At the same time we might ask: Is such a thing as a woman orator possible? With men it is the rarest of the arts, calling as it does for an unusual combination of inspiration and histrionics, both relying upon an exceptional larynx. Women can always be good speakers (such as Lady Violet Bonham-Carter), but while a woman's voice in singing can be one of the world's marvels raising us from the clods and the dust, it is not so well suited to the hustings, hardly capable of giving an oratorical rise. Yet in art there are no rules, no absolutes, and I have witnessed at least one exception to this. I twice heard Annie Besant speak. I had read about how she had been 'one of the greatest orators of the age', and one day in the twenties she was billed to speak at the Albert Hall, and I went to the meeting. She was an impressive figure, but too old now, it seemed, for this sort of thing. For some time her speech was ordinary, even ponderous and redundant. Suddenly she changed. She 'took off', as it were: she lifted up her voice so that it filled the enormous hall. She used a simple rhetorical construction '...the domination and exploitation of the poor by the rich – that is THE LAW OF THE JUNGLE! The robbing and the maiming of the weak by the strong – that is THE LAW OF THE JUNGLE!...' When she uttered these sentences her voice discovered a great volume, such as we do not associate with an ordinary or even extraordinary woman, and she did not just say LAW or JUNGLE in a normal way, she floated upon the words, especially upon the last syllable of JUNGLE in a manner which I cannot render phonetically. Instantly the audience was lifted and spellbound in the strict sense of the words. I have never experienced anything like it except when once again I heard her, this time in the Wigmore Hall. The subject was India. Once more there was nothing special about her speech at first, nothing arresting. And once again she suddenly took off and climbed up and brought us with her. She cried out loudly, her great voice sweeping across the hall like a wave, 'You have helped Garibaldi; you have helped Mazzini; now you must help the people of INDIA!' She made her voice float and rise upon Garibaldi and upon Mazzini and especially upon the first syllable of INDia, summoning up a spiritual power cast forward upon us in such a way that I wondered whether in her prime she may not have been one of the greatest orators who ever lived.

Thus, what I got most out of Oxford was my connection with the Union. I was also active at the Oxford Labour Club which was formed at this time, and in fact I became President of it, and discovered in myself a capacity during Committee for getting through the Agenda without waste of time, simply going on the assumption that it was never necessary to let time be frittered away upon piffling points on the periphery of business such as are always brought forward by the ditherers in every club – and I remember winning approval for this. It was a full and happy life I had then, not least because of the friends I made. Malcolm MacDonald was Secretary of the Club when I was President. He concealed his abilities with a lack of pretentiousness I have seldom encountered. Later he was to assume very responsible appointments in the Commonwealth without caring whether he got them or not: 'I would rather watch the ducks in St James's Park', he once said to me. And there was something convincing in the loyalty he always extended towards his father, 'whom, after all, I do know a bit better than most people', he said. Kenneth Lindsay was also a President of the Labour Club as well as of the Union. When he went down he began in Parliament as a Labour member, but later became an Independent – for even a no-party man must have a label. He had an open mind and a capacity to *listen* without apparent desire to contradict an idea in opposition to his own, which I have never found elsewhere among politicians, and it did him no good, Apart from his work for the Admiralty and Education, he brought a largeness of spirit into any gathering that amounted to an extra dimension.

In spite of the fact that I moved amongst politicians so much at this time, I never had the least desire to enter politics. Sir John Simon used to invite me to his place at Cadogan Square evidently regarding me as a likely recruit for the Liberal Party. But such an idea never crossed my mind.

1 See 'The New Alchemy' in my *Paths of Light*.
2 In a piece called 'The Plant, or Apostrophe to an Urban Gentleman' in my *Down to Earth*, I traced in two pages the whole history of a plant from seed to withered flower when a new seed is dropped. I flatter myself that it runs well, for no one ever notices that it is only *one* sentence.
3 Written before his death, see p. 106.
4 A very tall, well-built man. 'Hi, Mister', a cockney boy, impressed by his great height, called out to him: 'Hi, Mister! Would you mind handing us down the moon. It don't matter about the stars.'

THIRD MOVEMENT...

... SEARCHING

Ever since I grew up I have always felt myself bound upon a course determined less by outer circumstance than by inner impulse which I have blindly followed.

It seems that my religious impulse was very strong. In obedience to it, when I went down from Oxford I entered a theological college with the intention of becoming ordained! I have put that exclamation mark because it is such a strange fact to me and so seemingly out of character that even as I set it down here I can scarcely believe it. I do not suppose my impulse was pure. I had no desire to be a writer: I did not much fancy myself yet in that line. But I hankered after oratory. I pictured myself becoming a great preacher, and no doubt in an earlier age than ours that is what I would have become. Pure or impure, my religious impulse was strong enough to induce me to enter that theological college in 1923.

I had no real convictions, but I was unaware of this. I soon became aware of it at the college where there was a great deal of theological instruction, and a great deal of prayer. It then dawned upon me that you cannot half-believe, or a quarter-believe articles of faith, let alone thirty-nine of them. Every afternoon I took a motor bicycle to a certain place in the countryside. There I thought the matter out. It was more in the way of an experience than a cogitation. The more I looked at Nature the less I needed Theology. The more I loved the fields and skies the less I liked Doctrine. It was scarcely more complicated than that. Many years have passed since then, but I still recall the intensity of those feelings when I got off my motor bicycle there, the response to Nature that can best be described as ecstasy. It was Wordsworthian, though lacking in any complete mystic experience. Yet it was so clear a vision of Glory that I could no longer approach the matter from a theological angle. At the conclusion of my first term at the College I never returned to it.

Evidently I needed to take this concentrate of doctrine so as to learn that I could best do without it. It was to Nature that I turned for intimations of Truth. I cannot say exactly when this became a conscious response. One hardly knows these things. Even Wordsworth, whose sub-title to *The Prelude* is 'Growth of a Poet's Mind', made no attempt to pin it down. 'Who shall parcel out His intellect by geometric rules, Split the province into round and square?' he asked when telling how there came a time when at length Nature 'was sought for her own sake'. And he adds, 'Who knows the individual hour in which His habits were first sown, even as a seed? Who shall point as with a Wand and say – "This portion of the river of my mind Came from yon fountain"?' I am sure that seeds were sown in me by the influence of the Wicklow Mountains, while unaware; and a non-theological approach to religion was growing in me already while I was at Rugby. One of the things which schools often accomplish for a boy is the presence of one master who inspires him and helps to shape his mind and soul, a permanent influence. The boy gravitates to this man, the whole thing irrespective of lessons or exams or school knowledge. The influence is so great as to liberate the boy and clarify his advance in the way he should go.

I was particularly fortunate in this respect. I received special tuition for several terms from the poet, Norman Gale, ostensibly to learn Geek. He was not a master, but he lived at Rugby and gave some private tutorials. He seemed to me a wonderful man. This view of him was not peculiar to me, prone as I am to hero-worship. Everyone who came in contact with him was affected in much the same way. He was finely built, very handsome – a photograph of him in his youth is Adonis-like. I have never seen a man with larger eyes, or more gentle ones; his voice was deep but very soft. He had been a great cricketer in the Nineties and had made a name for his *Cricket Songs*. I was not interested in them, but in his small volume called *Country Lyrics*. It had been well received and Oscar Wilde had wanted to meet him (apparently he had not wished to meet Wilde.) Those lyrics meant a great deal to me for a number of years, and the little volume is still a precious possession. But the lyrics have not been included in many of the anthologies. His virtuosity and command over metre and rhyme were outstanding, but he allowed sentimentality to undermine nearly all of them. At that time I was naturally entirely uncritical. I liked some more than others but I read them all eagerly, many fine lines remaining with me all my life. I was already beginning to respond to Nature with a passion which, though I did not know it, was to be my only genuine religious experience. Norman Gale's poem, *A Walk*, though flawed here and there by a facile pastoralism and his tendency to preach after singing, in too obvious a way, still seems to me good, and at that time what it said meant a great deal to me. Especially these lines:

> 'We stood upon the forehead of the hills,
> And lifted up our hearts in prayer;
> And as we halted, reverent,
> Meseemed that Nature o'er us bent,
> That she did bid us sup
> From bread she gave and from her cup.
> There at her large communion did we feast,
> Herself the Substance and herself the Priest.
> The immaterial wine she poured,
> And standing on the Cotswold sward
> Administered to us
> Beneath the unsupported sky
> Her sacrament of scenery.'

At that time I had never heard the term, Pantheist, and would not have been particularly pleased to hear it, for with regard to a label like that I would probably have responded rather in the manner of Kitty in *Anna Karenina*. ' "What is a Pietist, papa?" asked Kitty, dismayed to find that what she praised so highly in Madame Stahl had a name.' That poem was just right for me at the time, for I was not mature enough to have taken in *The Prelude*.

I know nothing of Norman Gale's history. He clamped down at the slightest hint of inquiry. There was some tragic secret that had made a hermit of him. As I say, I went to him for Greek, but most of the time was spent in talk. He appeared to possess an effortless grasp of any subject, factual or otherwise. I think he had immense ability which could have been used in many directions, including the financial. But the chief thing was the goodness which emanated from him to an extraordinary degree, and it was clear that the war made him suffer intensely. We use the word good somewhat lightly, do we not? A good man is very rare, and to be one is perhaps a form of genius. My tutorials with him were the only truly educational assistance I have ever had. He either sowed seeds in me or helped seeds to grow which were incipient, and it was only necessary for that concentrate of doctrine at the theological college to press their growth to the surface.

On leaving the college I went to London. My father allowed me one hundred and fifty pounds a year, and I decided to see if I could support myself on this and what I could earn from freelance journalism.

Once when I was at Oxford I had visited a Boys' Club that was in Rotherhithe Street which runs for a long way by the side of the river in the Docks. On going inside and looking out of the window I had been enthralled by the river directly below, with ships passing up and down. *What* a place to live, I thought. So when I left the college and went to London I tried to get a room in that club, facing the river, and very nearly succeeded. In the end I did find a room in a pub, opposite the end of Elephant Lane, called The Torbay (which no longer exists). My window faced Wapping, and away to the left was Tower Bridge. Imagine seeing the river and the boats in every light from that room. I did well to live there. In my one and only novel I have described Rotherhithe in some details, and am unwilling to say more, now that the scene has changed so much. The street itself is scarcely subject to change. It margins the Thames for some miles, though while walking through it one can seldom see the river on account of the warehouses. But sudden clefts divide them at intervals, through which a glimpse of the water can be caught – clefts often ending in steps down to the water and to the shore when the tide is low. In the novel I wrote:

'Robert was fascinated by this street. The warehouses *on each side* made it a strange, dark walk. He did not like it in the daytime; it could not take the light of morning well. But in the evening the solitary lamp-posts gave those walls their opportunity, and beauty interfered at every turn, and the damp stones glistened in the reeking air. Very few people passed through that long, lost street then: there was a hush over everything; no chance visitors strayed in this land where he dwelt alone. Rotherhithe Street – he would not forget it: street of warehouses, of recurring pubs, of watery glimpses, unearthly street! Silent, empty, cobbled, cliffed-in path by day; by night a greater silence on the gleaming, filthy stones, an echoing chasm where no mountains are – a gorge lit up by lamp-posts.'[1]

Since then the surroundings and general atmosphere have changed a great deal. The blitz wiped out the 'slums', and high council houses have taken their place. Furthermore, the district has been 'discovered' by the rich, and the one-time labourers' pub, The Angel, so poshed up that if you go there at lunchtime you will be served by a waiter in evening dress. That pub was only a few yards up the street from where I lived. But in those days I did not drink, not even a pint of beer. So I did not go into the bar of The Torbay, nor did I go to The Angel. I could have made no greater mistake. Years later I realized that it had a balcony directly over the river, a more immediate view and experience than from my window. I could have had a lunchtime sandwich and beer nearly every day, but I never did. Still, I suppose I must accept myself for what I was in those days. Though always immensely susceptible to the beauty of women I did not pursue girls. I did not even know when they were pursuing me. One day the local beauty knocked at my door in The Torbay. She asked if I could spare her some stamps. I thought that that was what she really wanted, and gave her some. Greater greenery than this one can scarcely imagine. No doubt she thought I was haughty. But I never feel in the least haughty towards anyone – let alone a pretty girl.

I was taken for a bit of an eccentric. I was more eccentric than they knew. I am told that no sane man would go for a swim in this part of the Thames. Yet one summer evening I went down one of the steps and swam out. In the course of which I took a gulp of the poisonous water. It did me no harm. Once, after a terrible fire in the docks, I wanted to see a particular wharf, but I could only do so by swimming round a certain corner, which I did. Unfortunately an enormous amount of rubber had melted and was flowing in liquid form through the water. When I came out I found that I was black from head to foot. Again, one night I returned to The Torbay very late, and found that I had forgotten my key. It was low tide, and I went down the adjoining steps onto the shore. A high wall reached up to my window, but the stone knobs made it not impossible to climb. I took off my clothes – for I can accomplish physical feats naked which I could never do clothed. I managed to climb to my window and get into my room, after which I recovered my clothes from the shore. Luckily such eccentricities were unknown to the locality.

After eighteen months there I moved to a second floor flat at number 5 Guilford Street, Bloomsbury. I had been too isolated at Rotherhithe, and the terribly sordid Underground from Shadwell station began to depress me. Moreover, I had foolishly consented to pay a higher rent for my room than I should have done, and became so low in funds that not only did I appreciate the phrase, 'bang goes sixpence', but once caught myself saying, 'bang goes a penny'. At Guilford Street I was able to get that flat for thirty shillings a week, and after putting in some primitive furniture, regarded myself as well placed. I was able to get a little work for the Workers' Educational Association, and I took a Course for freelance journalists, run by Mr Gordon Meggy. It was useful but curious. One of the requirements was that no paragraph in an article should be more than four lines, on the ground that the newspaper reader would not be able to take a longer one without mental discomfort. As one who has witnessed for forty years the consequent murder of the paragraph (which is the unit of literature), and as one who could give some fantastic examples of this ruthless snipping-up of words into neat but senseless parcels, I would venture to say that the supposed semi-literate half-wit reading the piece must find it far more difficult to follow the article thus mutilated than if a modicum of intelligence were applied to this matter. At this journalistic school we were asked to write an article called 'Holiday Sounds', for which a prize would be given. By conforming to the rules I won the prize, and then sold it to *The Evening News*. During my life I have written a good many articles for a good many papers, but I think this is the only one in which I have managed to exclude any merit, any touch of personality, any fresh thought or truth or wit.

I made very little money then from journalism or from the teaching at the WEA, but with my £150 it may have amounted to £200 a year. That meant much more than now of course, but after deduction of rent it was not a lot. Still, one could get a good lunch in Museum Street for one and sixpence, which included soup, meat and two veg., a sweet, and coffee for twopence extra. Once a week I went to what was then the Stoll Cinema in Kingsway. You could go to the gallery for sixpence. There I saw many marvellous silent films, including the incomparable 'With Byrd to the South Pole'.

Guilford Street being only a short walk from the British Museum, which meant to me chiefly the Reading Room, I could get down to serious study and start trying to educate myself in earnest. Even in a capitalist society there is a degree of communism. In London the National Gallery and the Reading Room are good examples. On free days I could go to the National Gallery where all the schools of painting from the earliest Italians are so finely represented – and at that time I had two volumes of a catalogue with a whole page of commentary devoted to each picture, written by Ruskin! As for music, the radio came in, and for a tiny fee, literally worth thousands of pounds, one can hear all the great composers of the world over and over again, a communal gift of such priceless value to me personally that no words can express my gratitude.

The British Museum Reading Room is a unique institution. Provided you can justify a claim to receive a ticket of admission you can spend the whole of every weekday in the Reading Room for the rest of your life. And the wonderful thing about it is that you can get out any book that has been published (at least in the English language) – even R Zon's brochure on 'Forests and Water in the Light of Scientific Investigation', published by the Washington Government Printing Office. No doubt this policy will lead to disaster in the end. Meanwhile it is one of the wonders of the world. Recently it has been cleaned and modernized. In the old days it was more homely and cosy. There was no strip-lighting, but a lamp for each desk to be turned on as the reader desired. And lamps hung aloft from the dome, friendly and soothing in the winter dusk and dark. The atmosphere was less spick-and-span than now. The Room is in the form of a huge circle; the design best imagined by thinking of a wheel; the spokes as the rows of desks; the hub providing the space for the largest catalogue in the world.

Many great men from all parts of the world have used this mine of knowledge, and indeed it is associated with many mighty names, historic figures who have risen from their seats to go out into the world and change it. Karl Marx sat there for years planning the overthrow of capitalism, while both Lenin and Trotsky used the Room as quite a home from home until they were ready to blow up homes. Samuel Butler went there every day, always sitting in the same seat. In his early years Bernard Shaw did most of his reading there, and met William Archer who helped to start him on his career. It was pleasant to enter into such an atmosphere, and now and then look up to see some legendary figure lost in the anonymity of the place. I once found G K Chesterton beside me taking down a book from a shelf, and I noted his formidable head, his concentrated eye, and purposeful movement. I saw the classic profile and amazing head of hair of Havelock Ellis. I saw Cunningham-Graham consulting a catalogue; standing very erect, well-dressed, with sharp beard, every inch the gentleman, and Hero as Man of Action not unwilling to lend a hand to Literature. One of the habitués was Rose Macaulay, who had the face of a nineteenth-century governess combined with that of a lost child, and whose reputation as a novelist was second to her reputation as the worst driver that anyone had ever known; and personally I support this finding for she drove me once, and her lethal jerkiness in progression made me amazed that she continued to live.

Yet I think that the most appealing feature of the Reading Room was not so much that one might sometimes see there the aristocrats of the intellect; it was also the communal nature of the place which provided a harbour for many an outcast. This was not a club to which one belonged and paid a sub. every year. It was a home, a refuge, a workhouse, a retreat, an asylum for many people of whom the world has never heard. At all times there are a number of foreign readers and theses-maddened Americans and a heterogeneous multitude who come in for various reasons; but one's picture and memory of the place is coloured by a vision of the habitués who were often eccentric. I think some readers were, quite simply, tramps who came in for warmth and shelter, tramps of a special kind who loved to be surrounded by books and to see people studying, even if they didn't do much reading themselves. There were not many of them, and it was cheering to see how this great institution was open to them in this rough competitive world; no one interfered with them, they were treated with as much respect as anyone else. I think of one man in particular. There is a swing-door entrance opening into a corridor leading to another swing-door into the Reading Room. In this corridor there used to be hot-water pipes. One of the readers took up a position there for a great deal of the time, gazing down at the pipes as if carefully examining them. He was quite broken down in person and dress. He was slight and small with almost no shoulders, and with decayed trousers creased concertina-fashion from thigh to foot. A long piece of string always dangled from the pocket of a miserable overcoat. He had so little face and so much battered hat that it was like a mouse wearing a hat. Occasionally he would sit in the Reading Room, but nearly always he would be found standing in the corridor carefully studying the pipes.

There were strange characters not always easy to make out. Once when having obtained a place at one of the crowded seats in the aisles between the main desks, I sat opposite a man who was writing very fast in an exercise book. He was not copying anything, but wrote very fast in his book, paused for a second or so, and then pushed forward again. I had seen him before rather vaguely and had noticed a certain abstracted air about him which did not seem congruous with composition. Now sitting opposite him I became amazed not only at his ceaseless writing but at his manner of writing which seemed to me sheer *scribbling*. I got up and walked about a little and finally stood behind him. I knew that he was unaware of me and that it would be safe to observe what he was writing. On he went, at a great pace, his pen racing across the paper, writing – *nothing*. It was just like this 〰〰〰 〰〰〰〰, line after line with almost no variation, no letters formed. When he came to the end of his page he turned over and feverishly started on the next. I think he has been doing this for some time; he is doing it still, for I had another look only the other day, and there he was, in a kind of enchantment, still bent on this strange task.

When I first went to the Reading Room, I was attracted by one particular man who was always there. He was tall, dark-haired, and moved in a very calm, slightly lounging manner which argued an inner serenity which I though was reflected in the expression of his face upon which there rested always the foundation of a smile. He came early and stayed till closing time. I never went to the Reading Room without seeing him there. The twenties passed, and still he took up his position at a certain part of the circle near the door leading to the North Library. He always had a pile of books beside him from which he took notes. One day when he was out at lunch I looked at the titles of his books. I even wrote them down, but have lost the list; books such as 'New Aspects of Evolution'; 'The Future of Psychoanalysis'; 'Moral Force in Sociological Idealism'; 'The Philosophical Significance of Comparative Religion' and so on. His notes were written on rather small sheets of paper, and his handwriting was very small indeed and the letters crushed together. More years passed. I would be away for some time. I would return, and there he was; never, on any single occasion, absent from his station. He must, I felt, be writing a major work; he must have published some books. In the late thirties I noticed his name on one of his book slips, and decided to see if I could find him in the catalogue. Yes, there he was, two or three books to his credit. I filled in a slip and got them out. They were on Evolution and Religion and Morals; but they were very short and slight, and I had never seen a single review of any of them at any time. Still, I thought to myself, perhaps these are mere notes for the major work he is preparing. Again the years went by. The war came howling down, and like a great storm passed over, and when it had gone, the Museum was seen to be still standing – and there was my friend as before, still studying, still taking his notes. More years passed. Now his dark hair had become grey and his movements slow, but something of the old dignity remained. We entered the fifties, and still he came. When we entered the sixties I went to the catalogue again to see what was now listed in his name. But *nothing* more was there. He had added nothing to his published output for thirty years. His hair was now white, straggling untidily over the collar of an overcoat which he never removed; his beard was ragged; his pale face had turned grey-green; and now he wore black gloves, keeping them on when reading and even when writing his notes. It was only between long intervals that I visited the Museum then, but when I came I saw that he was still there, in the same part of the room, the same seat, with his pile of books and his notes. But he seldom remained for long reading or writing, and about every quarter of an hour would get up and take a little stroll. Glancing into his face once, I saw that there was no speculation in his eye and no longer purpose in his search. But still he came. Yet I knew that the day must come when I would enter the Reading Room and not find him there – and it did come. One day in 1966 I came in and saw no sign of him, and understood that I would see him no more.

As I have said, it was a short walk from my place in Guilford Street to the Museum, and I went there continuously in the twenties and off and on for many years after that. As I mounted the steps to the porch I was confronted by the figure of Hoa-Haka-Nana-Ia, a statue from Easter Island.[2] I gazed upon him always before going in. The sight of him lifted my spirits however drooping, however close to despair. That drastic presence, that steadfast countenance set in the everlasting stone, the great contemptuous lips, the high imperial brow, raised above the ephemeralities and follies of mankind, gave me strength to pursue my course.

Quite soon after going to Bloomsbury and attending at the Museum I wrote, rather quickly I think, a book on Bernard Shaw which was immediately accepted and soon after published by Jonathan Cape. As I think I should explain how this came about, I must go back a little in time.

2

I had come upon Shaw's work when I was sixteen, while at Rugby. By that time all but three of his major works had been written, but I had never heard of him since it was the policy of the masters to protect the boys from the intrusion of new ideas or the reading of living authors. I am far from complaining about this. It is better to discover living authors on one's own, for then it can be a real creative experience. One can then gravitate towards those writers who will best nourish us at a particular time. Thus when I was sixteen I saw Shaw's *John Bull's Other Island* at the Abbey Theatre, Dublin. I had never heard Shaw's name mentioned in our household. I knew nothing of his earlier work or style or anything of the man and his reputation. The result was that the play had a very powerful effect upon me. The cast of the author's mind made a direct appeal.

He was a contemporary of the Irish poets and playwrights who formed the Irish Literary and Dramatic Movement, but he played no part in it; in fact he was so afraid of the influence of the Celtic Twilight that he sough refuge in England. That Literary Movement did not influence me at all. I was too young when it was going strong, and in any case did not fancy myself as a literary man at that time. But when I grew up I did have slight contact with the Principals, notably George Russell and Yeats. And in so far as personal impressions have their interest, and even some value, I will pause before continuing with Shaw to say a few words about them.

Perhaps the most celebrated of the Dublin talkers was George Russell (known as AE), the poet, sage, and practical agriculturist. He was much revered. Now, Dublin has never been a place where people are easily revered in literary circles, in fact it is famous for the harsh remarks exchanged. I once asked Sean O'Faolain (who in a short story can, within the compass of a page, reveal the essentials of a person's character and background), whether he ever went into a certain pub. 'No,' he replied, 'for I know that someone would come up to me and say: "Now, I'll tell you just what's wrong with that last story of yours".' In this connection I recall a remark made by Shaw: 'A certain flippant, futile derision and belittlement that confuses the noble and serious with the base and ludicrous, seems to me peculiar to Dublin.'

As far as I know AE generally escaped the Dublin tendency towards denigration. He was not the subject of backbiting, no one sought to belittle him. He was regarded as a Sage, even an Avatar; and his firm belief, consciousness, he called it, that he had been on earth before in a number of incarnations, made him all the more impressive. People came to him for wisdom and would sometimes seek his blessing when parting. 'Give me a word of power,' requested L A G Strong once before going his way. For that was the sort of thing one said to AE, and without batting an eyelid he would come out with something at once. 'Seek on earth what you have found in heaven,' he replied. Strong was quite satisfied with this and went away happy. AE made himself felt by the spoken word rather than on paper. Everyone listened. He became famous for being listened to. This encouraged him to become a monologist, and at least one evening a week was given up to listening to him at his house at Rathgar where a roomful of people would foregather. There would be an exchange of views at first, then AE would come out with a dictum such as 'We become like the thing we hate,' or 'If a specialist is not intelligent upon general topics he is probably not to be trusted on his own subject either,' and then examine it in an exhaustive monologue. He was expected to do this, and he did it for many years with remarkable virtuosity and it was not thought proper to contradict him.

In my twenties I called on him at his house. He was a very approachable man. I remember him saying on a certain occasion that after all anyone who approached him by writing or otherwise did in some sense belong to him. A noble and endearing thing to say, though rash perhaps. I took up too much of his time that afternoon, and only realized at the end that he was longing for me to go. He was not a particularly striking personality: dim eyes, colourless hair, too much hair on his face in addition to a beard, and a carelessly acquired paunch, emphasized by the waistcoat which men always wore in those days. His speech was sonorous and flowing, and he always pronounced God as Gawd. He asked me almost as soon as I arrived whether I had read a certain pamphlet of his on the current Irish Situation. I said no. He then launched into a long and finely phrased account of that situation – and I realized afterwards that this was the pamphlet.

He had a repertoire of amusing reminiscences to be brought out as occasion demanded. He did not have a very high regard for many of his contemporaries, but he revered Shaw as a superior being, and told me a few things about him such as are not often heard. He related how he once told Shaw of a woman who was in hospital, a person of no particular consequence or beauty, who was lonely and depressed. 'Shaw went to her bedside, telling her stories, illustrating his anecdotes by assuming the particular accent which a man from Antrim, then from Dublin, then from Cork, would have used. He entertained her for about an hour, making no show of commiserating with her. This wonderful experience cured her almost on the spot. He did that sort of thing without people knowing about it.'

AE told me how he met Shaw for the first time. It was in the Dublin National Gallery. He wondered who he was – perhaps a high ranking Civil Servant? They fell into conversation, and soon were talking about Whistler and his famous lawsuit against Ruskin; and Shaw spoke in his characteristic man-of-the world way of approaching such things. 'Whistler made the mistake of talking about his "artistic conscience" and expecting damages on that account. In the opinion of the court his artistic conscience was only worth a farthing, so he got a farthing's damages. He should have claimed professional denigration and got a thousand pounds.'

I formed the impression that W B Yeats was rather under a cloud in AE's estimation. He did not mind saying to me, a young stranger, 'I lost interest in him when he adopted the Grand Manner.' As a man who gave himself no airs he was not impressed by those who promoted what today we would call a public image of themselves. He gave me an amusing account of what happened on the only occasion when James Joyce met Yeats. The established poet, assuming that he had an attentive listener in the young aspirant, laid down the law a good deal on the nature of poetry and the dangers of realism, and so forth. Joyce listened to him in silence, and finally after an awkward pause, said – '*I'm afraid that you are too old for me to be able to help you.*' Yeats was absolutely outraged – as well he might be at such bad manners. AE himself did not have much insight into James Joyce at this time. He told me how Joyce had shown him some of his first efforts which were short poems. He had thought them quite good but slight, and he had said to Joyce that he was afraid that he *hadn't enough chaos* in him to make a poet. 'I didn't know then,' said AE, 'that I was speaking to a man who had enough chaos in him to blow up the world.'

My only personal contact with Yeats was at that debate at the Oxford Union already described. I saw him again when he was a guest of an Oxford Poetry Society. He recited his poetry and talked in between whiles. At intervals he became excited, waved his arms about, raised his voice, and flashed his eyes. After the meeting I still recall the comment of an alarmingly clever, good-looking and self-possessed Balliol man, so well known now as A P Ryan. 'Yeats doesn't behave like that,' he said, 'when he goes to see his publisher.' The sophistication of this remark, and its truth, struck me forcibly. One thing about his person seemed strange to me. He had put on too much weight, and this slightly coarsened him. It surprised me that a man who had such a right to be vain should have allowed himself to develop a paunch.

I had another opportunity to witness his oratorical powers, and the way he could dominate an assembly. Once in the twenties I was travelling through Switzerland with my father in late autumn. On the notice board of a hotel in the mountains where we were to stay the night I read the information that at 3 p.m. W B Yeats, Laurence Housman, and Lennox Robinson would read extracts form their works. I turned up in the room arranged for this. I have forgotten what Lennox Robinson did; Housman read one of his Francis of Assisi dialogues. Then it was Yeats' turn. This hotel room was designed for anything but a poetry reading. It was too large, and the chairs, curtains and general appointments were garish and depressing. Whatever is done here, I thought, looking round at the meagre and straggling audience, no human being could effectively recite a poem, and the others had certainly found it heavy going. I had not reckoned with Yeats. Hardly had he spoken for two minutes before the atmosphere was changed. He did not bother to consider whether his audience was a good one or not; he was an orator who could change an atmosphere and lift us out of ourselves. Between his readings he made comments in his best manner. He recited *Innisfree* of course. And told us how he had composed it in the Strand, and we had the splendid *Irish Airman*. The plush chairs, the awful curtains, the poor audience, became of no account, we were enchanted, and one was left in no doubt regarding Yeats' stature.

In the course of the performance he told how an American woman at a meeting had once asked him why he recited his poems in the singular manner he adopted. 'Madam,' he represented himself as replying, 'all poets have read their poems like that since Homer to the present day!' True or false, indeed palpably false on reflection, it was swallowed by us without question as no doubt it was by all other audiences to whom he had addressed this crack.

It is natural that many people have thought that his incantatory manner of delivering his verse peculiar or even absurd. It was probably right for *him*, though not for anyone else to deliver the poems in that way; he had his theory and performed accordingly, indeed magnificently. It was right for Dylan Thomas to read his poems in his way, sometimes over-emphasizing his

71

lines. It is even right, and much in character, for Robert Graves (who says he declined to meet Yeats on the ground that he was phoney) to deadpan his poems in delivery. If he favours that brand of overemphasis in reverse, good luck to him.

It was just as well that Yeats was a man with theories, for they create motor activity. He preached a 'Back to the Folk and Folk History' theory for Irish drama, and this gave impetus to the Dramatic Movement. True, it went in the opposite direction as soon as a sufficient number of playwrights had climbed on the bandwagon. That did not matter, it is essential that a movement should move, and it went steadily in the direction of modern themes and a stylized realism. Yeats was the last man to mind this change of direction. He supported the Gaelic teaching in schools and rehearsed its merits, but when Gilbert Murray asked him if he could read Gaelic he replied, 'It is one of the sorrows of my life that I have never been able to understand a word of it.' It was entirely typical of him not to be evasive in making that reply, for there was nothing of the politician in him, though he was a really great Nationalist in the true meaning of the term. He had an acute and shrewd mind to balance his touch of twilightery. He was an extremely good critic of drama. He saw what John Synge could do, urged him on, and when he did it and put Yeats' own plays in the shade, no one was more delighted than Yeats himself. It is said that he ruined Sean O'Casey. He did nothing of the sort. O'Casey ruined himself. A man who is humble can never be humiliated. It was not Yeats' criticism but O'Casey's pride that was responsible for his self-appointed exile from Ireland.

The last time I saw Yeats was one day in 1947 when taking the mailboat to Holyhead. Out at sea I was about to go up to the stairs from the saloon to the deck, when I saw Yeats mounting the steps. He was not managing well. He was halfway up, standing still, quite rigid. He was feeling ill, and finding it difficult to go up. But everything Yeats did he did with style. He went up now, taking two steps and then stopping, standing absolutely erect like a soldier on parade; then two more steps upward, firmly and smartly executed, then another pause standing at attention, before proceeding again. His wife stood at the bottom of the stairs not daring to help him or say anything.

I saw him again on the platform at Holyhead. He stood still, others hurrying by. All the necessary things were being done for him. He just waited, an erect and splendid figure on the platform, doing nothing amidst the hurrying and anxious scurrying about. I heard one of the train restaurant-stewards say, 'See 'im? 'E's that poit. You can see 'e's got his head well up in the clouds.'

When the Irish Mail was pelting along I peeped into the first class carriage in which he was sitting. His face was in repose, and a profound melancholy had settled upon his countenance as he gazed from the window at the fleeting fields. This was his last journey from Ireland to England, for he was travelling towards the scene of his death.

Returning now to Bernard Shaw, that performance of *John Bull's Other Island* made me feel highly elated. In those days, before radio or TV, and little enough cinema, the theatre could make an impact seldom possible now. I'm not likely to forget my first experience, which was a performance at the Gaiety Theatre in Dublin of *The Only Way* (a dramatization of Dickens' *Tale of Two Cities*) when the great actor, Martin Harvey, took the lead, and when he finally uttered the words, 'It is a far, far better thing that I do than I have ever done, it is a far, far better rest that I go to than I have ever known', I thought it simply terrific (and probably would think the same today). Witnessing Shaw's play was an intellectual treat, the first of the kind that I had ever had. The play gets a lot of laughs. There is a curious Leaflet (preserved in the British Museum), which Shaw was obliged to have distributed amongst the audience requesting people to refrain from laughing and applauding till the end of the Acts – for there had been so much interruption that the play was running overtime and the actors were finding it difficult to speak their lines. Personally I have never found Shaw's plays particularly funny, though they are often amusing. In this Irish play it was the deeper notes that struck me most forcibly – the gentleness, the eloquence, the poetry, the understanding, the sadness. Many phrases have remained in my mind to this day: 'the hardest toil is a welcome refuge from the horror and tedium of pleasure'; the description of modern man as 'mighty in mischief, skillful in ruin, heroic in destruction'; the comment on efficiency as an end in itself, 'For four wicked centuries the world has dreamed this foolish dream of efficiency; and the end is not yet. But the end will come'; Keegan's grim reply to Nora who wonders how they can all laugh so much over the death of the pig at the car accident, 'Why not? There is danger, destruction, torment! What more do we want to make us merry?'; or the remark which he makes sadly to himself after Nora has gone to look for Larry, 'Aye, he's come to torment you; and you're driven already to torment him.'

I was lucky in seeing this play first since it provides the best clues to an understanding of Shaw. Then I came upon A G Gardiner's book called *Prophets, Priests, and Kings* which an exciting essay on Shaw and a Frontispiece of him which was very attractive (and which I have never seen elsewhere). In the course of the next eight years I read all his works. I passed through (during the rest of my life) various phases regarding him which were quite unusual. First an uncritical and hero-worship stage. Then a very critical attitude towards his severe shortcoming as sociologist, as prophet, and as philosopher. Then a final period when I saw his true stature in perspective. At all times his unhypocritical approach to everything, his tone, his spirit, his antiseptic assault upon the stables, have been an inspiration to me.

I attended at the height of his vogue. It was phenomenal. He was discussed ceaselessly. His detractors were many and virulent. His followers leapt to his defence, especially when his characters were called 'mere mouthpieces' or when people said that they 'didn't know when he was serious and when he was not' or when he was accused of being cynical, sarcastic, and unkind. I was terribly pleased when AE said to me that Shaw was really 'a sensitive suffering soul who shielded himself with a brass brand and the pseudonym of GBS' and that he was 'the last saint sent out from Ireland to save the world.' If in the end the mask stuck to him and he became insensitive and unsaintlike, that is chiefly because he had overworked and outlived himself. It will be allowed that the generation I speak of was fortunate in having as mentor this superior being who not only rose above spite, bitterness, rancour, resentment, and malice throughout his life but met these traits in others without apparently minding them. It is easy to understand why such a man as St John Ervine declared that it was the greatest privilege of his life to have been alive at the same time as Bernard Shaw, and to have been his friend. I recall how the justly famous Dr C E M Joad, who did not regard himself as either a great or a good man, absolutely worshipped Shaw. I think we glimpse the inner man best through that early beardless photograph in which there is such severity in the expression and such a lack of illusion in the eyes. He regarded mankind as for the most part composed of savages, He elected to face them with gaiety. Gaiety is courage. It is one great form of bravery. This may have come easily to him: it was a shield he never lowered. We are bound to admit that this told against him as a playwright. He evaded the harsher truths. An excessive *cordiality* runs through all his plays; and the element of anguish in life, though not wholly absent in his plays, is too much concealed by comedy. This makes them enjoyable, but it often detracts from truth. The vein of cordiality is never relaxed, and it included the accusers of Saint Joan, and he would doubtless have adhered to the same tone had he written on the Hitler gang. He must have known what certain bad men are like, but he could never face the truth on paper. It was the same when he staged the domestic front. You get a large slice of truth from Strindberg; and you may feel obliged as Gordon Craig did when witnessing *The Dance of Death*, to leave the theatre before the end because of the huge and terrible figures unsoftened by any touch of humour – but it was truth, and Shaw was too squeamish to stage it. Yet when all is said and done I think that he stands only second to Shakespeare in quantity and quality.

He made such an appeal to me that at the age of twenty-four I wrote a study on his work. He quite liked it, made comments on the MS, and I had some letters from him. They were partly concerned with technicalities about quotation licence and copyright laws. I quote one paragraph on that topic here as being so entirely typical of Shaw the business man of very legal mind (which he loved exercizing) clearing up a cloudy matter:

'The last Copyright Act made an end of the old twenty-three years joint copyright held by magazines and contributors. The acknowledgements still made in Prefaces etc. are pure superstitions except as courtesies. The copyright now belongs to the author in the absence of any agreement to the contrary. Some editors, however, use a rascally form of endorsement on their cheques by which careless authors are trapped into selling their copyright; but the normal assumption now is that the author is the sole proprietor.'

One letter contained a reply to some question I had asked him about what I should have said to a certain person who had threatened suicide; and an answer to a question I had put to him concerning the charge that he never took a walk in the country if he could help it. His reply was wholly characteristic and no one could mistake the style for that of anyone else:

'When people tell me that they will commit suicide in a certain event – which may be through a shock to their religious belief, a failure to let them have £50 by return of post, or a refusal to elope with her, I reply (when I reply at all) that they won't, because it is always easier to wait until tomorrow on the chance of something amusing turning up in the meanwhile. When I was a young man I received such a communication with warm interest, and explained elaborately how to do it painlessly with hydrocyanic acid. All the recipients of this prescription are still alive, or have died a natural death.

However your reply seems as good as any.

When I first came to England in 1876 I spent a little time in the Isle of Wight. I then went to 13 Victoria Grove, Fulham Road, since immortalised as Alexander Grove in one of Arnold Bennett's novels; and as far as I can remember, the weekend in Surrey described by me in the old Pall Mall gazette, entitled A Sunday in the Surrey Hills, in 1883 or thereabouts, records the first excursion I made from London during the seven years that intervened. However, at that time, West Brompton was on the edge of the country; the site of the present huge workhouse which now smothers it was open land; and the houses had not a second house crammed down their throats by building over the garden.

Still, it is notable that whenever I went out for a walk I turned towards Piccadilly, not towards Putney.'

I had raised some point concerning Wordsworth, and he wrote in reply:

'I have never put anyone "above" anyone else. There is certainly nothing of Byron's that I should put above Intimations of Immortality: it would be like putting Peter the Great, who was the most infernal blackguard, above King Alfred, who was a decent man. But there are differences; and though I should never dream of arranging those differences so as to award a Sunday School prize to the man with most marks, yet anyone who does not see that Ibsen was a much more penetrating and tenacious critic of morals than Shakespeare, or Byron a bolder or more vigorous one than Wordsworth, can hardly count as an essayist on either. Remember my hint: don't have Dulcineas: don't run about defending your favourites and belittling your aversions, like W E Henley, whose criticisms, accordingly, are not worth twopence in spite of the trenchancy of their expression.'

It will be admitted that that also is a highly characteristic piece, not least because it would never have entered the Shavian mind that no essayist on Wordsworth should be concerned with his homely ethical views but with the significance of his poetic experience, just as the last way to throw any light upon Shakespeare's genius would be to compare him as a moralist with Ibsen.

It is no minor point, I think, to note that when Shaw wrote a letter he did not dictate it or type it, nor did he even get his secretary to address the envelope, it was always in his own hand. It amused me to observe that one letter was dated 25 December. I once asked him what he thought of Christmas, did he like it. 'Like it! I am a civilized man,' he replied. He kept a Christmas card which ran, 'Courage friend! We all hate Christmas. But it is soon over.'

I would like to mention one other letter, though it does not belong to the same period. Shaw wanted people to think that he was mean. But he wasn't. Many people, including myself, can vouch for that. At one period when I was very hard up I asked for help. He sent me fifty pounds by return. Many years later I held out the hat again. This time I received a typed card on which was written:

'Please do not ask Mr Bernard Shaw for money. He has not enough to help the large number of his readers who are in urgent need of it. He can write for you: he cannot finance you.'

On my card there was a finger drawn pointing to the word Over. I turned over and found that he had written, carefully bolstering up my *amour propre* in the manner which he was master of:

'Dear Collis, When you reach the height of your career you will have to keep a printed card like this one. Mrs Shaw is in the same difficulty. Ninety-five per cent of authors are always in desperate crises of impecuniosity; and when they read in the papers that I am a multi-millionaire and that I have never sent a less fortunate author away empty (actually I seem to spend my life bawling No, No, No) they appeal to us to help them out. We should be destitute in a month or so if our hearts had not long ago become millstones. George Bernard Shaw.'

All the same he did not enclose ten pounds in the envelope.

The first time that I saw him was when he was speaking in the Albert Hall after the First World war on the Treaty of Versailles. Ramsay MacDonald and Arthur Henderson were the other speakers. In that enormous place it was difficult for anyone to make himself heard in those days. Everyone could hear Bernard Shaw. Dressed in a dark suit set against his white beard, erect and easy, his voice carried, not better than the others, but his elocution defined his words, which of course were simple. He was not an orator in the sense of emotionally lifting an audience, but he never failed to hold them. I remember two things. 'Monsieur Clemenceau's idea,' he said, 'sounded like a quotation from Tennyson, "half a league, half a league onward".' And when someone in the audience made a heckling remark which though inaudible to him raised laughter, he said: 'If the gentleman has a good joke to make, I wish he would make it so that I can hear it, for I like a good joke.'

The most interesting thing was the tone of his voice. Since *tone* is frightfully important as an indication of the character and essence of any person, it really astounds me that the gifted actors who have recently been representing Shaw on TV and in radio programmes, should not only fail to get this right but do it so wrong that it is as maddening as it is unnecessary. Whatever the subject may be they give him a jocular tone, an it's-all-so-amusing, lighthearted manner, and an over-Irish accent, which not only detracts from the whole thing but makes it all but impossible even to take in what is actually being said. Shaw's tone was never in the least like that: he was never jocose any more than he was belligerent or malicious, but spoke in a reasonable, sensible, friendly manner inviting agreement. 'If the gentleman has a good joke...' was spoken in a friendly as well as a rebuking way. 'Half a league, half a league onward...' relied upon his Irish accent, which was as slight as it was definite, for its effect – but it was not a stage effect. As I say, it astounds me that the actors make such a travesty of the man, for I can get the tone and accent right myself (as I have often been assured, I think rightly), and I possess absolutely no acting ability and little powers as a mimic. There are the BBC records of Shaw's speaking voice to be consulted – but one would think they did not exist! If on a radio programme his words were to be spoken in a straight English accent, say by Carleton Hobbs or Norman Shelly, the effect would be most refreshing. I wonder will they ever try it?

After the publication of my book on Shaw I met him on a few occasions which I will describe in immediate sequence here to avoid untidiness. The first time was a visit to Adelphi Terrace. My age was twenty-five and I was exceedingly nervous. It was a hot day in June, and being anxious that my right hand would not be too clammy when I shook hands with him, I kept wiping it on my trousers. I walked up and down a bit before I had the courage to go in. Then I mounted the stairs only to find an iron gate half way up, blocking progress. However, I rang a bell which brought down a maid who let me in and led me to a room w here I was left alone for a few minutes. On the bookshelves I saw Theobald's edition of Shakespeare, some volumes of Ruskin, Goethe, Schiller, and Gibbon's 'Decline and Fall'.

Presently Bernard Shaw came in moving soundlessly it seemed, as if he had no weight. There was a strange combination in him of ethereality and extreme solidity: seeing him so close I realized for the first time his great stature, for he almost had the frame of the one-time famous Dublin policeman. He handed me a letter addressed to myself c/o Bernard Shaw, and warned me not to get into communication with the man for he was 'as mad as a hatter'. I handed him my book, on the blank page of which I had written 'To the Subject from the Author', and he glanced at it and laughed politely. 'How do you like Cape?' he asked, and I made some equally banal reply.

There was an awkward pause. I had not come to interview Shaw. I had no intention of asking him questions and making an article about it. I was horrified at the bare suggestion that I might make money out of this meeting. This is the first time that I have written about it. I think he soon realized my attitude, for I learnt afterwards from his secretary, Miss Patch, that he had intended to give me a quarter of an hour, but I was with him for over an hour.

I asked him: 'Where is the inscription, "They say! What say they? Let them say!" which has so often been quoted against you?' He said it was engraved over the mantelpiece in the next room which he would show me in a minute, and then told me how he had got the house and how Mrs Shaw was responsible perhaps for letting the inscription remain there – he thought it 'tactful not to ask her about it'. 'You know don't you,' he added, 'that it comes from Holyrood. But heaven knows who engraved it on my mantelpiece.'

We went into the drawing room which had two big windows getting all the morning sun and looking down over the river and across London. We looked across at the Surrey hills. He told me how the first act of Granville Barker's play *The Madras House* (he had a great respect and much affection for Barker) in which all the daughters point out the Crystal Palace, was suggested by the view from this room. We examined Rodin's bust of Shaw which stood by the piano. The master sculptor, who knew nothing of Shaw's reputation, did not in any way extend or 'interpret' his sitter, he sculpted exactly what he say. We compared the original with the bronze, measuring the forehead, finding it absolutely correct. We looked at a fine photograph of Rodin, 'taken one morning when he was particularly fed up with me'. Then he said suddenly, 'Rodin had a remarkable habit when working of pushing his face right close to the face of his model, swiftly turning to the stone, then as swiftly again back and peering into the face.' While telling me this Shaw suited action to the words, peered into my face and turned away, then again thrust his face at me and turned away. Then I noticed for the first time the singularity about his eyes – one hard, the other soft, one shrewd, the other dreamy, one sane, the other mad.

We looked at various photographs. There was an interesting one of him and Wells taken together. He spoke of what a wonderful talker Wells was, 'the best talker in London. Talks better than his books. A very rare gift in a

79

literary man.' I mentioned something about Oscar Wilde as a talker, and he said, 'Wilde only told set stories and occasionally made an epigram; Wells is a much better talker.'

I was no longer nervous. The atmosphere was really relaxed, no obvious effort having been made to 'put me at my ease' and thus unsettle me. His manner was so easy and ungrand: no greatmanship act of any kind. We bent over the photographs together, he holding one part of the frame and I the other. I didn't take in all he said. As he spoke I was thinking – Here am I, in the centre of London, talking with the greatest writer in the world. I was saying to friends: No, I wasn't in this morning: as a matter of fact I was having a chat with Bernard Shaw.

A photograph reminded him of a meeting with Einstein. 'I did not know whether to address him in German or French – I can't speak either. I asked him in German what days he lectured on. "Lundi", he replied. I said to myself, Ah, French, I'll talk in French. I made some remark in French. He replied in German. This was too much for me; I flung him into the arms of my wife.'

He showed me a photograph of the actress who had played Mrs warren – a picture in which her head is between her hands. 'She was always so overcome with drink and drugs that she could not steady herself for a photograph unless she held her hands with her head, so to speak. At the last moment before a performance she would take something that would cause her to go down hopelessly; a frantic note would be sent to me saying how she had gone down, and the performance due in an hour or so! I would write her a desperate note, and she would appear on the stage just in time.' We referred to the Mrs Warren days, and he regretted how the play had now become uncensored– 'Its theme is not out of date, but the whole style of the thing is out of date.' I suggested how peculiar it was that in those days he never used a purple patch. 'It was later that I took up the libretto', he replied.

Which led him to talk of the early days of the new drama, and the general atmosphere then. His *You Never Can Tell* was considered to have not enough jokes. He told me the famous story of the play's ill-starred rehearsals and how he broke the camel's back by finally turning up in a new suit of clothes! He mentioned how then he did not want his plays to be performed. It was such a nuisance, rehearsals took up such a lot of time. I enquired if financial reasons would not have made it worth while. He said he got enough money by the time his plays began to go 'by criticising the other fellows'. But he admitted that 'before that I had an appalling time financially, and I was often in need of a meal.'

He showed me a photograph of himself which represented what he looked like in the *Saturday Review* days. I would hardly have recognized him, so much broader seemed the head. 'Is this really you?' 'Yes, my head during recent years has been changing its shape, getting thinner and higher.'

The receding of his hair had caused some trouble, it seemed. Mrs Shaw had made him go to an expensive man who 'knew how to make hair grow. The result was that a dreadful little tuft, like a moustache, began to grow on my forehead, which I had great difficulty in getting rid of.'

This meeting with him took place shortly after an illness which had reduced him to ten stone, a surprising weight for so tall and well-built a man. 'It was after the Shakespeare dinner,' he explained. 'I was feeling in very good form and made a special effort when saying what a scandal it was that Granville Barker did not write more plays. I sat down feeling well satisfied. When I got up again I was astonished at my condition. My back seemed to have given way and violent pains assailed the back of my head. The fact is Mrs Granville Barker had been sitting directly behind me. The suggestion, which I suppose she detected in my speech, that she, a rich woman, had been responsible for Granville's falling off in work, had infuriated her, and she summoned up a curse of will against me – and this bore right into my back as if she had used a knife. The effect was disastrous.[3] I was forced to bed again and again. This lasted for thirty days. On the thirty-first day I decided that I must go for a walk or I was done for. And then it left me as completely and suddenly as it had come.'

A public debate between Shaw and Belloc had taken place a short time ago in a theatre, which I had attended, and I referred to it. 'It was a bit of a strain giving that debate just on top of my illness,' he said. 'I wanted to speak second but Belloc absolutely refused to speak first; so I had to.' I made some remark about the contents of his speech, and he added, 'I dished up all his own stuff and waited for him to reply to it; but he didn't do so until the very end when he referred to that part of Roman Catholicism which nobody understands. But I am glad we spoke in the order we did; it would have been hopeless the other way. He was very amusing.'

We talked a bit about *Back to Methuselah* – never a favourite of mine.

'Are you really serious about this long-living business?' I asked finally.

'I don't know any more about it than you do yourself,' he replied. 'I only suggest that if we have got into the habit of living for a short time with bad results it might be a good thing to get into the habit of living for a longer time.' This seemed, and seems, to me a slender foundation for so ambitious a play.

I told him of my experience with *John Bull's Other Island*, which pleased him. I had thought Fred O'Donovan wonderful as Keegan, and thought he would make a fine Caesar. To my surprise he said, 'O'Donovan was too monotonous, too much on one key, he did not reveal the fires and depths within the character.' He praised Cedric Hardwick who had taken the part of Caesar in a recent revival of *Caesar and Cleopatra*. However, I was extremely interested to hear him refer to Keegan in those terms, which supported my view that a lot of Shaw himself was to be found in that creation.

He had recently been over in Ireland. I protested, 'You went to Ireland and walked in the Wicklow mountains, and then wrote a letter to *The Times* as if there was nothing interesting in the world except hotels!' 'I know when to be romantic and when not,' he said. 'That letter was written to revive the hotel trade in Ireland. Ireland has had quite enough romance lately. As I said to AE, if Patrick O'Reilley is seen gazing with a maudlin air into Loch Dan, have him thrown into it.'

I then rose to go, and he opened the door for me very politely and said goodbye.

When Adelphi Terrace was 'developed' Shaw moved to Whitehall Court, and I had a meeting with him there in the thirties. Before mentioning that, perhaps a vignette of him at the Fabian Society meetings might be of interest. There used to be a season of Fabian lectures at Kingsway Hall, and Shaw's lecture wound up the series. There was a little brochure sent out containing a précis of what the speakers would say. Shaw never adhered to a single word of his précis. He spoke extempore, but on these occasions he did not take very much trouble and sometimes he got tied up and at a loss for his verb. An amusing feature of these meetings occurred at question time. Shaw made a point of turning up at all the lectures and sitting on the platform with the other Fabians. At the conclusion of each lecture, in the course of question time, he rose and asked a question. He never failed to do this, knowing that it would have been regarded as an affront to the speaker if he had failed to do so. There was something touching about his never omitting to come up with something, and the Shaw Question became a recognized part of the evening's performance.

He was equally conscientious in attending the Fabian Summer Schools. I went to one. Shaw gave one lecture and sat through all the others on the uncomfortable school-chair-desk accommodation. Only once did I hear him make a criticism (not publicly) when he said of a lecture: 'too much information; one should never give information in a lecture.'

He always played the game according to the rules, giving all his attention to the Summer School apart from his afternoon swimming expedition – (I possess a photo of him in a Victoria bathing costume); visitors could not tempt him away. Celebrated Americans, hearing that he was there, sometimes turned up, and a circle was formed round him on the lawn. One day Sinclair Lewis came with some companions. I joined the circle. There was talk about the American book trade. 'In spite of my enormous reputation,' said Shaw, 'no one in America buys my books.' 'Let me recommend you to Mr —', said Sinclair Lewis, indicating an American publisher who was with the party, 'he knows how to sell my piffling efforts.' The publisher smiled a polite business smile and said nothing, biding a favourable moment later when he might possibly 'make a deal' with Shaw. Lewis was a very likeable character, a red head, bubbling with energy and tensely strung. The party were bent on getting Shaw to go out with them that evening. They kept trying to get him to accept, and without directly refusing he was not saying Yes. At one point he seemed to hesitate, and Sinclair Lewis, hoping to win him over, said in a jocular way, 'He's about to accept, about to, about to, a-b-o-u-t to!' But it didn't work. There was no particular reason why Shaw should not have left the Fabians for an hour or so and relaxed with the Americans; but for some reason he felt that he ought not to go. It is a small thing, yet strangely vivid to me in recollection – as was also one other thing. Cyril Joad was strong at getting girls to go to bed with him anywhere, and this still held good at Fabian Summer Schools. At this one his quarters were adjacent to Shaw's. One say, when passing by, Shaw perceived him in bed with a girl. When talking of this, Joad seemed very much impressed by the fact that when they met later Shaw never by the slightest look of amusement or disapproval, allowed Joad to feel the smallest embarrassment.

One day in the thirties when passing along the Embankment I felt a strong desire to go to Whitehall Court and call on Shaw – to cheer my drooping spirits. I had no invitation, no appointment, but I rang the bell and Miss Patch came to the door. Always friendly towards me, she told Shaw that I had called, and to my astonishment he invited me in. His delightful study had the same view of the river as from Adelphi Terrace. Everything was in good order in the room, all geared for the smooth running of the machine: the tidy desk, the proper sort of chair in which he sat erect, Miss Patch in the offing efficiently oiling the works. Mrs Shaw came into the room, and I was introduced. She was a brighter and warmer personality than I had imagined, not did she appear to me old – though the eighties had caught up with both of them. She produced a volume by Ouspensky, and advised me to read him.

Here was a surprise indeed. For this was very far from Shavian country. Knowing in which direction his gifts lay, Shaw's interests and even beliefs were largely governed by those gifts, and he instinctively kept clear of fields not suited to his pen.

Miss Patch and Mrs Shaw left the room to attend to something. Since he had been so good as to invite me in when I called thus unexpected I was anxious not to take advantage, and said I must now go. Seeing that I was not intending to hang on he said, 'We get a good view of the South Bank from here.' I guessed he was thinking of a possible National Theatre, and I said something about it. 'What we need,' he said, 'is not a National but an International Theatre. We want a theatre where plays could be seen which never are seen because of box office demands.' 'Such as Tolstoy's *The Power of Darkness*?' I suggested. 'Yes, a very good example. It is a very powerful play. Those Russians sometimes make me despair of my own stuff.' He continued in a way that is supposed to be uncharacteristic of him. 'Even Tolstoy, who was only an amateur in theatre work. He could reach a subtlety of situation and behaviour in a few words, which I can't. As for Chekhov, when I see a play of his I want to burn one of mine.' He did not say this for the records, and I had no intention of quoting it when I went away. But too much used to be made of Shaw's 'conceit' (especially with regard to Shakespeare in whose work he revelled, it should be needless to say). And one word here on his 'love of publicity'. How real was it? On the First Night of *Saint Joan* they tried to get him to take a curtain call. He would not do so. He would have had the whole of that audience cheering him sensationally. After 'Methuselah' he had despaired of writing another major work. Then he got the idea of Joan. It became the highest moment of his career. For any really limelight-loving man, to step forward and take that curtain call would have been irresistible. Yet he remained in the background leaving it to his actors to receive the applause.

In the thirties he couldn't get his plays accepted for the commercial theatre. 'There isn't a Manager in London who will touch my stuff', he said. I wasn't the only person he said this to at the time. He seemed really sorry for himself, as quite a Cinderella. He greatly boosted the egos of frustrated playwrights by saying this when they came to see him.

The subject of eye-witnesses came up, somehow, and I told him of a good example. His car had been seen outside a certain hotel in Devon. An eye-witness swore that he had as his number plate GBS. Of course it had simply been GB. But the eyewitness hearing that the car belonged to Shaw, either expected to see or wished to see GBS – and so he saw it. It was at a hotel in Devon, he told me, that one evening he was standing on the balcony looking at the moon. A man came up to him and asked how far away he thought the moon was. 'By the look of the thing,' replied Shaw, 'I should say about twenty miles.' The man received this answer gravely and then said, 'As a matter of fact you are very nearly right: it is exactly twenty-one miles away – I can prove it to you.' He had expected to get a rise out of Shaw but Shaw got a rise out of him. 'Subsequently I used to receive books from him elaborately proving that the moon was only twenty-one miles from the earth. And I found his proofs just as convincing as those which proved that it was so many thousand miles away.'

I think he was a quarter serious. He never could bring himself to believe that the sun was ninety-three million miles off, seeing that a little wisp of a cloud intervening between us and the orb was enough to make us shiver.

He was ninety-three when I visited him at Ayot St Lawrence in Hertfordshire. He had fallen from his high estate.

Thomas Mann, speaking of his idea of greatness during a talk on Bernard Shaw, said that 'it implies a degree of human tragedy, of suffering and sacrifice. The knotted muscles of Tolstoy bearing up the full burden of morality, Atlas-like; Strindberg who was in hell; the martyr's death Nietzsche died on the cross of thought; it is these that inspire us with the reverence of tragedy; but in Shaw there is nothing of all this. Was he beyond such things? or *were they beyond him?*'

It is a searching question. I defy anyone to reply to it convincingly one way or the other. But there was tragedy. Once I heard him say to a Fabian '...when I become a hopeless old dodderer...' He could never become that. But he outlived himself, and fell below himself. The flame and the flood, the high integrity and superior character, the truth-facer and exposer of canting insanities, the embattled warrior for the poor and the imprisoned and the abused, the voice for them that were afraid to speak – all passed away, and the towering figure tottered and fell.

He had never been a Contemplative, and his idea of contemplation is in any case distinctly odd in *Back to Methuselah* where his Ancients contemplate nothing, since nothing there is worth contemplating. He had retired from the world – but not to mediate, or even to sink quietly into the human life around him. Ayot St Lawrence is a small hamlet with few inhabitants, but Shaw did not become their friend, he was scarcely known to them: it would be fantastic to conceive of him going to the local pub, sitting down there with half a pint of bitter (or something less inebriating) and entering into the lives of the people, this village the centre of their lives, their problems and doings the central happenings and problems of the world. But he had not now, if he ever had, a quiet loving interest in simple human beings, however valiantly he had spent himself in fighting for Humanity at large.

He lived now a Solitary who did not make solitude a solace. He wandered round his study as in a prison, round and round, with the radio continually turned on. He stood for hours in the garden senselessly beating at the trees. He abandoned all desire to worry out the problems of the world and brood upon the mystery of life. Visitors, coming to him from as far away as India, hoping to find a sage, were received with a surprising lack of consideration, and sent away empty. One of the greatest pitfalls of the celebrated man is *complacency*. Shaw showed no originality in this respect and fell into that pit. He spoke always with cocksureness, without reflecting. He had no capacity now to listen to others quietly and perhaps agree or simply learn; instead of thoughtful quiet answers his replies were always debating-platform quips. In general everything that was brought up was referred back to himself in the strangest egotistic manner, as if he had become lost in himself. Material considerations seemed to rule his life, and the richer he became the nearer he felt to the workhouse.

I called now at the invitation of the Winstens, the charming and gifted family who lived close to Shaw's house – in the garden of which Clare Winsten's sculpture of Joan of Arc can still be seen. A little earlier Desmond MacCarthy had suggested to me that we call on Shaw, 'to see the dear old man once more'; but he wasn't sure for he felt so sore about Shaw's recent attitude to the Dictators and his evident failure to acquaint himself with the facts of the concentration camps. I asked him now, but he was still feeling sore – a fact which I mention as a measure of the estrangement Shaw had caused amongst some friends who had revered him most.

... He came to the hall door of the Winsten's house. Extremely ghost-like, I thought. Indeed I was reminded of some Ghost in *Hamlet* I have seen, with flowing cape and a vizor on head (he wore a cap like a vizor). He advanced soundlessly across the room and sat down shakily on the carefully cushioned chair prepared for him – and became quite solid. Once again one was struck by the *specialness* of his personality, the room-pervading aura of his charm – no photograph conveys this.

He turned to me and asked,

'Are you your son or your father?'

I paused before replying,

'Actually, I'm both.'

For after reflection I grasped that this question bore upon the one-time book of mine on him.

He carried with him a pail and a well.

Whatever subject was in hand he took his pail and lowered it into the well, and always came up with something. Somehow Horatio Bottomley was mentioned. At once he dipped his pail into the well and came up with 'Bottomley was not such a bad chap. An employee of his was caught doing something shady, and this was told to Bottomley. He didn't get angry and sack the man, but only said "Well, I suppose he must start somewhere".'

This led to the subject of crime, and dipping into memory again Shaw recalled the actor who took the part of Blanco in his play *The Shewing Up of Blanco Posnet*. 'The actor, it appeared, had committed a murder, but somehow was not charged, or not yet charged with it. However, this seemed to aid his histrionic abilities in playing Blanco, and I was well satisfied with his performance.' This in turn made him recall a murderess. 'I knew some people who went to a lodging house, and on asking the name of the proprietor, were told that it was Madeline Smith. Since she was known to have committed a murder, though she got off in court, they were too terrified to take the lodgings. Madeline Smith had character. A Doctor Simpson who attended her in the prison hospital, begged "to use the privilege of an old man", and speak to her seriously at parting. "My dear doctor, it is very good of you," she said. "But you mustn't trouble to give me advice, for I assure you I have quite made up my mind to turn over a new leaf!" '

Shaw had once written that the happiest day of his life was when his mother told him that they were going to live at Torca Cottage in Dalkey, County Dublin, overlooking Killiney Bay and the Wicklow Mountains. As I was born in Killiney and used to bathe at the same 'white rock' where Shaw sometimes did also, I wanted to get him onto these scenes. I succeeded, and he came up with some new things – not the old chestnuts about his uncle which was a recognized part of his repertoire. His pail brought up some really characteristic stuff. 'One day I was going over the railway bridge that leads to the rocks,' he said to my delight, for that bridge was bound up with so many of my childhood memories, 'when looking down I saw a man on the line. At the same time I saw a train coming up from Killiney. I shouted down to him to look out. At this he lay down beside the line and put his neck over it.'

Here the playwright appeared to have finished his story, for he stopped. Or perhaps he was waiting for a cue. Anyway the cue came. 'Did he remain there, Mr Shaw?' asked Theodora Winsten. 'No, he was playing for a dramatic effect, and took himself off the line just before the engine reached him. He went away quite cheerfully. I think he did it because he had an audience. Some people will do anything for an audience.' This dip of the bucket brought up another thing with it. 'One day when I was going to bathe with a towel over my shoulder a man said to me, "What are you carrying a towel for?" "To dry myself of course", I replied. "You don't need to dry yourself! You should let the water dry on you so that the magnesia of the sea can sink into your skin. You will benefit from that." I took his advice, and have never dried myself since.' This led to a further thought – about washing your eyes. 'The way to get clear eyes is to wash them just as you wash anything else.' 'But you can't take your eyes out and scrub them,' I said. 'No, but it is good enough to open them under water and let them wash that way. It is good for the sight as well as for the complexion of the eyes.' 'That is why you have such beautiful clear eyes', said Theodora. 'Unfortunately many people have clear eyes without washing them just as the people with the best teeth have generally never washed them at all.' This in turn brought out a memory about an American judge when he was once in the company of Hall Caine. 'The judge expected us to talk on high literary themes, but of course we discussed royalties and fees and that sort of thing. Then the American judge said to me suddenly, "Do you ever wash your face?" I said No, I did not wash my face, meaning that I did not put soap on it. Subsequently I learnt that the judge went about saying that "Mr Bernard Shaw declares that he never washes himself".'

These pleasing items were somewhat checked by the Tragedy of the Vegetable Machine being introduced into the conversation. It appeared that a remarkable vegetable machine was on the market which squashed out the essence of any given vegetable into a powerful liquid extract. 'The very thing to save my life' he said. But it had been forced on him in a cunning way by a certain firm, and he, a poor man, felt that he had been grossly overcharged and shamefully diddled. He represented himself as being much overcome by this, and enlarged upon the subject with an excess of detail. To me his emphasis upon this manner seemed ludicrous, and his anxiety about his finances unwarranted. He was afraid of being ruined if any more of his plays were bought by the film industry. I didn't follow this, thinking that at any rate he would get sixpence in the pound. He pointed out – which I recognize now as true when an income reaches a certain point – that if he made more money he would be fined for doing so. He would be taxed *more* than he received. This amused me. It did not amuse Shaw. 'A man is walking down a road,' he said, 'and a robber comes along and says, "I demand your money"; he takes it. But that does not satisfy him. He wants more: he takes away the man's jacket and shoes and shirt. It is no longer – Your money or your life, it is – Your money *and* your life. Moreover the robber does this not only in open daylight but with the approval and backing of the government.' Thinking on these things the great socialist and egalitarian who had for so long asserted that 'property is theft' now gloomily contemplated the idea following it, that theft is property.

There followed the Tragedy of the Neglected Playwright. This seemed to me equally wry. He represented himself as fruitlessly knocking at the door of various theatre managements in a vain endeavour to get his plays produced. In England they were always damned, he declared, the critics assuming that the play was a failure because it was by him. He spoke of the copies of one of the Old Masters (I forget which) with two angels in the picture, each with a squint. The squints were taken out. 'That's what they always want to do with my plays, to take out the squints.' It wasn't clear to me who 'they' were, or what plays he was referring to: if to his good plays, his groans were unjustified, if to the later ones, unrealistic. I tried to get him onto a pet point of mine about a big contradiction in his work, but he muttered, 'I never contradict myself', and we did not pursue the matter.

For my part, it was delightful just to be in his presence regardless of anything that was said, because of his strange personality, the tone of his Irish voice, and the trained clarity of his speech. To the end of his life he could come out with a strictly inimitable Shavian remark. Before closing I must give two. During his last years he corresponded with a Mother Superior. In his agreeable letters to her he played the game according to the rules, asking her to pray for him, and so forth. He said that he hoped that perhaps he could get into heaven by the back door, 'whereas a man like Judas Iscariot had to be damned as a matter of heavenly business.' That is what I mean by strictly inimitable, it could not have been said by anyone else, or mistaken for that of anyone else. The tone given to it, if he had spoken it aloud, would have been killing. I want to mention one other remark, for it would be a shame to let it pass into oblivion. In his ninety-fourth year, while 'pruning' – strictly in quotes – he fell down, injured himself, and was brought to Luton Hospital. Now, I truly believe that hospitals, more than almost any other institution, not excepting the Army, move in a mode of ritualistic fantasia. John Kennedy is assassinated and brought dying to Parkland Hospital. The clerks promptly escaped from reality and entered their land of paperwork ritual. 'Kennedy John F' was logged in and identified as 'a white male', and assigned to Room 24740. His 'chief complaint' was then docketed and described as GSW 'gun-shot wound'. When Shaw went to Luton he did not escape the fantasia of the clerks, and was subjected to *continuous washing*, which though a Rule of monumental absurdity and often cruelty, is adhered to with the insane persistence of people who so close to reality in the particular, lose sight of it in the general. They did not relax this ritual in Shaw's case, and he was constrained to complain about it, and spoke up for the whole of humanity in this vulnerable position. 'I want to take out a certificate', he said (in that tone and manner not subject to representation in print alone), 'I want to take out a certificate of having been washed.' It is as perfect a Shavianism as any I know, and it was nearly the last public utterance he made.

The last years of his life may have exhibited some failure in spirit and in sense, for his force was exhausted and he was very old. I cannot see that it matters at all. Just as everyone is dedicated to disaster of some sort sooner or later, so everyone fails at some time – at the beginning, or the middle, or the end. For half a century Shaw had fought the Monster. The Monster that must be exposed and must be slain in every generation. The triple-headed Monster that though it be slain yet rises from the dead in ever renewed disguises and forms to delude the simple, to betray the good, and to smooth the way for evil men and evil deeds. The Monster that always speaks so suavely in the name of religion or the name of duty or the name of legality or the name of love or the name of liberty or the name of country or the name of society. The Monster with three heads: cant and humbug and hypocrisy. He who can expose and slay the Monster, even for one generation, has the right to be numbered among the saviours of mankind.

3

Keeping the chronology of my own story well in hand – in spite of the above flash forward – we can now return to the British Museum Reading Room in 1925. I had met with no publisher-difficulty over this my first book; it was taken without hesitation. Cape had an engaging way with authors. He spoke to one in a fatherly manner, and at the same time thought it a good idea at the start to suggest the light in which he regarded royalties. There was a picture on his wall of a seedy-looking person, bedraggled and worn-down, a lugubrious expression establishing complete predominance over his features. Cape pointed him out to me and said 'That is the portrait of – *a publisher.*'

The book was very well received and soon went into three editions. Yet I paid little attention to this and ceased to care for it, and have never to this day dared even to glance into it (so jejune is the style), let alone reread it. Furthermore, I completely failed to do the usual thing and 'follow it up' with some other study or biography. I got a letter from Cape suggesting that I do a book on St Paul. I was quite shocked at the idea. It never crossed my mind that I could possibly be *given* a subject: it had to be a colossal inner compulsion! Today I could write upon any subject, if asked, without the slightest loss of integrity, but not then. This was not entirely priggishness and self-importance, it was a damaging and yet essential part of my character leading me on a course which eventually got somewhere. To hold to a course is the sole form of courage I possess, and even so I'm afraid I held on only because I always expected everything to come right in the literary way 'tomorrow' or 'next year', rather than about thirty years later. I became consumed at this time by two things. One was a growing passionate love of Nature. To take a train to Dunton Green in Kent and thence go by the little line to Chevening from where I went for a walk, frequently brought me to the verge of ecstasy. I got Cape to publish a Dramatic Dialogue called *Forward to Nature*. It has no literary merit. The other thing was a passion to achieve a philosophy of life and religion. These two passions came before sex or games. Every hour was precious to me. To the business man time is money. To me money was time. With what money I had I purchased time. I used to be amazed at the way so many people frittered away that commodity, calmly sitting back without tension. I set to work in the Reading Room to study the philosophers, the metaphysicians, the Eastern Sages, and, above all, the anthropologists, for to grasp the bearing of Frazer's *Golden Bough* upon the religious creeds and rituals was stimulating indeed – a real 'brain-wash', as Stephen Potter and I put it, years before the term was brought in to signify the opposite. Stephen Potter and I came together in this search. He had a very open mind. It was not comprehensive in understanding, but it was wide open and it never narrowed. He had no clear vision or really strong philosophical feelings, nothing passionate in the way of intellectual conviction. He wanted me to think that he could hit the nail on the head when he wrote about Coleridge or D H Lawrence, but I could not say so. He had been so coddled by his mother and his sister that he was vulnerable to any sort of resistance, and rather than read any review of his work which might be unfavourable, he would put them aside unread for a year before looking at them. In place of conviction he put affirmation: on all occasions, especially on the Radio programme, *The Critics*, speaking affirmatively and enthusiastically – a highly original attitude. Then he struck his Gamesmanship line. 'My little miracle book', as he called the first one after its successful publication, was conceived of at first as a possible little joke which might bring in a few shillings at Christmas. That is how so many good things start. Everyone knows how it grew, and how it grew internationally. One of the reasons why he could make the idea work was because he had such a knowledge of the 'mandarin' style and he could ironically adapt it to his needs and shape a style as firmly based as that of Wodehouse.[4] He created a world in which he could move easily, and he created an audience that moved easily with him. The work will therefore endure – and there are very few enduring humorists. Another element which will make it endure is the entirely mythological nature of the world created. The real joke of the whole thing is that it bears no relation to reality. Nobody getting out one of the books with a serious view of achieving an advantage over someone, would be helped in the slightest degree – that is the chief joke to me. I played many games of golf and tennis with Potter (being beaten by him in golf, and beating him at tennis) but it never occurred to either of us for an instant to mention gamesmanship, let alone attempt a ploy. I am speaking quite seriously. But at the same time I must admit that he did have a native attitude from which the gimmick could spring naturally. I used to play a tennis foursome with him and John Strachey and Cyril Joad. On a doubtful point Joad was expected to cheat. John Strachey was expected never to cheat. No one was sure whether I would cheat or not. Stephen Potter leant backwards so much against a ruling in his favour that we were bound to give him the point.

I write these words in the past tense, for yesterday I went to his funeral – 8 December, 1969. With no man have I ever been so close. I could confide anything in him, any skeleton in my cupboard, sexual or otherwise, for he was as utterly without moral attitude as he was totally devoid of cant in any form. We had a kind of code-language, seeing life in much the same way, though he was very English and my cast of mind is very Irish. No man has ever been so generous to me in deed and in thought, or so long and consistently responded to my literary endeavour. But a shadow fell between us. During the last few years I had seen little of him. I neglected him. He neglected me. Nothing was going right for me and I did not confide in him, I was too proud. He had wanted me to write some such book as this. I kept putting it off, thinking no one would be interested. Then I made a series of false starts, but I never told him about this. In August of this year (1969) when on a visit to Ireland I sent him a card with a picture of Killiney where he had once visited me. On my return I found a note from him. '... Your Killiney card gave me a big nostalgic pang. Two ends of one's life. Slight melancholy because I am slowly recovering from disease originally diagnosed as fatal. Marks? Huge meaty story when we meet. Please ring.' Against his shaky signature he wrote 'note partially paralysed hand.' His light way of referring to an illness was typical and habitual of him. I went to see him at once. Our meeting was good indeed. He had omitted sending me a copy of his *Golfmanship*, thinking I wouldn't value it! He now remedied this with an endearing inscription. After reading it with intense enjoyment I rang and told him so, noting the way in which he was now so at ease with his public, so sure of the line being taken, a very enviable position – a point which much pleased him. I still told him nothing of my own affairs, for I was still baulked and did not start this book till 1 November. I had seen death in his face. But when I rang up to say I was coming again, I gathered, or thought I gathered, that he was away for the weekend. This made me suppose that he was getting better. I got down to the book in earnest, and having reached the point of our first meeting at the OCB at Bushey in 1918, I decided that I would tell him about it and read him my passage on our time there, my bit on the strange man in the Reading Room, and then the part about himself – *in the present tense*. He died just before I had come to it. Such is life. Such rather is death. Such is the way our friends suddenly disappear from the surface of the earth, never to be talked with again. I am sorry for myself, not for him. He would have been pleased with the success of his ploy. *This* was for real, and put him one-up on me for ever.

I have referred to the studying of philosophic books at this time. I read attentively, trying to worry-out the problems of existence, and take the kingdom of heaven by intellectual storm. This cannot be done; but if you are clever and learned, or just learned, you can write a volume and throw out another handful of dust calling it Theory or Solution or Explanation. But the 'worrying-out' process is not entirely futile for the dedicated searcher – as opposed to academic re-searcher. Simone Weil, who said so many good things in short compass, has something cheering that bears upon this, I think. 'Never in any case whatever is a genuine effort of the attention wasted,' she wrote. There is little doubt that *attention* gets results. 'Quite apart from religious belief,' she wrote, 'every time that a human being succeeds in making an effort of attention with the sole idea of increasing his grasp of truth, he acquires a greater aptitude for grasping it, ever if his effort produces no visible fruit.' And again, 'Even if our efforts of attention seem for years to be producing no result, one day a light which is in exact proportion to them will flood the soul.'[5] I believe there is something in that. I spent some ten years giving my attention to the solving of the big problems, and after about twenty years they *dissolved*. This is not the best place to finish out my thought on these things; I would rather wind up my book with it in a compact statement in case I might possibly, in a small way, make a useful impact.

At the same time I must acknowledge that if I eventually got somewhere in this matter (if such a claim is at all justified) it was also due, perhaps chiefly so, to two poetic sages and one mystical poet – namely to Walt Whitman, Edward Carpenter, and Wordsworth. The first two were introduced to Stephen Potter and myself by our mutual friend and mentor,

93

G B Edwards, and I doubt if we would have come upon them at the right time otherwise. Whitman is a difficult man to cope with, not only because his Americanism is false prophecy, but because he doesn't give much pleasure from a literary point of view; but if *Leaves of Grass* is read with complete receptivity *as if it were Nature speaking*, then it works wonders in breaking down mental and moral barriers, and in clearing the obstacles to vision. And of course there is the man himself – that face – especially the picture of him at thirty-five, 'The Christ portrait' as it has been called – certainly that of a saviour. I got even more out of Edward Carpenter. It used to be said that his mystical poem, *Towards Democracy*, was merely a sort of carbon copy of Whitman, or 'Whitman and lemonade.' Such remarks were made, not out of stupidity or malice, but ignorance of the work. (Bad literary criticism is often due, quite simply, to ignorance of the work or works.) *Towards Democracy* contains passages which can get you further than *Leaves of Grass*. And Carpenter, unlike Whitman who could not write prose, was in command of a lucid style as good as any in the language, and was able to give clear intellectual commentary upon intuitional knowledge. His *Art of Creation* and his *Christian and Pagan Creeds* are extraordinarily illuminating, the latter especially with regard to the upshot of Frazer's *The Golden Bough*. Then again there was the man himself, a bright particular star of the English genius.

A reader might complain that there is little point in praising these writers, since no one reads them now. Well, just now, no one reads the mystics much, or any works falling under the head of *scripture* (a useful category proposed by A R Orage). This is not because they belong to the past but because they belong to the future when religion will have taken the place of theology.

The most compulsive reading experience for me at this time was Wordsworth. Again I must express gratitude to my schoolmasters for having kept me off reading works which as a boy I would not have responded to. It did me no harm to be made to learn *The Daffodils*. I'm sorry to say that they did include *The Ode...*, but anyway they concealed the existence of *Tintern Abbey* and *The Prelude*, and for that I can never be too thankful. I came to these works now, and I think that my response to them was almost as great as Wordsworth's response to Nature!

I must add here that one of the reasons why we should not have 'The Ode' forced on us as children is because of the passage about the 'vision splendid' dying away. It is not a good thing to accept that without question. It was true for Wordsworth, but not generally so. I sometimes hear people say of so-and-so that 'he has retained the child's sense of wonder'. But the child does not have a sense of wonder. That comes, if ever, years later. He may have a bit of fancy, which can eventually grow into imagination. The main characteristic of a child is that he takes every damn thing for granted: whether an industrial plant or a natural plant. He has endless piffling curiosity but no vision splendid. As for seeing a view, take children to a high place and they will be as blind as a bat to the scenery, but if they find a good place for a slide they will have fun there. Surely that is how it should be. This is not to say that as the youth grows up he doesn't lose things which he can never recapture. The sight of a girl's handwriting on the envelope of a love letter, at the age of fifteen – we can never know a thrill of that kind later on; or the sight of a Christmas stocking; or the taste of strawberries and cream; or the joy on first riding a bicycle; everyone could make a list of blisses which have faded. But the fading of bliss should not be confused with the passing of wonder. I remember feeling very reassured when I once heard AE say that his own experience was the opposite to that of Wordsworth. For that goes for me also.

I am aware that according to the *zeitgeist*, and to the fashion game, I had no business in the twenties of this century to be inspired by Wordsworth. I should have been helping myself to large and regular spoonfuls of Eliot's *The Waste Land*. Now, if an autobiography is to avoid tediousness or distastefulness or immense length, the artist can only give bits and pieces of his experience; but what he does elect to speak about should be honest and not evasive. Thus I am obliged to confess that *The Prelude* meant more to me than *The Waste Land* which I positively disliked – much as I do like *Ash Wednesday*, one of his plays, all his profound prose observations on social matters, and I get some fun and games out of the Quartets. My lack of response to *The Waste Land* is not a question of literary criticism but of personal need. I find in myself such a need for the *lyrical element* in poets that if it is not present I do not go for them – (not that I want it on the surface; I am happy with that element as found in a James Thompson or a Thomas Hardy). In this I'm rather like an animal, like a cat going for its essential nourishment, lapping up milk, and not being terribly keen about what look like nails or sawdust. I feel the same about James Joyce's later works. I cannot read *Ulysses*. I formed the impression that Joyce had, at bottom, an uninteresting mind, with nothing really fresh to say, but elected nevertheless to say it at enormous length, and invent a new language into the bargain. Adhering to the tradition of Anglo-Irish writers from Swift to Shaw, I hold that the subtlety of the English language is such as to be equal to anything and yet give the reader a smooth run. So no doubt there is an element of personal prejudice in my attitude to Joyce; but I do think that the critical apparatus built upon *Ulysses* is as deplorably tedious as that built

95

upon *The Waste Land*, and, for that matter, upon the poems of Gerald Manley Hopkins: he had a rhythm certainly, and it may have been 'sprung', but it is evident that he believed that poetry consists of *battering* the reader with words, chiefly adjectives – though under the circumstances no human being could possibly follow what he is saying... But I digress. I will only add that turning back, this minute, and rereading the first three Books of *The Prelude*, I am not surprised at the effect it had upon me on the first reading, seeing the effect it still has upon me now.

As dusk fell during the winter in the Reading Room the atmosphere was very appealing (one day when I was sitting there at such an hour, the light over my desk was turned on, and looking up I saw the receding figure of Stephen) and a kind of echoing hush informed the place. The atmosphere was also at all times conducive to sleep. I never could read for long there without dozing off. Often on a winter afternoon feeling sleep overcoming me I would cup my forehead in my palms resting on the desk, having put an overcoat over my shoulders and perhaps over my head as well. A slacker sight it would have been hard to find. I tend to go to extremes and this was one of them. But I could also be overcome by an overpowering restlessness; and one day, going to the other extreme, I got up from my desk and climbed Mount Etna. I was able to command funds for this because just then there happened to be a good market for Shaviana and I decided to sell the MS of my Shaw book upon which GBS had made comments in the margin, together with the letters I have quoted. A dealer offered me fifty pounds, but once every ten years or so I become business-like and practical, and this was such an occasion. Seeing how interested he was I turned the offer down and accepted one hundred and fifty pounds elsewhere. Etna's volcano being in eruption I decided to go to Sicily at once and climb the mountain up to the crater if possible. Taking hardly more than a satchel and entirely the wrong footwear I set out without delay. I had never heard of the famous village of Taormina but by fluke I got out at the right station after I had taken the train at Messina. A number of hotels are dotted on the hillside leading to Taormina, but by another fluke I chose a taxi that would take me to Victoria Hotel which is in the centre of the enchanting village and from which I could see Mount Etna. After several false starts and vain attempts to reach the mountain from Taormina I met a German journalist who was attempting the same thing with the aid of guides, but after we had taken a car to a certain place and then climbed some distance up the mountain beside the lava, the guides declared that it was dangerous to proceed farther, and went back with the German journalist. I refused to retire and continued to climb, eventually reaching the very verge of the crater. I saw nothing, for the sulphurous smoke was too thick, but I heard a sound rather like gravel being poured into a ship from a wharf, sounds of men at work where no men could be at work. I was satisfied with this, and now only wanted to find the town of Mascali which was rumoured to have been destroyed. I raced down the mountain on an eerie quest but came upon no such town until, meeting some people, I was told that it was *beneath my feet*. I returned home content with my expedition, especially as I learnt that I was the only man in Europe who had evaded the guides and reached the crater of the volcano. Entering the Reading Room I was pleased to see our friend, the everlasting student, still at his seat with his pile of books, still taking his notes.

Thus my headquarters was Bloomsbury at this time. I think that the famous Bloomsbury Group had more or less dispersed by then. I never set eyes upon any of them. Was there ever such a concentrate of brilliance? If they looked upon the rest of the world slightly *de haut en bas*, we can scarcely blame them. The only man in the district whom I knew at all well, R H Tawney, lived in Mecklenburgh Square, and belonged to a very different sort of camp. He was held in great esteem by a whole generation, ruling supreme at the London School of Economics, while his book *The Sickness of an Acquisitive Society* made an impact on his age almost equal to the *Fabian Essays*. For he was a stylist. He took much trouble with his prose, finding it difficult to write more than two hundred words a day. I think he was too fond of the clever phrase, and could have said a thing or two more simply, but it was an attractive fault. In person he was no stylist. He cared nothing for his appearance, not for dress, nor money, nor grandeur, nor wine, women, and song. He sat in his study at Mecklenburgh square for forty years. The blitz caused him to change house but not square, and when at length he saw the Bloomsbury housescape changed by certain appalling buildings, the phrases that would do justice to his feelings eluded him, though he did his best, which was pretty good. He sat in his room there, a squat, broadly built man, wearing the same old Tommy's khaki jacket for at least thirty years (he had enlisted in 1914 as a Tommy, disdaining to take a commission). But I think there was more of pride than humility in his character. His study was a shambles of untidiness, a kind of compost heap of papers, as Kingsley Martin — whom I knew in those days when he was climbing and very far from sure of himself — used to say. Tawney was unable to bestow order upon these papers; they gained upon him however much his wife strove against them. I used to visit him quite often, and he was extremely helpful and kind to me. Years later I sometimes brought flowers to him and his wife from the country, and I was touched to find that they were touched at my remembering their kindness.

Not far away in space – in fact not more than a hundred yards from Mecklenburgh Square – but as far from Tawney's world as the Bloomsbury Group, lived Epstein, in Guilford Street. Beyond shaking hands with him I did not know him but to this moment I recall the iron handshake of an iron man. At that time he had two Indian models whose friendship I enjoyed, and whose fascination and dusky beauty completely threw the English girls. But one day Rabindranath Tagore turned up in Guildford Street in regal splendour, frowning upon the girls, so they said, for being models in London instead of remaining in their own country! Tagore had a majestically poetic personality. He had more Appearance than Power. Gandhi, whom I also saw twice in London at this time, struck me as having too pinched a look for a holy man. Dispensing with Appearance he was chiefly Will. I saw him sitting on the floor in a Knightsbridge drawing room, a ball of coiled-up *will* that could destroy Empires while he remained as still as a cat. It is a troubling fact that great men do not always look the part. Occasionally the features of a Lincoln, a Churchill, or a Bernard Shaw are perfectly cast for their role. But it is not always so. We can tell a fool at a glance, but we cannot certainly discern the man of genius. I was once brought to visit Rudyard Kipling at Burwash. Seeing him as an unknown quantity one might think that here was a sharp man from the Inland Revenue. But as I did know who he was I felt Authority. 'You want to know how we got the Indian Empire?' he said to me. 'I'll tell you. The British arrived at a given place in the midst of squabbling tribes. And wherever they were the tribes could have their breakfast in peace and go to sleep without fear. The British moved on to a further place, and once again there was security and peace. And so it went on. We couldn't help it.' He was quite apologetic about this.

Looking back, I mention these names as of interest. But I do not really think of them, but of myself, in days of difficulty, darkness, and obscurity; and of those who shared them with me; of Stephen Potter before he struck gold; of a dear friend, Pauline Short, a Jewess, from whose love and belief in me I drew strength beyond anything I have ever known, and who disappeared into the void in the war, so that to this day I do not know whether she is alive or dead, and have grieved over it for thirty years. Few people look back in anger: it is more often in anguish.

4

It happened that at this time Stephen Potter and I became acquainted with Middleton Murry, for he was living in London then and was working on his *Shakespeare* which caused him to study in the Reading Room sometimes. He had already created *The Adelphi*, a much alive magazine which ran for nearly twenty years – an achievement which gives the measure of Murry's ability. Much influenced by D H Lawrence he wrote with great crusading zeal, attracting many admirers and followers who when under his spell felt that there was no one like him.

In about 1927 he had bought the Old Coastguard Station on the Chesil Beach in Dorset. It was a very isolated station midway between Bridport and Abbotsbury, with only a pathway by the sea leading to it. It was the usual long-terraced building, and Murry could let out two independent quarters. He let one quarter to H M Tomlinson. I persuaded him to let me have the other – the rent per year was incredibly small. I spent over a year there. What a contrast to Guilford Street and the Reading Room! The house was almost on the beach, so close that an exceptional storm would drive waves into the garden. The scene made a simple scheme: in front, if you looked south-westwards there was the ocean with nothing between us and the West Indies (as Tomlinson put it); behind, green Dorset hills rose up; to left and to right a long semicircle of brown shingle rising into headlands made dark blue by distance. That was all. Not much change, probably, since the days of Julius Caesar. I was born by the sea, but never before had seen such light upon the horizon. The whole sky would be grey and gloomy on a bleak winter afternoon, answered by a sea as sombre, but a great wall of light lined the horizon, and in the growing gloom gloriously englamoured the congregation of the clouds with sunset hues. Many years have passed since I gazed with rapture upon those gleams, and still they roof my memory. It is not a wall of light out there, I would say to myself, it is an *entrance* to the heavenly land; see that ship go sailing towards it! – into the paradise regained regions of the visionary mind. I still see the October sun setting on the sea and laying a water-path first of silver, then of gold, and last of red, till the ball sank without a sound – in such contrast with the cold and lonely beauty of the moon-lane in the night. From my window I could watch the alien light of dawn upon the waves, the seagulls swerving and pouncing for fish, while sometimes two or three swans from the Abbotsbury swannery would pass skimming the waves, heads thrust forward, legs tucked away, and wings making a loud swishing noise. There were the heatwave days with the liquid glass lip-lapping on the pebbles. I preferred the windy times when the waves were exciting, though it was then exceedingly dangerous to take a swim, for the shelving was terribly steep and immediate, and the backwash overpowering. I always looked forward to the storms when the waves were as exhilarating as Atlantic rollers; while on some rare occasions there would be a real tempest which provided as untamed a scene as might have been beheld at any time since the foundation of the world.

As I have mentioned, H M Tomlinson rented one portion of the Coastguard Station. He was meagre in frame and not distinguished in face save in so far as there is something particularly appealing and comforting about a Cockney face. He was unpretentious, uncomplicated, not much concerned with philosophy or religion, and an artist: he had written *The Sea and The Jungle*, one of the few great travel books written with a touch of magic. He had won a name for himself as a 1914-18 war correspondent. Later he tried novels. One of them had a good title, *All Our Yesterdays*, but that is all it had; novels were not in his line. 'I don't know anything about women,' he complained to me, and that did make it difficult for him to write novels, and foolish. He was comfortable married: he addressed his wife simply as 'Mums'. His *The Sea and The Jungle* remains. After all the wind-baggery and traveloguery of our age has been washed away, that little rock will stay behind on the riverbed of literature. For the only really hard thing is poetry.

In contrast Middleton Murry was a decided personality. One can see from early photographs that he was an exceptionally bright-eyed and beautiful schoolboy. Then the handsome dark young man with the fine head indicative of great ability. 'It is my belief,' says Mr Rayner Heppenstall in his penetrating book on Murry, that apart from his literary activities 'he might quite as successfully have practised law, divinity, statesmanship, or naval command.' Yes indeed; and he was as good at healing with an agricultural financial sheet as with a Greek text. When finally he took up farming he knew what to do – which astonishes me. A further photograph shows him as the emotionally stricken intellectual brooding upon the miseries of mankind. At all times a person with whom both men and women would fall in love – and be hurt. 'They are the eyes of Goethe,' said a German woman, greatly struck by his remarkable grey-green eyes. One day when I was speaking with him I saw a strange light in his eyes; not so much in them, as playing around them, a kind of haze or aura. Perhaps it was an illusion. But I was startled.

He did not impress me as being all of a piece. He could not look you straight in the face with those eyes, he always turned them aside. His walk was ungainly. His drawling manner of speech was incongruous with the intensity of his thought and emotion. He had a defective sense of comedy, but a dazzling smile which was full or mirth, with a touch of the devilish in it, not excluding the elements of a sneer. On paper he passionately poured himself out, seeking the way and the truth and the life; he was chock-full of idealism, love, comradeship, dreams of the perfect commonwealth, and so on, together with much wearing upon his sleeve personal privacies and agonisings which most people would keep to themselves. Off paper, so far from being expansive he was extremely aloof and withdrawn, so that young admirers calling on him for cheer or advice or with the hope that he might help them to 'find themselves' went away disillusioned and hurt by his coldness, and put out by his stickiness in conversation. He was not really cold of course, but he could not let go of himself in a free and easy way, and he was a man of such veracity that he could never bring himself to say anything which he did not really mean. Years later his fourth wife told me that he had so little self-conceit that it never occurred to him that younger men might hang on his words or good opinion or treasure a crumb of literary praise and encouragement. There may have been some truth in that. It is difficult for young unknown men to realize that the senior 'known' and 'famous' men who they look up to as such, often do not see themselves in that light at all. Even so I did find him unduly sticky. Once I borrowed some gramophone records from him. When he wanted them back he didn't ask me for them, but left a note. 'How typical,' said F L Lea, his searching biographer, when I mentioned this to him. 'I never gave you a chance,' he said to me at a later date, and added that I had been too wrapped up in myself. That also was true.

No doubt he was harmed by his association with Lawrence, becoming overshadowed by the stronger force and allowing himself to be drawn into unseemly saviour histrionics. As is well known one of the main characteristics about Lawrence was his personal influence on people. In one of his most autobiographical novels, *Aaron's Rod*, a man called Jim hits another man in the stomach. That character is supposed to represent Lawrence himself and is incredibly named Lilly. One day a man called on me announcing himself as Captain White. He declared that he was the person who had hit Lawrence in the stomach. This incident is quite a famous passage in the book since so little action takes place. White was proud of this: equally for appearing in the book and for having hit Lawrence – as well he might be. He had found Lawrence an uncomfortable person to know, and I was much struck by one observation he made 'Lawrence had a disconcerting power of *scenting out the carrion in a man.*'

Intellectual men in particular feared his judgement. Bertrand Russell, after hearing Lawrence's opinion of him, turned over in his mind whether he should continue living. On the other hand Aldous Huxley was so cerebral that faced with Lawrence he welcomed his corrective influence. Both Huxley and Lawrence tended to denigrate Murry, Huxley satirising him in *Point Counter Point* when true traits were mixed with false ones – an unsavoury way of telling lies about a person. (Huxley's beautiful personality and manner of speech were strangely incongruous with the ugliness of his fiction.)

I feel sure that Lawrence's relentless earnestness, lack of wit, and his abhorrence of the light touch when dealing with heavy things encouraged Murry's tendency to dispense with humour as a method of bringing perspective to bear upon tragic themes. But no one can deny that he wrote powerfully and wove an artistic pattern out of each theme, for he combined with his emotion an analytical drive which drew the work together. He preferred to write about the great sufferers rather than those who took suffering in their stride with a jest, for the slightest degree of levity was painful to him. He liked best writing about those who suffered and raved and died. He enjoyed it. He made them go through it properly. He created a world of his own in his books with a line of heroes all conforming to the same pattern of martyrdom and saviourhood. After the death of Lawrence he pulled out all his stops. He transmuted him. He worked him up, higher and higher, in a kind of frenzy, until he became hero, martyr, saviour, saint, betrayed (by Murry himself), disabused, crowned with sorrows and thorns. There was a good deal of dross in all this. And when he got going as a sociological crusader his pen ran away with him, preaching the Necessity of this and then the Necessity of that (often the opposite), and during the war contending that Laval was a good chap and Churchill a villain, and editing a paper called *Peace News* while battles were raging in every direction – a state of mind which argued a lack of sense of humour amounting to insanity... But I must note here, however, that if one put a criticism to him in private there was absolutely nothing of the arrogant zealot in his manner of taking it. I once suggested to him (meeting him a few years before his death in the London Library) that he tended to make all his clients conform to the same pattern and 'come full circle', a favourite phrase of his; and that he overdid adjectives like 'timeless' and 'inevitable'. He laughed and agreed with me, and said that he had so little of the artist in him that he didn't realize that he was using certain adjectives in a reckless way. He was the last man to get onto a high horse with regard to a critical comment.

And he has certainly left some rocks behind. There are some in his God, his Jesus, and his Shakespeare. The firmest rock is his *Keats and Shakespeare*. The creatively analytical power with which he interpreted Keats' *Letters* is a lasting illumination. He wrote a kind of appendix to that book called *Studies in Keats*. In the course of it he wrote the following words: 'Since every existence has its part in the realm of Being, any existence may become a symbol for us of that totality of Being to which it also belongs. So soon as we contemplate any existing thing without desire or regret, without belief or anxiety, without the stirring of any animal impulse towards it, in a pure experience of it as a thing which simply is, we have gained our entrance into the world of Being: the first gleam of that which can become, if we will suffer it, a total vision, is ours.' It will be allowed, I hope, by all who do not consider theology to be the only approach to religion, that that paragraph is as profound as it is powerful.

I am sure that Murry was sounder on Keats' philosophy than he was on the poet's love story with Fanny Brawne. He was not at his best on the subject of love. He was very sensitive; but I came to believe that like many sensitive persons the sense was more for himself than for others. He fell in love with a French girl called Marguérite whom he jilted, and failing to keep a final promised tryst with her called this, 'falling out of love and into pity'. He then married Katherine Mansfield, and when she died of consumption he declared that it was a law of life that true love must end in disaster. In the following year he married Violet le Maistre who dressed and looked like Katherine, talked in the same idiom, and also wrote short stories. Murry gave her a pearl ring which he had once given Katherine, called his daughter Katherine, and embroidered KM on the napkins. Mr Lea maintains that it took him three years to discover that Violet was not Katherine. Then she also caught consumption. He assured her that he would pull her through by the power of love. This caused her to declare that she was actually glad that she had caught it, for now, she thought, he would love her as much as Katherine. He could not see that this was quite natural. He did see it as 'a grim cosmic joke', for he always saw things that way. The joke was completed when after he had nursed her for four years she left him to die in another man's arms. Murry then married his housekeeper. She was illiterate and truculent and gave him such a bad time that he nearly lost his reason. At length he fled from her to live with Mary Gamble until Betty (the housekeeper) died, and Mary became his fourth wife. With her he found peace and happiness.

He had a passion right up to the end to preach in high terms about love, recklessly, on the foundation of his personal experience. When Katherine died 'love was inevitably attended with disaster'. When Violet was dying he wrote 'Oh, you who come after me, don't let a woman become your sweetheart. It's unbearable – unbearable: just unbearable. For she will die and the world will stand still, and your heart will burst. I have had two sweethearts.' Anyone might write something like that in a letter. It throws light on Murry that he could actually print it, and talk about 'you who come after me'. Later, when he was happy in marriage he sent out another message to mankind: 'The one thing of permanent value and significance I have achieved,' he wrote, 'the one thing worth listening to which I have to say, is that man-woman love is the supreme felicity, and that it is attainable.' In which case he might just as well have held his tongue when he laid down the law on the other occasions. And he knew as well as anyone that what is attainable by good fortune is not obtainable by any known means. So the 'one thing worth listening to' amounts to no more than would the glee of a child boastfully displaying a sugar-plum to others.

His current wife at the Old Coastguard Station was Violet. She remained out of sight in bed in their upper room overlooking the sea. Murry did not encourage her to receive visitors and I only once went up to see her. She was sitting up in bed; dark hair, striking features, the bright eyes of the consumptive, and an almost waxen complexion. But I had not idea how seriously ill she was, and she showed no inkling of her impending doom. Had I realized this and also thought how lonely she must have been there with Murry at work downstairs for long periods, I might have put deference aside and suggested to Murry that I go and talk with her sometimes – he did not suggest it himself, no doubt thinking I might be told things he would not want me to know. However, I was too shy to suggest it, and shyness so often takes the form of thoughtlessness and lack of imagination where others are concerned. In retrospect this one meeting with Violet Murry was a very sad occasion in my life.

5

Thus, having the flat in Guilford Street and these quarters on the Chesil Bank, I was a house-in-town-and-country man, roughly millionaire class, though I hardly exceeded two hundred a year. But in 1929 I was obliged to abandon both these places and to live, first in three consecutive flats in Hampstead and then in a house in Kent. This was because of marriage. I sometimes hear people say that they are bored at reading about love affairs in autobiographies. I am not bored by this myself, but I find it impossible to write about it – and that's flat. Early in my twenties I became engaged, but the girl was much too sensible to keep it up. Later I was to be married to an American girl. She had to return to America (or I let her return) and then she wrote to me in Dorset from New York to say that she did not wish to marry me. I borrowed – rather, I was given by a kind friend – the passage money and took the boat to America to see if I could get her back. I was unsuccessful. After a week I returned to the Chesil Bank. Murry was interested in this. 'Everything will come right as soon as you meet her again,' he had said. So it should have been, but a quality of dream hung over the whole thing, and there was no question of her accepting me since she was awake. The going, the staying, and the returning took little over a fortnight, and this struck Murry rather forcibly – 'fantastic', he said (before that word had become pop). Shortly after this I met my wife in London and got married after a week.

It is really extraordinary the way people talk about marriage as if it were a problem that could be solved, or even discouraged from existing at all. Elaborate discussions on it are held on TV, one of them even asking: 'Why Marriage?' 'Is it good or bad?', and so on. As if it were not, in inception, as natural as a bird's nest – about which we do not ask whether it is good or bad, or whether it should have a future. There will always be a lot of people who want to get together and make a nest for themselves and their children. Some are really gifted in this creation, a few men as well as more women, have a positive genius for it. Many need it without being able to preserve its naturalness, and turn it into a prison. Many think they need it and find they don't, while others fall into it in a fit of absence of mind. Any discussion on the subject is mostly subjective and could go in indefinitely, for there will always be as many views as there are marriages, since each marriage is different. What is becoming generally felt, perhaps for the first time in history by both sexes – as the economic aspect alters – is the absurdity of two people taking out a licence in one another for the rest of their lives. If we all lived for about one hundred and fifty years it *couldn't* be faced; (imagine someone saying bitterly, '...and to think that I have given you the best one hundred and twenty years of my life!'). That licence would certainly be discarded if economics ever became of no account. Already among the rich no one is surprised when a man has four wives or a woman has four husbands, so long as they have them consecutively. If the 'I will love you for ever' vow is dropped, it will not mean the end of marriage in the least, for those who have a capacity or a genius for it will be in exactly the same enviable position as they have always been; though even in their case the behaviour towards one another could be improved, while generally speaking behaviour would be bound to improve since possessive bullying and financially inspired ill-temper would no longer be sanctified by the Church and legalised by the State.

In my own case I was ludicrously unsuited for keeping a nest, and my wife suffered accordingly. I had not allowed for the financial cost, and expected to be able to continue my work, and was in fact as bent upon doing so as if it were as important as that of a Beethoven, a Michelangelo, or a Shakespeare. And I did stick to it because I always imagined that success was just round the corner, and for years the financial problem was so appalling and so humiliating that I could not even look at the flowers in spring so much did bills come between me and them. I could not really relax and enjoy the company of my two beautiful daughters; and the time to really enjoy children is before the age of ten. There is no question as to the truth of this: the time to make the best of your children, and unquestionably the time when the enjoy your company best, is before the age of ten. I realize that I am stating the obvious, and that I am preaching; but I have a firm grasp of the obvious – when it is too late. We should always listen carefully to the man who preaches what he has not practised. He is the man to attend to, not the good man, who so seldom feels the urge to preach. I do not say that I wholly failed in this. 'Tell us a story, Daddy' they would plead in bed in the evening, and on the spot I would begin, 'There was a hare who...' and would blindly carry forward – successfully enough for the insistence of another instalment next evening. But I am far from sure whether to have not entirely failed when one could have wholly succeeded does not make matters worse when the opportunity has passed and the children have ceased to care.

I have always been struck by Dr Johnson's refusal to talk about his early struggles and financial difficulties: he could not *bear* to think of it, he said. So it is with me regarding the next ten years after 1929. No words can describe the awfulness in terms of money-anxiety. What! The reader may feel, you the son of a well-to-do solicitor who could send you to Rugby and Oxford, what do you know of such things? A good deal, I think. Your impecunious literary man, with family, is a pitiable object. And the 1931 financial depression, so disastrous in America, was bad enough over here, making jobs scarce while cuts in pay were made in every direction. In money matters I am very punctilious: if I borrow I always pay back. And to ask my father for more than the £150 I regarded as the ultimate in humiliation, as I had done nothing to justify myself in his eyes. In any case he did buy us (after the births of children had driven us from place to place in Hampstead) a house in Kent which was going for six hundred pounds – and which after the war fetched thirteen hundred. We struggled on somehow, but I do not like to think of those days. I love to be able to *give*, but I couldn't give, and the incapacity of having the power to give, financially, I regard as an almighty curse. I have *received* from time to time – with good grace, I think. It is a strange thing, but it is supposed to be common (especially among literary men) that a person who receives help subsequently feels resentment towards his benefactor. This has always seemed to me a monstrously unnecessary attitude. I remember wrongs. I feel resentment. I bear malice. But I never forget a kindness. Any good thing that is ever done me I cherish with never diminishing gratitude. I sometimes hear people say, to me or to others, 'Why drag all that up now, it's ancient history!' Well, I obstinately hold to the belief that what is true on Monday is equally true on Tuesday. And I have not observed the people who raise this objection making the slightest complaint if one brings up something good that they have done, and remembers it with gratitude.

One of the people that I remember with most gratitude at this time is A R Orage, first famous as the editor of *The New Age*, and then in the thirties as editor of *The New English Weekly*. He was much more than an editor, he was a great human being in the largeness of whose heart and understanding young writers received solace. And the comprehensiveness of his mind was acknowledged by his peers. AE, who came to live in London at this time, frequently talked with him and the last thing that he wrote was an obituary of Orage, setting forth his greatness. T S Eliot, who supported and contributed to *The New English Weekly* said that 'even if one did not see him often, it was a comfort to know that he was *there*.' G K Chesterton wrote at the time of his sudden death, 'The news came to me like a thunderclap that Orage, whose very name was The Storm, had passed as suddenly as he appeared in the stormy times of old.' He said that in relation to Wells and Shaw there was sometimes a kind of paralysis of modernism which hampered them, but that he had no such feeling about Orage who 'could be reactionary as well as revolutionary.' After quoting a passage from him, GKC lamented that prose such as his should be stacked away in the files of a newspaper. AE was attracted to him because he was both a philosopher and an economist, and he was attracted to him also because of his insistence that a writer is a man *speaking* to the public, and that if his words cannot be heard by the reader as well as seen, if they cannot be spoken, then he who touches a book will not touch a man. He will only touch literature. You will get not speech but words. AE held this view just as strongly as Orage did – and as I do myself.

About once a week Orage and AE would meet at an ABC café in Chancery Lane, and other contributors could join in. There was an element of comfort in seeing these two men, two of the choicest spirits of the day, meeting not in a grand salon or Café Royal, but in an ABC, paying sixpence for a bun and cup of coffee – for that was about as much as either could afford. I was living in Kent then and did not often join them. Sometimes I met there other contributors such as the brilliant Rayner Heppenstal, Hugh Macdiarmid, and Pamela Travers whose creation of Mary Poppins eclipsed her own name! Ruth Pitter also came. AE's monologuery was less encouraged in those days,

107

he had the wrong audience for it. In any case Ruth Pitter far surpassed him, or anyone else, in conversation, her talk having in it so much of surprise and freshness, enriched by an ever-ready particular example, and never giving the impression that she had made the same remark before. It is very rare to find a poet talking as well as the poems warrant, but she did and does. Although as long ago as 1936, James Stephens wrote of her as in stature 'the companion poet to W B Yeats', it is only recently that she has come into her own. Her remarkable *range*, and the subtlety of her oblique lyrical assault always stagger me, and support my contention that technique is genius. Most people are inspired from time to time, some often, some at infrequent periods; but they cannot communicate it. This calls for extraordinary powers, and I call it genius, and doubt very much if any genius would object.

T S Eliot appeared at meetings dealing with the N.E.W. but I do not remember ever seeing him in the company of AE – it would have made a strange contrast. It was difficult to realize that Eliot was an American, though he did have a touch of the Emerson-eagle kind of countenance. And his extreme politeness struck me as American. Cultivated Americans are the politest people in the world. Eliot was courteous rather than forthcoming with acquaintances, but he was less ostentatious than anyone, and seemed to have nothing of the charlatan in him – (though that is not wholly true of anyone). Two remarks which he made to me strike me as characteristic of the man. He said that during the Abdication Crisis he changed his mind on the subject several times a day. How many would admit to that? The second remark was the psychological effect on a poet in getting a poem into print. If a poem was accepted and printed it became more real to the poet; and if it was paid for it became still more real, even if he were only paid ten shillings. A great remark, coming from him of all people. The last glimpse I had of him was in that great leveller of humanity, an Underground lift. I came upon him crammed in one at Kensington. He said How are you? and I said I was well, and had just been to a cocktail party. There was a pause, for he may have thought that I had said 'the cocktail party' as his play by that name was then running. Then 'How long are you staying in town?' I said a few days, and he said 'I'm sorry it isn't longer.' I mention this banality as it is a typical example of failure in communication I often experience when a little less diffidence on my part could have effected a reasonable exchange – instead of working in me as a damaging recollection.

Orage's sudden death was hard for me to face. He had been very fatherly towards me. He could not as a rule pay contributors, but he always paid me two guineas, and I possess (tied together in a bundle) a series of letters to me about my articles which did more for my morale than anything in my life. Later on I did a lot for *Time & Tide* till death of Lady Rhondda put paid to that. Then a lot for *The Observer* under Viola Garvin till suddenly, overnight, the paper changed hands and I was out in the cold. I'm not very good at hopping from one paper to another, I've never known how to do it. Poor old Easterbrook, I once thought when *The News Chronicle* closed overnight. I need not have worried – he was on another paper next week. I didn't know enough people, I didn't mix enough. Stephen Potter, who was very good at the gentle art of not making enemies, was concerned about this, but though I always made friends when I went out I didn't follow it up. I used to be told in early days 'The way to get on, Collis, is to get to know people, to lunch with everyone.' But I didn't know how to do this, for no one asked me in the first place. I once asked John Betjeman to lunch. He replied that he 'didn't want to sound like a Prima Donna, but he was booked for lunch for the next two months.' I did think he sounded like a Prima Donna, and should have written back to say so, but I was too polite; after which I regretted my politeness, just as I have often regretted my restraint, and just as I have often regretted behaving like the perfect Christian gent when it would have been much better if I had behaved roughly. I am slow to anger. This is not a good trait in me, for a bit later I become angry that I was not angry and get extremely angry, when it is too late. The roots of this restraint are in my childhood, I'm sure, for then I was obliged to habitually restrain myself. It is often plain caution and prudence (very strong in me), and sometimes just cool condescension – never guessed as such by the other person – more often than simple good nature. All the same I do advocate restraint and I regard it is utterly preposterous when car drivers abandon restraint towards each other in a manner they would never dream of on the pavement.

One source of income for me at this time and for many years before and after the war was that of Tutor in Adult Education classes under the auspices of the Extra-Mural department of the University of London, and also, though less often, under Oxford and Cambridge. Here is a field of education that does not become subject to class or other controversies, is not in need of any 'solution', nor cursed with great 'problems' (apart from technical matters that is, for the Ministry of Education imposes upon this Department of the universities certain regulations, of which some are not only ludicrous and useless but decrease by thousands the number of those who would join and gain enormously from this great movement). It consists of grown people, of any age or class, whose attendance is *voluntary*; of people who have escaped from school knowledge and ask things they want answered, and discuss whatever they are most interested in. That is a wonderful atmosphere for a tutor. In any case, who is really fit to start his education (by which I mean self-education) much before the age of twenty? 'Until I was twenty-five I had no development at all', wrote Herman Melville (who, I sometimes think, means more to me even than Shakespeare or Dickens or Tolstoy, than Shaw or Wordsworth or Thomas Hardy). 'From my twenty-fifth year I date my life. Three weeks have scarcely passed at any time between then and now, that I have not unfolded within myself.' Inspiring words for the young.

I believe that this extra-mural education for grown people is only in its infancy, though it started many years ago as The Workers' Education Association. But when the workers became better off most of them abandoned it. *'Their souls are hungry because their bodies are full'*, says Shaw's Undershaft in *Major Barbara*, in 1906. Was there ever such a non-sequitur? Since they became affluent to a degree never envisaged by Shaw their minds have become ever less hungry. When in the nineteenth century Ruskin dedicated *Fors* to 'The Working Men of England'; when Henry Millar's famous *Old Red Sandstone* was first given as lectures to a Working Men's Institute; when Thomas Huxley read a paper to them 'On a Piece of Chalk', that was quite in order. Today the idea would be laughable. The English working man does not now hate matters of the mind and spirit any more than an animal does; he merely has a bestial indifference to them. Why should this matter, it may be asked. Well, it doesn't matter to me a scrap. But by God it matters to them! Because not only is an educated person far more interesting than an uneducated one, but apart from ill health and financial problems, he has nothing to fear until the day of his death. Just consider. We are continually being asked to be sorry for 'the old people', how unhappy they are, how lonely, how bored, how they have nothing to do, and so on. The truth is never faced, it is never stated, it is always evaded: namely, that it is *their own fault*. If at the age of sixteen, seventeen, or eighteen a person elects to be a boor and a bore, then at the age of sixty, seventy, or eighty he will be far worse off than an old horse or an old goat or an old sheep or an old pig and they are never observed to be wallowing in self-pity. Oceans and empires of interest, door after door after door, window after window after window, of fascinating vista regarding the universe can be thrown open to all who bother to cultivate their minds. If they choose, after they have grown up, to read but two pages a day from the literary classics or the sciences, or both, then life would become far too short for them, old age a priceless chance, and solitude their greatest blessing. Even bad health and poor finance would be largely conquered by the spirit. The fact that they miss this chance and then think themselves victims of mischance is appalling because it is unnecessary. I will only add this: when I see right, left, and centre young thugs and thugesses, flaunting themselves and exhibiting an open contempt for what they call book-learning, I feel like crying out, Beware! Look what's coming! Take caution! Remember that a young person is an old person who has not yet become old just as an old person is a young person who has not remained young; very soon your faces will be knifed and your bodies enfeebled, but the one thing that is not eroded by Time, the mind, will not exist for you, and you will come to hate the world and detest each other.

Now that illiteracy has made such rapid strides, how about the middle and lower-middle classes (awful terms, but it's not my fault), are they much better in this matter? No, not much. A great sigh of relief went up the other day when the advent of television made it unnecessary for them ever to read a book again. 'Ten years of cheap reading', wrote Shaw in 1900, 'have changed the English from the most stolid nation in Europe to the most theatrical and hysterical.' Ten years of television (in addition to a mountainous pile of journalism) have swept away the necessity for even a bookshelf in a house. Go into a home in suburbia and you will find tasteful appointments, perfect curtains, congruous carpets, wonderful kitchen, everything spotlessly clean (not that we can equate cleanliness as being next to godliness, since the mind of the dust-sweeping housewife is often in a ferment of corruption), but without a single book in sight. I do not blame them. I have a personal interest at stake, and yet I often find TV compulsive even when it is repulsive; enthralling on nature subjects, absorbing on interviews and discussion programmes, irresistible on any of the sports in which we may be interested, and entirely new in its power to ceaselessly educate people about people. Those who refer to the screen as the goggle-box are merely describing themselves, while those (with exceptions) who declare that they never watch TV are nearly always as dull and unimaginative as they are conceited. But Literature (as opposed to journalism which is often first rate) is put in a very vulnerable position – not applicable to music or painting, since you cannot play snippets of a symphony or show bits of a picture. It is not in the interests of TV to support Literature, but to promote the new medium and keep people away from reading books exactly as it is in the interests of Fleet Street to do so. It is no light matter to see, day by day, the inner eye of the imagination that forms moving pictures in the mind exchanged for the outer eye that merely gazes at a moving picture on a screen. This is now virtually how all the classics are taken by the people – *seen*, not read and imagined. I shall doubtless be told that I am quite wrong about this: 'on the contrary, Mr Collis' (when someone says 'on the contrary' it always means that he is lying), 'on the contrary, after a film or a TV production of a great classic there is an unprecedented demand for it at the libraries, as statistics will show.' I fear such people deceive themselves with their silly statistics. Oh yes, the books are asked for and taken out. But they are not *read* – only the few are capable of that art any more. The incomparably brilliant 'stage-directions' of Dickens; the descriptions of Thomas Hardy where the vision of beauty is built upon endless particulars of arresting exactitude; the unexampled penetration and candour of Tolstoy's commentary in the course of his story, all this and much more must be omitted in the pictured version.[6] The library reader does not get out of the book for these things, but in order to read the complete story again and see if it matches up to the film or TV production – which in its own terms is often very good indeed.

Further, both TV and Radio discourage anything in the way of solid reading in relation to the essay on general themes or on philosophy or on religion. That can all be taken care of by Talks – to which roughly *half* one's attention is given, if as much, because of the conditions in which one listens, and you cannot ask the speaker to repeat what he has just said... I have enlarged about all this for I have used both radio and TV a very great deal, and also have been associated with the Adult Education or Extra-Mural Movement – terribly dull names for which I hope something more exciting will be found – during forty years, and I know what I'm talking about. I believe that if we really want to create a solid nucleus of readers independent of the popular mediums, say one million out of the fifty millions, it could be done – and that would be enough.

6

In the thirties I was too crushed by the weight of personal problems to be able to take in much of what was happening in the world outside my own narrow sphere, and thus, for example, I understood nothing about the Spanish Civil War, and did not follow it. (Though I am glad to say that I did grasp, and quite thoroughly, what was happening in the German concentration camps.) But one thing at home interested me so much that I took notes, and can make a small personal contribution to the history of the period.

Coming from 'over the border', whether from Wales or Scotland or Ireland, a person will be struck by certain characteristics which he may consider as essentially English: for example the adherence to rules (observe this in any club or society) at the expense of conduct-as-an-art which can mean the breaking of rules sometimes; the principle of free speech being considered as of greater importance than the thing said; the mistaking of sincerity for seriousness, of ethics for religion, of vulgarity for comedy, and of lack of convictions for tolerance; and of a startling addiction to sheer *silliness*. I notice with regret that these are negative reflections only – perhaps because they are more amusing than positive ones – and they may be just personal quirks, their worth appraised by the fact that I could never enjoy more than one or two items in the programme called 'Itma' which set the whole nation yelling with laughter, and I have never had anything but contempt for the Goons. However, this is all by the way: what particularly interests me is the attitude towards Monarchy in England, and indeed the need for it. I'm not sure whether the intelligentsia quite realize the simplicities upon which it rests. I mean, we hear about it as 'an essential link with the Commonwealth', or as something useful 'above Party', or in some way 'stabilizing' the Constitution. But these are largely empty claims, since Constitutions in many countries get on without a Monarchy. The thing rests, rather simply, upon *affection*. Monarchy in England thrives if affection is felt; if it is not felt, or if it is withdrawn, for good or dubious reasons, its support dwindles. (The fact that no one could fail to like Princess Anne or Prince Charles assures a bright future for the Monarchy.) What is gained by this? it may be asked. A good deal is gained by affection being felt for a noble line, a royal family whose entire activity is concerned with the life of the people. There is no question but that it adds dignity and prestige to the nation – a prestige which is felt abroad, especially in America. It also happens that the English, above all others, have a genius for the organization of ritualistic occasions on a large scale: funerals, coronations, weddings. It is a form of theatre in which they excel, and which they need – at least they certainly give every indication of needing it. It is theatre, a play, not impinging upon anything that can really help or hurt them in the manner of political or economic events, but which has theatrical value, and who will deny value to theatre? Certainly these plays are very well done, the best productions being in relation to the Monarchy.

The Dying Scene of George V was one of the best. The announcement from the BBC made by Stuart Hibbert (whose early retirement was never explained) was masterly work. The long silence when the News was due, and then at last the Voice:

'This is London. The following bulletin has been received from Sandringham: *The King's life is moving peacefully towards its close. Another bulletin will be made at 10.00 p.m.'

Then precisely the same words at ten o'clock, at 10.15, at 10.30, at 10.45, at 11.00 p.m., at 11.15, at 11.30, at 11.45, till almost as Big Ben struck midnight, the King expired.

It was very enjoyable. The people, drawn together by means of the wireless, bent their thoughts upon this single mystery. The concert, the talk, the normal theatre, the dance tune, the news of the world, all silenced for the one announcement: 'The King's life is moving peacefully towards its close.' And thus the nation, in public places, in family groups, in lonely rooms, unified with that single thought, stood waiting for the death of one old man.

I felt moved next day when I came upon people still living in the drama and touched with the semblance of grief. 'We Mourn Our Beloved King', I read over the portal of a tobacconist's shop. 'We Grieve Not As They Who Mourn Without Hope', was chalked on the window of a shoemaker. 'I feel as if I had lost a father', a man selling socks said to me. The Lying-in-State must have commanded the longest theatre queue in the history of monarchy.

But it was not till I entered the suburban railway carriage that I really made contact with one of the audience. I was alone in the carriage when at Knockholt a man got in – an old-young little clerky man with a washed-away pale face almost the colour of a sheet. There was no not-speaking-to-a-stranger just now. He immediately addressed me, saying, 'Sir, our Beloved King has taken his last journey today' (for this was after the Funeral). 'Not long ago', he continued, 'I took a snapshot of His Majesty on the balcony of Buckingham Palace. I treasure that, I treasure that!' I rose to the occasion. 'Sir', I replied, 'in the past and up till modern times it has been possible for a king to be one of four things: he could be a Ruler or a Conqueror or an Emperor or a Tyrant. None of these roles is now possible. Unless a king has a genius to create a new role he is washed out or kicked out.' Here the little man winced. 'Alone among all latter day sovereigns George V was inspired to create a new thing, he became – a *father*. Not a false and insincere Father like the Tsars of Russia, but a real one who rejoiced in the joy and shared in the sorrows of his people. But mark you,' I continued with emphasis, 'such a new role could not have been created by guile, it could not have been created by mere cleverness, nor even by the desire to be a Father. It was created almost unconsciously by a *good man*, and was accepted by the people because he was good.' These words were received by my companion with ill-concealed emotion. He rose higher to the occasion. Plucking at his collar a bit, nervously coughing at the audacity of his utterance, he jerked out, 'I... er...think that he was the greatest man since – Jesus Christ.'

If the drama of the death of George V was a fine performance, the drama of his son's Abdication was stupendous. These works, both performed in the same year, served as a vindication and justification of British Monarchy which still holds good.

Entering the theatre for a whole week to watch this morality play called 'The Crisis' they escaped from the real world. What they saw had no roots in the real issues of the day, it had nothing that could substantially touch their lives. It was a Play. But it was absorbing. It held attention. The world outside did indeed cease to exist for one whole happy week, and it may well be doubted whether any other Sovereign ever achieved so much for his people.

What they witnessed was a Tragedy. It was not a pure tragedy. That is the worst of life. It is the privilege of Art alone to present us with the image of a perfectly tragic event and to exclude the elements of absurdity which in real life shoot through the theme and spoil the even step and steadfast countenance of the hero. Even the King's speech before the fall of the curtain contained an element of the absurd greater than the element of the tragic.

In a sermon preached on 1 December, 1936, the Bishop of Bradford while speaking about the coming Coronation made a few mild exhortations to the King. Since the Church lays the crown upon the Monarch's head it was natural that the bishops should express the hope that His Majesty should play the game according to the rules and approach the event in a pious spirit. The national papers made no comment, but nine local papers in the north wrote leaders about it.

At this point the King made known his wish to enter into a state of holy matrimony and to say farewell to ephemeral gallantries.

Then the entire Press started up in full fore and like a Greek Chorus did its best to tell the audience what was going on in the play.

Edward VIII was extremely popular with the public at large. People still thought of him as the Prince of Wales, for which post he had possessed all the right qualities. But it was now becoming necessary for him to settle down to the role of devoted public servant with a background of sound family life. For, while the English like their Princes to be Prince Hals, they like their Kings to be Henry the Fifths.

Unfortunately he showed no inclination to conform, and actually announced his intention to marry a lady who had already experienced marriage. An uproar followed for six days; for the people, willing to identify with what is loose through images on the screen, wish to identify with what is secure through the image of the Monarchy. The Press and the public threw the affair into a question of dramatic choice – between this marriage and giving up the throne, between love and duty.

The nation was held in suspense. What would the King decide? Very few went to the theatres or cinemas that week, for who would want to see another play just then? The shops also suffered, especially the book trade, publishers declaring that they had only one seventh of their usual sales that week. The conversation, everywhere and all the time, was entirely confined to this subject. The people visualized the King sitting at home, thinking, questioning, searching his heart. They pictured him trying to decide between Love and Duty. They supposed him to be bracing himself to the Renunciation of Love.

On big occasions, when no element of commerce is in question, the English people are ruled by two things – sentimentality and morality. At first the former presides, but the latter prevails. We see the force of sentiment slowly giving way before the ardour of ethics. This occasion was no exception. While the King was thinking things out, for three days the people gave way to Sentiment, and it seemed as if the Prime Minister, Mr Baldwin – who could read the public mind more astutely than any editor, and was therefore against the marriage – was at fault. The idea of Love was triumphant. A Monarch puts Love before a Throne. For three days the people responded to so great a theme. For three days the typist, the clerk, the workman, the tradesman, the bus conductor, the businessman, the housewife, the journalist, were for the King. On the fourth day the force of sentiment began to wane and the movement towards morality set in. On the fifth day the idea of Duty triumphed over the idea of Love. On the sixth day Duty alone prevailed and they were against the King. On the seventh day his popularity had waned so much that at South Wales the audiences in the cinemas witnessed in cold silence his recent visit to the distressed valleys when their cheers for him had seemed as genuine as his concern for them.

Thus when 'The Crisis' drew towards its climax and Baldwin brought the King's Message of Abdication to the House, and made an extremely astute speech, the Press declared that his voice was the voice of England. It was. The minority of sympathisers could be disregarded, and Baldwin could count upon full support. Some people hinted that he made a deal with the Labour Opposition lest it might use the opportunity to force an election and seize power. This was unnecessary. Labour would rather not take office than be associated with a King contemplating marrying a commoner. After all what was he but 'a poor weak creature', as Mr Buchanan from the extreme Left, put it, 'a man in a mess', and who instead of being treated like a common man was treated as if he were the King of England.

The climax was over and the tension slackened. Everyone waited for the King's speech which was to be broadcast the following night. Morality and

Duty having triumphed, they could now listen with sympathy to what the King had to say himself.

His first words were remarkable. 'At long last I can say a few words of my own.' We were confronted at once with the element of absurdity in the position of the monarchy. The King was not allowed to choose his wife, and he was prevented from speaking to his people until they had ceased to be his subjects. The *assumption* that he should say nothing until there was no point in his saying anything, would have been impossible to maintain if the proceedings had not been so theatrical, with unlikely assumptions accepted for the sake of the play. There is no reason why a King should not speak to his people if he chooses, not why he should subject himself to the dictates of his own subjects, without saying a word – even Charles I had plenty to say before they cut off his head. Edward VIII acted without spirit and therefore could command no support. It certainly argues a feeble state of mind for a King of England to throw in his hand just when his country is beating up against a second world war; and one wonders what his thoughts eventually were when the bombs were falling around his brother on Buckingham Palace while he himself was but an exile cast upon an alien shore.

Anyway now, the people thought, he was going to explain to them his side of the problem. In this expectation they were disappointed. He said little and only spoke for a few minutes. There was an element of indignity in a Sovereign having to talk about a love affair to his subjects. Perhaps this irked him, for he soon concluded, and then immediately left England, flying 'out into the night'.

Still, this broadcast moved the people. They wept. They swung back from the ethical to the sentimental plane. Love had prevailed over Duty. And was not this lover, they asked themselves, even more sincere in his belief in marriage than any of them; did he not more than all others yearn for the blessedness of the home and rehearse the sanctity of the hearth?

The BBC noticed this movement back to Love, and decided that it should not be encouraged. The Abdication was treated as a Funeral and all stations were closed down. Next evening, lest this dangerous spirit of sentiment should betray the people into regrettable reflections, the following numbers were struck out of Ambrose's late-night broadcast – *No Regrets*; *Crazy with Love*; *I Don't Want To Get Hot*; and *We Go Well Together*.

Not realizing that the tide of moral fervour had already subsided, the Archbishop of Canterbury attempted to round off the affair by a public rebuke against the departed King. This utterance contained a touch of poetry. 'In darkness he left these shores'; a touch of rhetoric, 'Strange and sad it is' etc; almost a touch of reality. But it created a further reaction in the King's favour. It was not 'fair play'. The man was 'down'. Nevertheless the Archbishop, thinking that the unpopularity of his words showed that the public conscience had been awakened, decided on the following Sunday to use the occasion to make a plea for a religious revival. Apologizing at intervals for his own lack of spirit, he said that the best way to bring this about would be for each man to love one woman and to hate all Russians. A shudder ran through the country, and next week there was a phenomenally small attendance in church throughout the land. This brought the curtain down.

It only remained for praise to be distributed among both actors and audience. This was done with a generosity never found wanting after big occasions in England. With one accord the Press said that everyone had been splendid. Mr Baldwin was the most splendid of all, but the man in the street had also been simply marvellous. It was another triumph for Britain. With the eyes of the whole world upon them the people of England by their calmness, their fortitude, their judgement, their good sense, their balance, had proved themselves to be exceptional. Mr Eden, the Foreign Secretary, in striking phrases witnessing to the originality of his mind, declared that 'the most remarkable feature of the Crisis has been the steadfastness and forbearance of the British public. They have again displayed those qualities of coolness, dignity, wisdom, and restraint which have characterized them at critical moments in the Empire's history. They have given expression to that innate political instinct which is, perhaps, their greatest gift.' Mr Eden was closely emulated in penetration of analysis and humility by the Bishop of St Albans who said that 'during these last terrible days, however accustomed we have grown to all sorts of things, yet the heart of the nation rang true.'

I asked a member of the Savile Club in what way exactly the people were splendid. He was a *Times* man: very able, and very grave. He was what the world calls 'a safe man'. He could be trusted as a sure guide in all matters of expediency and permissible behaviour of those in 'responsible positions'. He said that the people of England had acted wisely in averting the possibility of a King's Party being formed. He said that *The Times* had drawn attention 'to the danger of a King's Party being formed over the weekend.' The gravity of his tone was impressive. His phrase was well chosen. 'A number of people taking the King's side', is nothing; but a King's party is different. The capital letter gives an importance to Party impossible to mere sympathisers just as in certain Oriental poems an Ass becomes possessed of a significance impossible to a mere donkey; while 'over the weekend' gives a suggestion of underground intrigue not associated with an ordinary week day.

About forty million people in England were making remarks upon this subject at the rate of one every five minutes for a week. I heard a few observations. When I came up to town on the famous Abdication Thursday I was unprepared for the power of the moral feeling against the King which had gathered after the first days of sympathy. I entered a tobacconist's shop. A young proprietor was speaking to a taxi driver. 'Frankly, I'm ashamed of him, I really am', said the young man. 'I think he's dirt, that's my opinion.' He was terribly indignant. 'You're right', said the taxi man, 'it is shameful. It's the end of Monarchy, that's wot I say. I'm older than wot you are, and I tell you I've seen this coming, and it'll do no good to nobody, mark my words!' 'They've been trying to save him from himself', said the tobacconist, 'but it's now a good job he's going.' I suggested that Baldwin had gone too far. He looked surprised. 'How do you mean?' he asked in perplexity. 'But I *mean!*' he went on, 'it may seem a strange thing to say, but, well, er, there's things you and I could do that a king can't do.' (I thought of the kings in the past who could do things *we* couldn't do!) In the City, of course, the conversation was more sophisticated and more heartless. A City man sitting opposite me in a bus exclaimed to his neighbour: 'Have you heard the latest? Lord Nuffield has bought Mrs Simpson for the nation.'

I walked down Whitehall during the last hours of this drama. The faces around me were sad now. But the people were not in pain, they were enjoying themselves in the way they knew best. This was drama, this was history, to be taken sadly with pleasure. They pointed to the place where Charles I is said to have 'stepped out', and observed to their companions, 'Edward VIII is now stepping out. How sad it is. And all for a woman,' At Parliament Square there was such congestion that mounted police were engaged in requesting people to 'keep moving'.

Two men were standing on the kerb selling a paper called *Action* sponsored by Sir Oswald Mosley. These two young men kept shouting, 'Stand by the King! Stand by the King!' Touched by this I bought a copy of their paper, and opening it at a leading article I read:

'The past week has been a sad one for the English-speaking races, and also for that great circle of friends His Majesty, Edward VIII, has made for himself throughout the world. This unwarrantable attempt to hustle a loved and respected monarch off the Throne during the week-end of political intrigue has, fortunately, failed. Had there been the slightest chance of its success the prompt action taken by Sir Oswald Mosley and the British Union would have defeated it.'

119

This being so I wondered why these sellers of the paper were troubling to shout 'Stand by the King!' However, it was a useful slogan for drawing out the essential attitude of the crowd. Each time one of the young men cried out 'Stand by the King!' an old woman, determined in mien, resonant in voice, and histrionic in gesture, shouted back – 'Stand by the King's *mother*! stand by his *mother* I tell you!' She kept this up for a considerable time, for after walking right round the Square and coming back to the same spot, I still found her there, right arm upraised, hurling back the words, 'Stand by the King's *mother!*'

Though the aspect of this woman amused rather than impressed the crowd, her words were not without significance. Many people seemed to be concerned for Queen Mary. 'We'll stand by the King if he stands by us!' shouted one of his subjects who were being so splendid. 'What exactly do you mean?' I asked him innocently. His reply was startling. 'Do you mean to say that you would have Queen Mary *curtsey to Mrs Simpson?*' I admit to surprise at this. It had not occurred to me that Queen Mary would have to curtsey to anyone. Yet I could not help admiring the bold imagery of this splendid man's mind.

The crowd began to disperse. As they went away I heard people saying sadly to one another, 'It would not have done, it would never have done.'

7

Much fewer people had motor cars in the thirties than now of course, but they were less expensive second-hand. At the garages along the Maidstone Road one could pick up a serviceable car for five pounds, and I got a 'snub-nose' Morris-Cowley for £1.10s. which, though it might not pass the present-day Ministry of Transport test, moved along and was a great joy. At the outbreak of war I sold an Austin for £3, lacking the foresight to realize that after the war it would fetch £300. In 1937 we got a car which made it possible for my wife and I to have a break and take a journey. By means of charging two people for the back seats we were able to drive across Europe to Budapest to stay there with an Hungarian friend of mine, Kalman Gyarfas. I mention this because at about this time I had an invitation from Count Keyserling to dine with him at Darmstadt.

In the thirties Count Herman Keyserling published his *Travel Diary of a Philosopher*, a great work which was to 'transform him almost overnight from a writer esteemed in philosophical circles in Germany and a welcome guest in Parisian salons into a figure of worldwide fame and importance.[7] The translation of this work of art by Holyroyd Reece is itself a work of art, and it makes one of the most enriching books of our period. Enriching is the right word, I think, for every page has something arresting. The receptivity of Keyserling was so great that he could get into the skin of the kind of person produced by each country, as he went round the world, the attitude towards life, the beliefs held according to each environment. For window-opening and mental barrier-breaking it is an unsurpassed *tour de force*, calling for the energy and comprehension of a superman, one felt. And, indeed, the man behind the book was interesting enough. A Baltic Baron (born 1880), dispossessed of his estates by revolution, he became the cult of the German intelligentsia. His family line was aristocratic and scholastic in the highest degree, one branch through Caesar Keyserling celebrated a close friendship with Frederick the Great and Voltaire, while his grandfather, Count Alexander, who had a strain of primitive Tartar blood, was a friend of Bismark.

His other books, as they came out now, also fascinated me, though they had not the same literary appeal as the *Travel Diary*. His approach was from the opposite end to that of Bernard Shaw. As a German intellectual, he had a particular loathing for politics. 'Who can doubt, especially in our days, the essentially hellish nature of politics', he said. 'Blind urge to power, blind instinct of possession, and blind ecstasy of bloodshedding are the profoundest motives which animate statesmen.'

He addressed himself to the problem of changing the person rather than the economic problems caused by the nature of persons. His exhortations are always to the inner man, the inner life, and its development. His long sentences may sometimes daunt us but it is all written with such passion, such fervent ferment of intellectual drive that we are carried forward and frequently rewarded when he deviates into the short sentence or the pregnant utterance, as for example: 'More important things are done by a smile, a light gesture, a brief conversation among a very few, than owe their existence to hosts of armed men'; 'Courtesy is more important and means more before God than not to kill, not to commit adultery, and not to steal'; 'He who cannot stand the tension between the inner demand to do good and the impossibility of fulfilling it; he who refuses to take up his cross – this man is truly damned'; 'Only he who is ready at every moment to lose his soul, that is, to renounce the whole of what he was or is; only he *who never contends with others for what he is*, but only with himself for what he may become in time – this man only is on the way to progress.' He could never make an epigram, but his aphorisms are far from banal. Thus, 'A man can rise to the very pinnacle of greatness without having actually existed', a remark as profound as it is arresting; or 'Satan comes as terror and cruelty.

Also as comfort'; or 'Quantitative points of view are ruled out of court in matters of love', 'passion exaggerates isolated facts', 'That which is not given is lost', everyday truths which we always evade; or 'One may know everything without understanding anything at all', an ordinary truth made extraordinary by our neglect of it just as his 'It is not possible without loving surrender to understand anything at all' is as neglected as it is obvious, and yet as worth our attention as another remark, 'The mere existence of a saint is more beneficent than all the good actions of the world.' In using the word obvious I only mean that an aphorism shows us that it is so obvious. Thus we should realize, though we don't, that 'of course the substance of thought is much more formative than that which constitutes mountains', while it is a sobering consideration that 'Our highest virtues have arisen as reactive sublimations from the foundations of our worst predispositions.' I include one more remark, for it is typical of the man's powerful spirit. 'Life is always a tragedy; no one has ever escaped outward misfortunes and disappoint-ments. But the spiritualized man is joyful amidst his sorrow, he never finds reason to complain.'

I reviewed a good many of his books[8] in *The Observer* and several other journals, and since I did so affirmatively and with some enthusiasm, he sent me that invitation to dine with him at Darmstadt, which I eagerly accepted when taking the European journey. In his letter of invitation he requested me to arrive dressed for dinner. When I mentioned this to English friends they were astonished at such a demand to a man motoring through Europe. I thought it pernickety, but I never let a thing like that put me off and I packed my dinner jacket, relying upon the beauty of my wife to make up for any deficiencies in my appearance. He had also expressed the hope that I would arrive punctually at 7.30 p.m. As the Countess – who was Bismarck's granddaughter – had hinted in a letter to my wife that the Count was in a difficult mood these days, I saw to it that we arrived exactly on time, in fact at 7.29. I am always inclined to be punctual, but I do think that this was an achievement, taking into consideration the difficulties of foreign travel, and the confusing streets of a strange town at the last lap.

This masterly effort in punctuality and adaptability regarding dress met with appreciation and we passed a wonderful evening. The Countess was an exceedingly charming and calm person with a touch of the Mona Lisa in her countenance, without the superior smirk, and doubtless she possessed something of the iron of the Iron Chancellor. The Count had a personality which fully lived up to my expectations: the head of a Chinaman, the body of a German, the hands of an artist, he provided the combination of a Baltic

Baron, a Teutonic philosopher, and Eastern sage, a galloping Tartar, and a Hebrew prophet.

In England there would have been preliminary conversation about the journey and finding the way, and so on. All this was dispensed with. We went straight into dinner and straight into conversation. Keyserling talked at a tremendous rate in very good English, while his phenomenal vitality seemed to me equal to a number of men put together. He was like a suddenly uncorked bottle which instead of fizzing for a second fizzes for hours. 'I feel reborn!' he cried.

'I feel rejuvenated. The more I am made to suffer, the younger and stronger I feel. They can't hold me down. They may take away my passport, they may make me a prisoner in Germany, but the energy I shall generate by being held prisoner will blow up the country! Yes, I am a prisoner,' he repeated with considerable drama.

'I am watched day and night. All Germany knows that you are dining here tonight.'

'I do not quite see', I said, 'exactly how your work impinges on the political situation. What can they put their finger on for suppression?'

'The Nazis are good psychologists', he replied.

'They fear the Spirit. They feel the power of my spirit against them. Ah yes, a party came here the other day and tried to frighten and overawe me, but I frightened and overawed them. They like to see courage, you know, they are really afraid of bravery.'

'You said little about Germany in your latest book, *From Suffering to Fulfilment.*'

'That was the English edition. But in the German edition I have. I don't choose to tell the outside world what I think of the German soul, but in my German edition I have done so. I have laid bare the German soul. It is a Bible for Germany. When it came out Hitler suppressed it. I instantly wrote to him and told him that if he suppressed it that would prove that my influence was too strong for him. In two days after that the ban was lifted.'

The Count raised his voice to a shout.

'For I am more necessary to the German people! I am more powerful than Hitler!'

At this point the Countess took a tea cosy and placed it over the telephone – as guard against spies who had a device for listening-in. The philosopher's spirits were rising; he went on:

'Hitler has gifts, he knows the moment to do a thing. Anything can be done if it is done at the right moment – that's the essence of magic. But he has mistaken himself for God.'

I knew well, and he knew well, what was brewing in this city and in all
the cities of the land. The storm was beating up, it was plain for all to see
and to feel in passing through the country. Fearful decisions had been taken
by fearless and violent men, and who could tell the outcome? We did not
even know whether we would get back to England.

The dinner was not a large one, there was little food in the house, but
quantities of wine. People had a way of sending him bottles of burgundy and
champagne, he told us. My wife was not drinking much. The Countess
pressed champagne on her.

'I want to be able to listen to the Count', she said. This pleased him, and
glancing at her with admiration, he said:

'We must bow to your ruling in all things, Mrs Collis.'

However, presently an exiled Russian Princess came in, and my wife then
joined her and the Countess in a corner of the delightful room taking coffee,
while I remained at the table with Keyserling.

It was very stimulating for me to witness the resources of so vital a spirit.
'As a discipline I have just fasted for ten days', he informed me, delighted
with himself and pointing out a tremendous improvement in waist girth.

'I have often promised myself the luxury of fasting', I said, 'but have never
got round to it. There is also the luxury of not sleeping and watching the
dawn. But one doesn't do it, though one has all eternity to rest in!'

'It is a good thing even to be denied eyesight for a period.'

'You were once blind?'

'Oh yes, for some months, and I was surprised to find that a man without
sight knows no boredom. It is even an advantage to the inner life. Goethe
believed that.'

'I was struck by two reference of yours to Goethe in your *Travel Diary*. You
say that once on the death of a not very elderly man, who was a truly great
spirit, he said, "I cannot understand why he *consented to die*".'

'Yes, Goethe knew that in a spiritual man health depends largely on
spiritual conditions. If spirit is dominant then spiritual law determines the
life. The man governed by spirit does not grow older but younger with the
years and can stand an excess of work and a lack of food and sleep which
appear to contradict the laws of nature. Spirit grows, or can grow, as physical
life decays.'

He paused, perhaps thinking I was puzzled, though I wasn't.

'From this vantage point', he continued, for he was fond of that phrase,
and often used it to go forward.

'From this vantage point we can say that man does not die of a particular
disease until he is ready to do so, but when he has lost meaning and melody

in his life, he will succumb to any, even the most contemptible bacillus which happens to be at hand. Does this surprise you?'

'No, not in the least', I answered, for it certainly did not. 'The other striking reference to Goethe you made was his gospel of reverence as the sure way to *learn*.'

'I did. And I pointed out that so long as reverence is the primal attitude, even the greatest can learn, and always does learn even from the humblest. It is an effect which is as much a natural quality as the property of electricity.'

'What I was most struck by were the three kinds of reverence, or courtesy, recommended to those who wish to grow: "for that which is above us; for that which is below us; and for that which is like us." That's right, isn't it?'

'Yes, but remember that it is an *aristocratic* attitude. It has nothing to do with familiarity. It does not encourage the I'm-as-good-as-you attitude. The greatest distance is not created by harshness but by courtesy. That is why socialists resent polite forms. It is Comrade so-and-so all the time. But that doesn't do any good: it neither makes for growth nor for comradeship.'

'Yes', I said. 'I've noticed that in my own experience in England. The old slogan was Liberty, Equality, Fraternity. But I have observed how as soon as Equality sets in, then Fraternity begins to wane post perceptibly. It is each man for himself more than before.'

'Not only Fraternity, but Liberty also suffers. An overdose of Equality is very dangerous. Rights given to men who have no inner freedom are useless.'

'Would you agree that though the evil in us is stronger than the good, the will to good is stronger than the will to evil?'

'No. The accent is not on "good" and "evil". It is weakness of Spirit. What is needed is an *accepted metaphysic of inner growth*. Otherwise what ultimate use is political freedom? If mere slaves are unfettered, all the spirits of the netherworld, as I have pointed out, the spirits of malice, envy, pettiness, theft, treachery, cowardice, lying, rage, and delight in violence break loose.'

'In England', I said, 'there has been no sudden unfettering of the slave. The unfettering has been gradual and has produced the Average Man. There was a newspaper competition this year for the best example of the Average Man. The entries were enormous, and the man who won the prize was glad to be photographed and acclaimed.'

'In England the accent is still on individuality. It is not yet on conformity, as in America.'

'In your wonderful *Travel Diary* you appeared to me to be in a bit of a difficulty when you finally got to America. You were able to adapt and identify everywhere you went with the person and the viewpoint; but I wonder whether there was a forced note when you got to America? For instance you mentioned the slaugherhouse in Chicago. At first you were horrified. Then, having noted that a pig is dispatched in twenty minutes from life into a sausage, and that a single butcher could kill five hundred pigs that rush past him in an hour, you declared that such skill possessed metaphysical significance. That was surely going a bit far! It was leaning over backwards to be fair to America.'

I did not like to suggest that he had been dishonest, but he guessed that I thought it. 'You forget', he said, 'that I meant it in the sense in which Prince Wen Hui's cook spoke in a fable I mention. The cook was a great hand at dismembering an ox. "That's what I call skill!" said Prince Wen Hui to him one day. The cook put down the knife, and replied, "It is significance (Tao) which thy servant loves".'

'But if you think I wished to make myself agreeable to the Americans because they paid me more dollars for a lecture than was ever paid before, you should read the reviews of my book, *America Set Free*. I should have called it America in Chains. They were not pleased when I said that they thought they could cure bad marriage by better divorce; or that in America the women are not confined as in the Orient, but that the men are; or that if a man idealizes childhood to the exclusion of all other periods he will remain a child all his life, and America may *never* grow up in spite of the exceptional quality of their true adults.'

Keyserling talked for a long time and in high spirits, roughly from 7.30 to 12.30. He did not exhaust me, for nothing is less tiring than vital conversation, and I have experienced nothing better than this, and was acutely conscious of the honour he was doing me, as I sat there in the great tragic country beating up against the Forces of the Netherworld. He declared that I was the only critic in England who understood him – a remark which greatly cheered me, though I knew it was very far from the truth.

What he calls the 'In-break of Spirit' is his main plank, and I got him to return to it again that evening.

'We must face the fact', he said, 'that two-thirds or more of any man is at the bidding of blind original hunger and blind original fear, that he is dominated by the forces of earth and the evil of the underworld. Yet into this Man, this Man-animal, a new un-earth-tied thing has entered. There has been a break-in of Spirit – a Principle not tied to earth, a magical force, a miracle worker. It has been called by some the God in man, by others, the final Self.'

'Didn't you yourself call it man's freedom?' I asked.

'I called it *the what is free* in man. Whatever we call it we can *use* this power to bestow significance upon the facts. We can lay the accent upon any given stratum of our subjectivity. If a man puts the accent on his mineral nature he will become a stone; if he puts it on his reptilian being he will become a serpent or a toad – but he is *free* to lay the accent on the highest value.'

It depends on who it is that utters such things. They could be just intellectual or pretentious dark sayings, or even academic theory. But Keyserling made his affirmations as one who *felt* them, who *saw* them as truths, not as a philosopher or literary performer, but as one who spoke, whatever his faults and failings, from out of the heart of the universe.

The evening drew to a close and the Count was still going strong.

'I want to live one hundred and fifty years more,' he declared. 'I have seen so many revolutions. I was present at the Chinese and first Spanish revolution. I have so much more to see.'

Apparently he did not fell that war was a certainty. The last letter I had from him was in 1938 when he was still hopeful. (His handwriting was practically unreadable: purposefully so, he explained, conditions being what they were.) He believed that life was a polar phenomenon, and that the materialistic forces at work both in Russia and in Germany would bring about a deeper spirituality than ever before. As a short term prophet he was disastrously deluded, but in the long run his prophecies may yet be fulfilled. He died in 1945 – I do not know the details. What were the conditions that made him despair, so that at last he 'consented to die'?

8

In 1938 most intelligent people could see the war coming, but I'm afraid I did not, nor was I thrown into indignation over Munich, even rejoicing in it until I learnt that this was wicked of me. Yet there was a contradiction in this. For I did grasp to some extent what was happening in the concentration camps and I'm sure that Mr Philip Toynbee was right in saying recently in a discussion that the one central fact about our time that we must face, is the existence of such things. When war broke out I felt spontaneous relief, 'This is the end of *that* horror!' – the only really unselfish thought I can claim throughout the war.

Though lacking in any kind of foresight, I sometimes showed a little insight. In 1937, Orage published in The *New English Weekly* a thing of mine called 'Any European Dictator Talking In His Sleep.' It ran:

'They say that I am not great. Measuring me by the rule of historical standards they find me lacking. They read what I have written and they search in vain for the word of wisdom no less than the evocative phrase. They read my autobiography and in it they find no largeness of expression, no bigness of soul, no knowledge of self. They feel that I am almost dull as a person. There is something about me that puts them off. They think that if they found themselves alone with me in a room, stripped of the robes of glory and power I would seem very ordinary and my conversation commonplace. Obsessed with the idea of a Caesar, a Cromwell, a Napoleon, a Robespierre, a Bismark, a Lincoln, they would not shrink in my presence, nor bow the mind, nor would their hearts beat faster. They would say that I am not great.

'They observe my deeds. They watch me wobbling from one stage to another on the tight-rope of opportunity. Every minute they expect me to fall. They see no progress in my plans for the solving of fundamental problems. As an economist they find everything about me superficial. As a lawgiver they laugh at me. As a financier they regard me as the slave of financiers. As a religious man they dismiss me with contempt. As a moral being they make a helpless gesture of outrage against one who wots not that theme. They see in me no greatness, I am not great.

'And yet I am great. This is the age of the Many. This is the hour of the crowd, the mob, the mass, the multitude – no longer of the Father, nor of the Son, nor of the Holy Ghost. I am not an individual. I have no self. I am upheld by the people. I am what they wish me to be. I am the Image of their desire. I belong to the historic moment. I flow on the river of Necessity. My faculties are few, my senses feeble – save one. The heart, the mind, the soul, the presence, the artistic eye, the religious gleam, the moral impulse within me are all together nothing compared with my sense of the *Multitude's movement*. I know what It is doing, where It is going – that thus and thus and not otherwise will It go. I lead the way. I liberate the imperative lusts of the people. I give rein to their sadism and at the same time absolve them from sin. Through me their humiliation is avenged. Through me their highest goal is sighted, as also through me their netherworld vomits its spleen across the shuddering earth. So long as I retain this Sense I cannot fall to the ground. I am History. I am the very hands of God. Therefore I am great with a new greatness.

'I am great – so long as I retain my seat. Even as a person now I am great. The virtues that I had not now I have, and the evil that I once would not do but did is now not done by me. Chastity, sobriety, discipline, cleanliness, frugality, hard work, self-sacrifice, eternal vigilance – these now are mine. Alone I could never achieve this. As a simple married man it would be impossible for me. As a soldier, a follower of a leader, I would chafe at such virtues. But as Dictator it is easy. I am surrounded by such a spell of reverence and belief, I am upheld by such a wave of awe that I can actually rest upon the people's wish as if it were a concrete thing. They see me as a god, and as a god I find it possible to behave. I am freed from the curse of my individuality. My path is so clear. My duty is so obviously worth while. My personal problems cease to exist. No longer covered by the four-fold black cloth of ambition, hatred, fear, and greed, my ego rests in peace.

'Think of those last four things and measure me by my measurement of them! I have no ambition now but to serve the multitude. I have no need to think in terms of hatred, but only of that which must be done. As a private individual I used to be afraid; not, upheld by Destiny I know nothing of fear, neither knife nor bullet nor poison can touch me which I remain true to the historic moment – for I am history, and history cannot be stayed. What greed is left to me? I can rise above the body, for I am so held by the people that I am absolved from the frailties of the body no less than from the restlessness of the mind. It is granted that I achieve the ancient idea of sainthood and that I can even channel my lust into the energy of ceaseless work. I truly desire nothing save to serve the multitude. For I am the Image of the multitude's desire, and the moment I cease to be that I am finished. Therefore in that service there is perfect freedom. Therefore I am great.

'Seek no longer to compare me with others who have gone before. There have been men of Will – I am not one of those. There have been men of God – I am not one of those. There have been men of Wisdom – I am not one of those. There have been men of the fixed and burning Idea – I am not one of those. Each of such men by himself in a room would make you feel small; for in himself each was great. By myself I am not great. But because I am an empty vessel that is filled with the Multitude's desire, I am, even now, greater than the greatest of those. I am all that the people say that I am. They have given me the power to be what I am not. I am proud of the emptiness that can thus be filled. I await the coming of the end when by some folly I shall fail and fall from power. Then I shall no longer be great. I shall no longer be a god. I shall shrink. I shall become small again, I shall be mean to look upon. I shall be nothing!'

Making allowance for the rhetorical flourish of the piece I think its main point was eventually justified when Hitler crept into his bunker to die, and Mussolini was hung upside-down like a turkey in that Italian market place.

A personal anecdote attaches to that article. After its publication I received a letter from a strange woman. She declared that only a superman could have written it, and coupled my name with Nietzsche. Now, authors who strike out an original line are accustomed to extravagant remarks in praise or dispraise, and if they have any balance they do not bat an eyelid. But there was a peculiar circumstance about this, making it stand out. The lady *enclosed five pounds*. This was phenomenal. I expressed my gratitude and sent her a copy of a book which I had recently had published called *Farewell to Argument*, which in those days I imagined to be good. Here my troubles began. She now unloaded upon me letter after letter of violent vituperation, and eventually sent back the book ironically subtitled – 'Farewell to Socrates the Second', and every margin filled with query and exclamatory comment. I could not follow any of this and I protested mildly, but it only added to her fury. She said I was ready enough to take her five pounds but not her annotation and exhortation to a better life, and she declared that with all the power of her soul she had pronounced a curse against me that would injure me for fifty years. I do not know what I should have done. It was fatal to have accepted the five pounds, but would it have been less so if I had declined it?

I used to enjoy Hitler's speeches very much. There is no question that he was a great orator. I did not understand a word he said but I could never hear enough of him, and in later years when watching documentary films I was always disappointed at how soon he was cut short. In this he was great. It was clear that his secret was *anger*. I think that Martin Luther throws some light on this: 'I never work better', he said, 'than when I am inspired with anger; when I am angry I can write well, pray well, preach well. My whole temperament is quickened and my understanding sharpened; the vexations of the world and the temptations of the Devil depart from me.' It 'refreshed his blood', he declared, and it was in his most extravagant outbursts of hatred that he felt 'most conscious of the presence of God'; and especially stimulating to his spirit were his famous 'Hymns of Hate'. Anger is a very infectious and powerful weapon. Hitler spoke in a fury, his voice often breaking with excitement into a scream; and this carried him to power and sustained him in power. His anger obviously gave him a great deal of pleasure and was the cause of pleasure in his vast audiences.

Many of these speeches, especially those delivered at the Nuremberg rallies, were listened to all over this country. Hitler, we may be sure, was well aware of this and made it part of his 'war of nerves'. What was he saying this time? Was it peace or war? After his orations there would be a report from the stock exchange. People declared that his speeches gave them 'the jitters'. Unaccustomed to violence of statement, they became very apprehensive – though as soon as the uncertainty was over and war broke out they cheered up instantly and became active in happy unison. I admit to having been greatly fascinated by Hitler's ferocious periods, the massive plaudits of the multitude, the swelling tribal rumblings of the *Sieg Heil*. A violent spirit was being cast abroad, and a great wind blowing. This was the first time in history that it had been possible to sit in a cottage in the English countryside and *hear* an enemy from beyond the sea roaring and ranting. The miracle of this, the historic drama of it, greatly appealed to me. Thus, living in Kent with my wife and daughters, on some of these occasions I used to turn up the sound and step into the garden, and from there listen to these invisible spirits uttering their incantations.

At last war was declared. There was a general feeling of relief. I have mentioned my own particular relief, and perhaps for that reason one poem of the time deeply impressed me, and has remained with me. The poet died young by his own hand, and seems to have been somewhat unworthily neglected, if not wholly rejected. This poem, by Brian Howard, is called 'A Prayer for the Fuehrer', and here are some lines from it:

> In happy America, on the useless roads of Europe, in thousands of small,
>   far streets,
> In ditches, in prisons, in hundreds of thousands of furnished rooms,
> There lives a silent, separated people, with a few pennies, and no plan
> A father without a child, say, or a lost sister,
> Or a soldier, or just an unknown, furious old man,
> Their two hands grind together every night, and again in the
>   warring morning
> As they kneel on the carpet, grass, stone; as they've knelt since it all began,
> And their fingers crack like the prophecy of shooting,
> Their eyes burst with tears, and liquid sounds burst through their breath.
> They are saying their prayers. Their prayers are for our death.

1 *The Sounding Cataract*

2 Alas, now removed somewhere indoors.

3 'Hatred is mortal; it kills at ten miles – at ten thousand miles. All the people I ever hated died. A deadly and horrible emanation comes from the hater to his victim, and stays.' G B Shaw to Mrs Packenham Beatty, October 1885.

4 In his straight style *Steps to Immaturity* is a masterpiece of autobiography, and his *Minnow Among Tritons* one of the best things he ever did.
5 *Waiting on God* by Simone Weil.
6 In the case of Raymond Chandler it is not too much to say that the entire essence of his genius is extracted and thrown away.
7 *Introduction to Keyserling* by Mercedes Gallagher Parks.
8 Such as *The World in the Making; The Recovery of Truth; Creative Understanding; From Suffering to Fulfilment; The Art of Life; Europe; The Book of Marriage; America Set Free; South American Meditations.*

FOURTH MOVEMENT…

... DOING

1

I often think that the most critical moments – even the turning points – in anyone's life are seldom outwardly dramatic. An onlooker would see nothing but a man knocking at a door, or looking at a house, or coming before a board, or standing on a station platform.

On a certain day in April, 1940, I had gone to interview Mr J G Maynard who owned a farm at Stonegate on the border of Sussex. To work as a labourer on the land (not as a responsible farmer) had become a great desire of mine, and as my age group for being called up by the Army was not nearly due, I seized a chance that opened. I had my interview; I overcame objections regarding my inadequacy, and achieved the appointment that I would start work on the following Monday.

But before setting out on that Monday morning I received a letter from Maynard saying that after all he regretted to inform me that my services would not be required.

This was a fearful blow. The letter put me into a fury of frustration. I must not accept this cancellation! I *must* reverse it! It must and would be done, somehow, someway. I would go and see Maynard and force myself upon him. And I took the train to go there that same morning.

I was obliged to wait on Sevenoaks station platform for a train that would take me to Stonegate. I walked up and down that platform, and as I did so I said to myself that I would remember for ever these minutes at this station. I was *resolved* not to be defeated in my quest, for I felt that my life depended upon it. I would bring to bear upon him the full force of my determination. Nevertheless I walked up and down in a turmoil of apprehension, in the cold wind on that harsh April day in which, as so often, there was no touch of gladness or feeling of Spring.

I need not have worried. Determination overcomes most things. If any man has slightly more backbone than a jellyfish and knows clearly enough what he wants to do he can do it; resolution is a spear, and resistance, unless ready in advance, is seldom equal to the attack. I said that I would work on approval for £1 a week for a month. This was accepted. I had succeeded in my quest.

This launched an agricultural experience which lasted for nearly six years, because when I was called up I asked a military board before which I appeared if I might be allowed to stay on the land, and this was granted. I could have had pay and position as an Officer (having left that OCB as an Hon. Lieutenant) but I could see only some hopeless clerical military job being allotted to me, for which I would have been quite unfitted. Thus the clear positivity I showed at my interview regarding my greater usefulness on the land made an impression, and I was released from the military for ever.

I did not remain for more than one year at this first farm. I gave an account in my book *While Following the Plough*, but since I wanted to stick to the agricultural experience alone, I omitted an exciting aspect of our situation. A decisive decision was being reached in the sky. The Battle of Britain was fought directly over our heads. We had a front-seat view of the fun. The following Notice was once posted up in the village:

STONEGATE ENTERTAINMENT TAX
£3. 15s. 3d.
COLLECTED FOR SPITFIRE FUND
FROM ONLOOKERS OF THE SCRAP
SEPTEMBER 16th 1940

The entertainment value came as a surprise. For fighting had reached such a pass that soldiers actually fought children. Men armed with weapons of enormous power took on children – a bomber did that as part of his duty. Yet at the very hour when fighting had arrived at this absurdity the balance was restored and we beheld battle as an entertainment for the spectators and a tournament for the airmen.

The best show provided for me was on 16 September. At seven o'clock the glorious September morning spread around and below, the mist not yet having risen from the valleys. The embattled island was still that gem encircled by the sea – yet now every day invaded. At eight o'clock the repose was broken and across the land was heard the sound of the siren, so alarming and so strangely exhilarating, warning us that the enemy was approaching. Soon a thundering noise gradually gathered into the threatening volume that heralded the advance of the heavenly hordes. Surely nothing can stop them this time, I thought, the whole sky is in league against us, the end is at hand. I could discern them clearly now, squadrons in close formation protected by fighters circling round them like seagulls following a flotilla.

Then I saw a white snake growing in the blue like the act of creation on the first day. Soon similar snakes began to grow everywhere, and I knew that spitfires were climbing up to intercept the invasion. The battle began. The enemy formations were broken up. The sky became fully of fighters, everyone firing at everyone else it seemed. The mounting scream of the zooming dives and the falling bullets alarmed me very much, and I crawled under a cart. It became a question of single combats, not 'dog-fights'! – what an image to describe these encounters of the air men, the sky men, who hold acquaintance with the clouds! Rather did I see the beauty of birds more graceful than seagulls in their wing-work. Were it not for the firing and the falling one would not know that those two beauties up there were fighting at all, as one glides towards another almost tipping its wing, only foiled by a falling dive of unbelievable skill and beauty. It seems to us on earth that this is not war – it is the new Jousting, it is the modern Tournament.

And so, at the hour when war seemed to have reached its worst the balance is restored here with the sky-soldiers in the South East and we see it at its best. We return to the Middle Ages. Once more the Knights go forth, the few fight and the many applaud. The field of contest is changed; the heroes have the sky for the arena, their steeds have wings, their shields are clouds, and they plunge at each other 'from out the sun'; but the principle is the same whereby a few chosen champions take it upon themselves to liberate the multitude's desire for excitement and to redeem the lust for destruction.

The battle is over. I crawl from under my cart. I see others in the distance get out of a ditch. And soon the sum of £3.15s.3d is collected as Entertainment Tax.

Many of the battles were invisible. We heard a great deal and saw nothing till after some eye-straining it was possible to catch sight of a few white flies who surely could not be making all that noise. On days when the sky was blue and interspersed with radiant rocks of cumuli we could discern the fighters passing across the blue sky-lakes, appearing and disappearing, white wraiths, bird-ghosts, pursuing or pursued in a game impossible to comprehend. Sometimes one of them would come low and drop a bomb; a new kind of bird laying a new kind of egg; or a man would be seen slowly descending from the clouds holding a white umbrella.

One day a battle took place overhead when the clouds were thick and we could see nothing at all. The firing was very loud, bombs fell in the adjoining fields, the clash of arms in the empyrean seemed to be on a supernatural scale. Raised high above the earth in this way, the extraordinary occasion pertained to the condition of myth and belonged to the place of legend. Was this the Battle of the Angels rehearsed by Milton? Suddenly a flaming Messerschmitt was expelled from the clouds and crashed to earth with a tragic splendour that would have done justice to the Fall of Lucifer.

There are many ways of taking things and seeing things, as many angles of approach as there are seeing eyes and feeling hearts, and I must support my angle with a few lines from Sylvia Lynd published in the *News Chronicle* at this time:

THE RAF
I heard the squadrons flying home
At midnight among the stars;
Never did tale of Greece or Rome
Tell of such heroes or such wars.

Legend nor boast nor history
Proclaim such deeds as these achieve
Who daily fight Thermopylae,
Who snatch the glove from Death, and win.

Perseus and Bellerophon
They, too, were fighters and had wings,
They fought with monsters and they won,
And in the stars their glory rings.

Castor and Pollux keep their station,
Neither do we dispute their claim
If a more glorious constellation
Denote a still more glorious fame.

Instead of Bear or Wain or Plough,
Splendid to see in night's great Dome,
Give to those stars a new name now,
Call them the Squadron Flying Home.

We were also well situated to appreciate the concentrated bombing of London. As soon as it was dark the bombers thundered over our heads towards the city. Surely by morning, I thought, nothing will be left of the place. 'Poor old London', our neighbouring farmer, Mr Luxford, used to say, 'poor old London. It's like waiting for death. It's a queer turnout, a terrible queer turnout.'

'We are all living under delusions these days', said a labourer's wife to me. She did not mean that she was disillusioned in any way but rather that the Deluge had come at last, or a series of Deluges, and we could no longer hope to say with Louis XV, 'Après moi le déluge'.

The bombers kept their goods chiefly for London but they let us have some of them, and quite often would drop about fourteen in a row – I can't think why. In the country, bombs made a most alarming noise. You heard them coming, one, two, three, as if right into the garden, shaking the house. I slept upstairs lest I might be buried by debris and not rescued if I stayed below. In bed on these occasions I became really frightened and put the sheet over my head for protection. This fright on my part made me feel ashamed, till I found that when I was in company I did not mind.

I was very struck by a remark made to me by another farmer, Mr Top. On one of our worse nights, bombs fell killing a dozen of his cows and edging nearer and nearer to his door. He heard the whistle of their approach – (that whistle sometimes being so loud that once I mistook one for the swish of an aeroplane). He lay in his bed too petrified to try and get to the cellar. He told me that he said to himself, '*I'll take it here. I'll take it where I am.*' It was an arresting remark. I thought of how easily exhortations and boastings come to the lips of politicians. 'We can take it! England can take it!' and so on. Here was one man, one individual in the storm, quite inadvertently using the very same verb with an exactitude of meaning which made the public rhetorical flourish appear slightly unreal.

This is not the place, nor the book, to gather all my impressions of the war; but one further single thing I would like to mention. Dunkirk occurred. I sat one evening alone in the Old House. I hope I shall never grow so accustomed to modern marvels as to lose my sense of wonder. As I sat there I heard a voice. It spoke to me from Africa. It was the voice of General Smuts. Anyone, with any sense for greatness, always listened to this man with a concentration accorded to no other. One had no desire to hear from him an emotional appeal, or a literary frill, still less a joke or witticism: one just wanted to hear what he had to *say*. The massive intelligence of this great man, his comprehension of the forces at work in the world, was such that I listened to him breathlessly, literally so. It was such a comfort to hear him.

'It is truly a *comfort* to have him in our midst', said Churchill when he came over to address the Houses of Parliament. As I sat in that lonely place I heard Smuts explain, in that meticulous manner of his, just exactly why Dunkirk was not a disaster which would tell against us in the end, and just why the enemy would eventually be overcome. No memory is more present to me, none more strange or exhilarating, than this disembodied Voice coming across to me from a far country, with its comprehensive analysis and message of hope.

2

In 1940 – when 'evacuation' was so much in the air – my wife and daughters went to America at the invitation of the parents of the girl I had failed to marry. This unexpected and extraordinary act of goodness made a circle of sense with what had happened in the past, truly amazing to me.

Meanwhile I had let the house in Kent, and gone to live in an old empty house in a far corner of Maynard's farm.

This farm was chiefly concerned with fruit, not requiring much staff all the year round, and Maynard had to dispense with my services. I was able to arrange to work for Mr Rolf Gardiner on his Estate at Fontmell Magna in Dorset. Accommodation having been found for me there, the day for departure was fixed, in the Spring of 1941. So once again a van came to load up all my possessions, my furniture, books, everything, in preparation for leaving at dawn the next day. This van was two-thirds loaded when a messenger came with a telegram. Rolf Gardiner had discovered that he could not have me, so he sent this telegram to cancel the engagement he had made.

I ignored it.

The last bit of loading proceeded. I made no effort to check it, and did not divulge the contents of the telegram. I have seldom reasoned my chief actions. I did not reason them now. Instinctively I blindly went forward. If I have never calculated my moves in life I have at least not gone astray through *mis*calculation. Yet, if I have advanced with stubborn instinct I have never done so in a happy, confident frame of mind, but always with misgiving and fear.

So it was now. At four o'clock next morning, I went to Burwash and climbed into the van beside the driver, with my beloved dog, Bindo, and drove into the dark. The driver was a young man, sour and ill-mannered in the extreme, which scarcely helped my own mood. What would he say when, arriving at our destination, there was nowhere to put the contents of his van? It was a gloomy prospect, a gloomy drive into the bleak dawn. That gloom was certainly justified, for when we did arrive we were not expected and far from welcomed. It was a low moment in my life. In the context of the world's troubles it was a small thing, but one does not think or feel in terms of a world context, and the subsequent hours were amongst the very lowest of my life, the most miserable... However, in the end I was allowed to unload my stuff into an outhouse of Gardiner's estate, and told that if I went up to Gore Farm, on the upper Shaftesbury Road, which was run for Rolf Gardiner by Sigvart Godeseth, I might be able to stay the night there, and then look around for employment. I went up there and was indeed able to stay the night (a memory emphasized by a cow which bellowed directly below me all night long) and was made welcome by Sigvart Godeseth, and two others, Stanley Godman and Alan Clack – three gifted and strange characters with whom I made permanent friends. I searched for some time in vain to find a place, and then Alan Clack said that he thought that there was a small farmer named Mr Law at Tarrant Gunville (not far away) who owned an empty bungalow and might need labour. I instantly went to see him, found that he did have an empty bungalow, and was willing to give me temporary work. It was fantastic: the house might have been let down from heaven for my benefit. All was well. My blind journey down to Dorset had been justified.

It was a great pleasure working for Mr Law, and also he allowed the house to be my headquarters regardless of whether I was working for him or not (and there was not a great deal to be done on his farm by an extra hand). I soon found it possible to work for Rolf Gardiner in the forestry part of his estate. Rolf was and is a man with an immense drive and has for nearly half a century channelled his energy into practising and preaching the philosophy or organic farming, and in drawing together culture and agriculture, humanity and industry, tradition and modernism. A man of commanding build and clearly articulated speech, he is a flamboyant personality and a complicated character with so many strains running in his blood that he is not easy in himself, and not at once understood by others. Combining the agrarian philosopher, the musician, the preacher, the poet, the scholar, he might not seem to belong to any recognized branch of the English tradition. But he does belong to the line of British *idealists* who have fought to save the land from spoliation and the soil from erosion. Though much involved in the scene he has always seemed to me a lonely and embattled figure in the midst of many who are hostile or cold, yet never resting, never giving in, keeping alive by practice and by pen the idea of agriculture as a manner of living as well as a commercial undertaking, and ever holding onto the noble words of Nicholas Berdyaev 'There are two

141

symbols, bread and money; and there are two mysteries, the eucharistic mystery of bread and the satanic mystery of money. We are faced with the great task: to overthrow the rule of money and to establish in its place the rule of bread.'

By an extraordinary piece of luck this place of mine at Tarrant Gunville was very close to one part of his woodland estate, and at one time formed part of the extensive area known so well as Cranborne Chase. During the six years that I worked on the land, there were two periods when I undertook a forestry job for Rolf; the thinning, clearing and general reconstruction of a considerable acreage now entered in the books of the Estate as Collis Piece. Twenty-one years after writing about it in Part II of my book *Down to Earth* I open the *New Statesman* to find my last words in that book quoted by Bernard Levin in a Centrepiece article about making a bid for immortality.

'I look across at the growing and maturing trees now free from all entanglements. I had come to a wild entanglement, and now, as far as I can see in any direction, a free plantation meets my eye, accomplished by the labour of my hands alone. Nothing that I have ever done has given me more satisfaction than this, nor shall I hope to find again so great a happiness. Realizing something of what the work meant to me, and perhaps truthfully saying that he was very pleased with the result, Rolf entered this area of about twelve acres, in the books of the Estate, as COLLIS PIECE, and by that name it is now known. Thus then do I achieve what had never occurred to me could possibly happen, that a piece of English earth and forest would carry my name into the future. Nobody is ever likely to confer upon me Honours or Titles or City Freedoms, not will any Monument be raised to perpetuate and repeat my name. But this plot of earth will do it, these trees will do it: in the summer they will glitter and shine for me, and in the winter, mourn.'

'Yes', wrote Levin, 'that would do; that would do handsomely.' It does so well for me that often I go and have a look at 'my' wood to see how it is getting on, and find it always different, for it is always at work, and always the same in its seclusion and silence enwalled from the world's turmoil. And as a matter of fact my account of this bit of forestry work did bring me an honour, for in 1947 when *Down to Earth* was published it received the Heinemann Foundation Award For Literature, the cheque being handed to me by Lord Wavell. While working in that wood I could scarcely have imagined so strange a thing as that a time would come when a Field Marshal, whose way of life had been cast among the greatest battle fields of the world, should praise me and hand me a cheque for writing upon the flowers of the world.

Working in that wood was a wonderful experience, but I was anxious to join a large mixed farm and do all the various jobs entailed. Above all I wanted to plough. To achieve the status of being able to go onto a field by myself with a plough, as a paid workman, and plough that field, was something which I wanted to do more than anything else: it would give me more pleasure, more satisfaction, than anything, even than writing or reading – and as much pride as any job however high up in the scale of prestige or pay.

It was difficult to find the mixed farm I needed, but I learnt that it was possible to work for Contractors who sent out ploughmen with tractors to certain farms that required work done from outside. I applied for this and was accepted – heaven knows how! It meant that I would have to live at Fordingbridge in Wiltshire. I went there to see if I could find lodgings, and eventually found a place which I booked, and the date of my coming was fixed.

A few days before that date arrived I got a letter from the landlady informing me that relatives of hers were coming to stay and that she could not have me. I took this third occasion of being baulked pretty calmly. And almost immediately a man told me to try Mr Hannan, a farmer at Tarrant Hinton, the village at the other side of Tarrant Gunville, which could be reached daily by bicycle. I went to see Mr Hannan immediately, putting my best foot forward, saying that I was 'quick at the uptake' (which is the very reverse of the truth in practical matters), and he took me on. This proved a very fruitful engagement. The letter of cancellation from Fordingbridge had been a godsend (in the strict sense of a well-meaning god, sending messengers hurrying along to put me in the way I should go).

Hannan's farm was one of the most difficult I could have found anywhere, and on that account one of the most interesting. He created an atmosphere of continual crisis, to the extent that something akin to neurosis ran through the staff. I do not remember a single day when calm prevailed. For me the hours were particularly long, often from 6.00 a.m. when I had to rise, to 9.00 p.m. before getting home when it was a question of overtime (and as for food, it was far more difficult to make the weekly rations last for one person in the country than in towns, and I was often reduced to milk and biscuits). Hannan's behaviour was extreme but not unique. I called him 'E in my book *While following the Plough*, and expected to be accused of exaggeration, but I found that he was regarded as a universal character, and I got letters from all over the world acknowledging him. I had a great literary chance to bring together the Fact, the Idea, the Process, and the Person. I took advantage of this and made a whole, and was rewarded – in full measure – by the response on publication, and since – from the general public, I mean. But if one writes a book with living persons in it, those persons will read it just to see what is said about themselves. 'E could not read, but he was heard to say, 'A book has been written about I.' I used to dread any of the others reading it, not because I had written anything particularly critical of them but because the only purpose of their attempting to read it would have been to see 'What has he said about I? Is it good enough for I?' And of course it is never good enough for I. But here a surprise. In Part I of *The Plough* I had written about my experience at Maynard's farm, and I had been rather unpleasant about one person – Maynard himself. The fact is he had offended me, he had, unnecessarily I thought, wounded my *amour propre* on several occasions and one in particular. I did not forgive him. Whenever I mentioned him in my account I said nothing pleasant. Some time after the publication of the book he read it. (He was an educated man who read widely.) He wrote to me to congratulate me on it in warm and sincere terms, making no reference, no small complaint regarding my treatment of himself. I greatly admired him for this magnanimity and generosity and thus was able to write back at once to thank him and explain why I had written about him in that way. Ever since then we have kept in friendly touch.

At Hannan's farm I had got what I wanted at last, a complete participation in the ordinary work of the world, and that work of truly vital importance to everyone. This belonging to a body of men working together was very satisfactory for me – never experienced before. The physical-working man in Britain has a high opinion of himself – only class-conscious intellectuals imagine that he has any feeling of inferiority. He looks down upon 'posh' people, not always fairly, as slackers and incapable of doing anything. Land workers are particularly prone to this haughty attitude. I became somewhat infected with it myself and when I went up to town I became aware for the first time, and amazed, at the businessman's 'business lunches', and the general ease of life in comparison with farm workers.

I recall an enlightening example of this attitude of mine. Returning from one of my occasional visits to London, and about to enter a carriage of the Salisbury train at Waterloo, my attention was held by a man standing on the platform before boarding the train. He looked so distinguished that a person beside him seemed extinguished in consequence. Soon there was a group surrounding him. He was exceedingly well dressed, indeed with such perfect taste that he could not even be called a dandy. Everyone who spoke with him smiled in a happy and deferential manner, and in his turn he regarded them with pleasing benignity. He was tall, middle-aged, slim, and handsome, not unaware of his own consequence nor unwilling to accept homage, while presenting a gracious front that could scarcely be called condescension. I wondered who on earth he was, and for some reason got it into my head that he must be the Director of some Ballet company or a famous impresario of some sort. Later on while we were travelling along I went towards the carriage where I knew the celebrity was sitting, for I wanted to see how he was getting on. I peeped in unobtrusively. He was engaged in conversation, an indulgent smile playing upon his lips, his spotless white shirt cuffs protruding the exact right amount from the arms of his perfectly cut suit of pale grey. And again his travelling companions regarded him with respectful attention, and bent their heads towards him slightly nodding and slightly sideways at that angle which denotes deference. He got out at Salisbury, and I saw him step into the right sort of car waiting for him. Then I realized that of course it was Mr Cecil Beaton, who had a house in Wiltshire. But my haughty attitude in the role of world's worker was such that I regarded that admirable artist with a feeling akin to disdain!

What was so wonderful for me at this time was not only the farewell to that isolation, that feeling of 'non belonging' which an author has to endure, but the financial aspect. I was paid regularly. I was paid whatever happened, even when rain drove us into the barn and there was little to do. I could hardly believe that money was still coming in while I was doing nothing. The pay was not much but its regularity was a pleasure beyond description – and it gives me quite a turn nowadays when I hear that such-and-such workers are on strike though their basic pay is thirty pounds a week. One other thing. For the first time I knew freedom. The author, this one anyway, having failed during most of the day to solve his literary problem, may see the light, if lucky, by about 5.30, when he can at last go forward. He cannot happily knock off at 5.30. But as an agricultural labourer I was free at a given hour. One other thing: I was free to read for *pleasure*.

3

As I had so much to do I could find time to do more. I could sometimes take my bicycle and look round the nearby countryside. My own place, Tarrant Gunville, is about four miles from Blandford. Had I been a village-fancier coming upon it as an idle journeying spectator, I might not have been particularly struck by the village street. But for a long time it was the centre of my activities, the centre of my world, just as every place, no matter how much it may seem to hang upon the circumference of the globe or to be desolately lost in some forsaken hole, is yet the centre from which the world radiates for those who live there. Thus every cottage in Tarrant Gunville has more interest for me than other cottages elsewhere, however beautiful. In any case the village had everything: the avenue of trees; the creeper-clothed Manor House; the Church from whose graveyard wall you could look down upon the houses; the pub, with a garden behind and a row of chestnut trees in front, with an orchard on one side and on the other an ancient beech gloriously witnessing to the calendar. And there were the items of interest. Upon the gravestone of Sir Thomas Daccombe, a sixteenth century philosopher who was less interested in the Trinity than in the twentieth century's conception of Unity, is inscribed:

> Here lieth S.T.D. Parson
> All four be but one:
> Earth, Flesh, Worm, and Bone.

There is also a tablet laid to the memory of Thomas Wedgwood, who in 1791, observing that nitrate of silver is blackened by the effect of sunlight, became the father of photography. Less worthy was George Bubb Dodington who two hundred years ago asked Sir John Vanbrugh to build him a house costing £840,000. In order to approach their host, visitors were obliged to pass through a series of apartments with painted ceilings and walls hung with velvet. His bed was canopied with peacock feathers, and his wardrobe contained one hundred 'rich and flaring suits'. But soon after the house had been put up it was pulled down on account of lack of money, and Dodington lives now only in Browning's lines – '…folk see but one More fool, as well as knave, in Dodington'. One wing was left standing, which is called Eastbury House. I chain-harrowed the lawns around it. I could not help feeling better off than the original owner – in position and in cash.

The silent revolutions of England are so sweeping that the idea of a Dodington hardly enters a modern mind. Still less the idea of a Damer. When I began to cycle round to places I visited Milton Abbas. An attractive village. Indeed quite special. A spacious street sloping up a hill. And between each cottage, on both sides all the way up the street, a chestnut tree. Such planning is somewhat unusual. But then the history of the village is remarkable. This is its second life. Its first life was in a different place – a short distance from where an eighteenth century house now stands. When that house had been built by Joseph Damer, he decided that the village was too close to him. So he pulled it down. It was a big place then, with many street and taverns and over a hundred houses, together with a brewery and a Grammar School founded in 1521. Joseph Damer decreed that 'the town was too close to his residence, and proved an annoyance to him'. So he fell upon it as effectively as Vesuvius on Pompeii and swept away the whole of this settlement, its rectory, its school, its almshouses, and its inns. Not being oversentimental he caused all the headstones in the churchyard to be removed, broken up, or buried, and was much pained when bones occasionally appeared in his gardens. He was kind enough, however, to rebuild a portion of it further off – the Milton Abbas which we see today. That was two hundred years ago. Not so very unusual for those days. Exactly the same thing was done by another man at Tetbury in Gloucestershire. But in England the evolutions of society accomplish far more than the revolutions of other nations. A bicycle ride in many directions will remind us of this. We so often come upon a Big House abominably neglected and disgraced, its interior scarred by penury, its windows closed like the lids of death, standing in the solitude of gardens rank with weeds and with lawns lost in meadow grass – empty and desolate vessels waiting to be filled.

Choosing another way home from Milton Abbas, I mounted the high ridge of Bulbarrow from where a sweeping view can be held for long distances in all directions. At the top I was uncertain which road to take, but as I am fond of coming upon lonely villages I thought I would choose the way leading past a place called Stoke Wake. I went down a steep wooded hill and soon arrived there. It seemed to consist of only two vicarages, one of which was empty. It was getting late, and finding that I was on the wrong track for going home I knocked at the inhabited vicarage to ask the way. There was a bite and nervous tautness in the air. Was this really the centre of the world for these people? I wondered.

The vicar's wife came to the door and told me how by crossing a certain field I could join the right road. Then she added, while I stood there in the silent, chill, and darkening day, 'Himmler is dead!'

I pushed my bicycle across the field and over some fences, filled with the mystery of life and the drama of these days. Many a time during the war I had thought of that hour when Wordsworth, walking on the public way in Westmoreland, suddenly saw a man afar off hastening towards him who cried out, 'Robespierre is dead!' And I wondered when at last we should hear the like of Hitler. This was good enough.

One day I came upon a very lonely wood. Most are. Some are downright creepy. This was made more so by a number of yew trees. I have always liked this tree; not because of its foliage which somehow one hardly looks at, but on account of the gloomy peace that it bestows in churchyards, far better than more graceful or happier trees would do if ever they appeared there. It suits the melancholy of the grave. It never seems to have been young. Its funeral trunk, so riddled and fluted by Time's tool, goes well with Death and soothingly takes the sting out of it.

The first one I came to in this particular wood was so ancient that some of its branches were themselves trunk sized. In such a tree we do not expect nests or song of birds; but as I gazed into the nooks and cavities of the bark I wondered how many empires of insects had here set up their race and built their Jerusalem. The next one I came to was carrying on in a manner I had never witnessed before. It also was old and drooping. All its principal branches had curved down to join the ground and bury themselves in it. In fact they had firmly taken root there. Thus the original trunk was so well supported by its offspring on all sides that no tempest could possibly floor it as it defied the centuries.

But this was not all. From these props new trees had grown. The branches had *taken root* so completely that new trees grew up. And the process had not stopped there: these new trees had carried on the good work and had done the same thing themselves, sending down branches farther on from which *more* new trees were growing. A considerable area was being covered in this way, making a little forest of yew trees – which was yet one tree. Given time and circumstance it would be possible for a huge forest to exist somewhere – all composed of one tree.

I have always sought out village churches, finding there peace or inspiration. I now turned in one day to glance at Compton Abbas, a small place next to Fontmell Magna. There I found a tower standing alone – the church having disappeared. It was covered by a colossal cloak of ivy. That in itself was a good spectacle: but the ivy did more than cover the tower; having reached the top it proceeded to go down inside, down the steps to the bottom again. In attempting to go up the steps myself I was so impeded by the down-going creepers that it was almost like climbing a tree. Given time it would be interesting to watch the end of the story: the softer substance of wood eating into the hard substance of stone; the pedestal upon which the parasite flourished becoming loose in its joints; and eventually the tower tottering to destruction while the still robust ivy would be involved in its fall and floored with its ruin.

Another tower which I came upon at Childe Okeford drew my attention. There I beheld one of the best things I have ever seen and spent an hour in which I entered a slightly higher state of consciousness than the normal. A creeper was growing up one side of the tower. A very thick root, soon branching out, spread up the wall. Its colouring *exactly* matched the weathered stone – there was no difference. The sheer beauty of congruity startled me and fixed me. The month was October, and this climbing plant – I do not know its name – half-way up the tower opened into beautifully tinted leaves. Birds nests were exposed in many places, and every time that a bird alighted on or flew from a nest then one or two of the big leaves sailed slowly to the ground. Higher up birds perched on the gargoyles, also with astonishing congruity of colour and shape. The tower was leaning against the blue sky, and precisely towards this part the sun shone and the wind did not blow. I had entered into a corner of beauty and peace where nothing was wrong, nothing was stained, where there was no evil and no problem. And I said to myself – How pale the pearl of art beside this! No cutting out of anything here necessary, no selection needed; art, but art real; art as life and not as art; not Utopia, an idea; nor another idea, the Golden Age; nor an Eden that has been, nor a Heaven to be: but a NOW, a thing HERE before my eyes, more promising, more uplifting, more soul-saving than any scheme of salvation, or tormented Saviour salvaging sin!

We live in progressive days. This was 1944. I had been observed standing there, and had been seen using a pencil and a piece of paper (for this was one of the rare occasions when I endeavoured to seize what I experienced on the spot and get it down, however crudely, as above). In a few minutes I found myself surrounded by the military. It was clear that I was up to no good. Where was my Identity Card? I hadn't got it on me of course. Armed with rifles they marched me off to the local ARP (Air Raid Precautions) quarters. A Warden came out, and with a countenance graver than I have seen before on a human being, conducted me to the police station – from which place it took me over an hour to satisfy the police and military that I had meant no harm. Going home at last, I consoled myself with the reflection that this finish to my hour in Paradise was most proper, was itself perfectly congruous with men's activity upon earth.

4

It was a particularly delightful thing for me to find myself working at agriculture in Thomas Hardy's Wessex. I would not say that the modern farm workers bear much resemblance to Hardy's remarkable peasants – but they are larger than life and as highly stylized as the peasants of Synge or the Dubliners of O'Casey. Still, as I widened my acquaintance I began to realize how full of life and individuality the farming community is.

I was able to make this wider acquaintance because a few farmers wrote to me after reading some articles of mine in *Time & Tide*. Incidentally, two sisters, living at Cranborne, also wrote to me saying that they lived in the house where Thomas Hardy's Tess had spent her fatal bridal night. They went further: they were convinced that not only had this woman who never existed stayed there, but that she also haunted the house. They declared that on certain nights their cheeks were gently stroked by the ghost of Tess. They were not alarmed by this, the stroking was friendly. In earlier days, when at the Old Coastguard Station, I had visited as many of the Hardy sites (with the aid of a guidebook devoted to this, *The Hardy Country*) as I could. It was delightful now to visit these courteous sisters and be shown this particular house regarding his most famous book. They also claimed that on certain nights a coach-and-four would rattle down the street outside their house making a great clatter, and then disappear at the bottom. Others had the same experience, for it is a recognized phenomenon in certain old places in England.

I got to know farmers farther afield, as far as Ebbesbourne Wake in Wiltshire for instance, where a very fine farm was run by the Belfields, a gifted and remarkable family whose friendship added an extra dimension to my life, and at whose farm I often assisted at a later date. Through them I met other farmers in the district, notably Ralph Coward at Donhead. He used to conduct ferocious agricultural arguments, chiefly on the great question of organic versus artificial manure. At that time in the farming world such discussions were carried out with as much fervour and rancour and conviction as were given to theological heresies in the past, and the man who suggested that potash, say, was not an entirely unnatural preparation, would be regarded from one side as a person qualifying for damnation just as the tree zealots would put down all the erosions and all the deserts and even all the collapses of civilizations to the neglect of forestry. I secured a balanced view from Edwin Hooper, another friend at Tarrant Hinton.

Thus if you leave the towns in England and go into the country you still find behind any hedgerow a variety of lively individuals. It was at Coward's farm at Donhead that I entered a theatre. A barn had been used, for the afternoon, as an auditorium. There were two entrances to this barn, and at one end the big fully open door served as stage scenery. Have I made myself clear? That door at the far end of the auditorium was open and in the space was framed the countryside beyond; it was an unglassed window if you like, or a canvas that was not a canvas upon which was painted the real rural scenery. The barn was on a rise and commanded a view of the valley below with its Church and its cottages and meadows and clumps of trees and summer clouds.

We took our seats in the auditorium and soon the play began. It was a Fable belonging to the times. Enter a Poet in whom contemplation without participation had caused sterility in the Muse. Meeting some peasants, and finding that they seemed happier and wiser than himself, he decided to turn his back on poetry and cultivate the earth. He approaches a Farmer. But this is in the black days of agriculture, and the farmer replies that it is useless to engage labour as all his land is buried under Tins – symbol of the false standards, the false food, the false economy of our day. The Poet is surprised.

> 'I thought there was a queer crop growing.
> I felt perhaps it needed hoeing.
> But now I see its hills and hills
> Of rusty tins and empty bottles of pills.'

The farmer explains that this is because

> '...all folk now get their food from tins
> And have to push it down with medicines.'

Perhaps they can get the tins removed? Together they decide to appeal to the Parish Council. They do so, but that Body refers them to the Rural District Council. The Council refers them to the Agricultural Committee. This body also turns them down, the Chairman saying,

> 'You see you've lost your case Sir, unless you like to summons.
> Enough audacity to face the House of Commons.'

Once more the Farmer makes an appeal, this time before the Bar of the House. And again he is turned away.

But just as the House is about to adjourn for lunch a telegram arrives – symbol of World Catastrophe – declaring that food supplies from overseas have stopped. Sensation. Complete change of Governmental attitude. The Land is now the thing. All hands to the hoe. God speed the plough. The farmers are splendid. Thus the situation is changed; the tins are swept away; the harvest is gathered amidst rejoicing and song, and the Poet feels the return of inspiration.

Such was the theme. The author, Basil Hembry, who was dairyman of the farm at this time, took the part of the poet, and Ralph Coward the farmer, and a very striking pair they made, though an impassioned speech to the Councillors was slightly spoilt by the grunting of a pig and the neighing of a

151

horse just off stage. They were supported by a cast which included all the labourers on the farm. The whole entertainment passed without a dull moment. The stage scenery, as we have seen, copied nature by being nature, the changing light and the moving clouds over the quiet vale blending perfectly with the play.

As I sat there in the barn that was an auditorium, I reflected how after reading about agriculture I have often turned with relief to agriculture itself to become submerged in its grind. And since one so often reads about 'The Future of the Village' or 'The Problem of Rural Education' or 'Leisure and Culture', it is refreshing to turn from the book to the deed instead of the hope, the idea, the ideal, the could-be. Here work and play, culture and agriculture, action and contemplation had come together.

The most unusual man whom I came to know at this time was Sigvart Godeseth of Gore Farm, already mentioned. Here was a man whom everyone liked – to the point of loving. I recall an amusing example showing the regard in which he was held. At one time Jimmy Edwards worked for him. In due course Mr Edwards left the land exchanging Shaftesbury for Shaftesbury Avenue. One day when Sigvart was in London he decided to look him up at the theatre. He went to the stage door. 'I want to see Mr Jimmy Edwards.' 'Have you an appointment with him?' the doorman demanded. 'No, but I'm sure he will see me.' 'That is quite out of the question, Mr Edwards never sees anyone who comes to the stage door.' 'He will see me if you give him my name.' 'Who do you think you are!? It cannot be done, and that is final, Sir.' Sigvart wrote something on the back of an envelope and handed it to the doorman, saying, 'If you send this up to him he will come down.' The man assured him that it was useless but he sent a boy upstairs. In a moment down came Jimmy Edwards with an open-armed welcome to Sigvart, and a loudly expressed hope that he had not been kept waiting.

He was a Norwegian, but his command of English was as remarkable as his voice was pleasant. His handsome face could have been that of an actor or painter or poet, while his powerful hands were unmistakably those of a peasant. Of course the word peasant is a very difficult one nowadays, and in any case he bore no resemblance to a British farmer or farm labourer. As everyone knows, the old time labourer was an exceptional man, and when he allowed a Hardy in England or a Synge in Ireland or a Burns in Scotland to present him, he was also a philosopher and a poet. Today he does not differ very greatly from the industrial worker, certainly not in attitudes and valuations. Sigvart was a strange bird to be found amongst the English. His mind was naturally comprehensive and enlightened without being undermined by school knowledge. One day, picking up a fossil turned up by his plough he graphically pictured to me what the earth was like when this book of stone was first inscribed. Knowing him, I was not surprised at his grasp of geology. He could speak five languages, and when he went for a European holiday on his bicycle he hardly ever had to pay for a night's lodging, for he seemed to have friends strewed all over Europe, and he seldom met a stranger whom he did not leave a friend.

When he left Gore Farm he took a farm of his own at Semley, the other side of Shaftesbury, and I have visited him there from time to time in recent years. He disliked machinery, never even got a tractor – on the ground that it did not produce young. With his wife and family he did all the work himself, and as far as I could see almost anything would grow for him. He often had voluntary assistants, for the idea spread abroad that to give Sigvart a hand was a sufficient honour in itself – though if no one turned up he would carry the wheat or bring in the whole potato crop himself, enjoying it very much. His enjoyment in this hard work was very striking. Equally so, more so, was his *warmth*. Whenever I have gone down to Dorset in recent years, or an any time since I left agriculture, I have made my way to Sigvart's farm, having made no arrangement, written no letter in advance. Arriving, I would see him in the distance somewhere, perhaps at the far end of a potato crop, and I would walk towards him. When at least he saw me coming he would instantly abandon his work and welcome me with open arms. It didn't matter how busy he was, humanity came first, affection came first.

While I had my headquarters at Law's bungalow, I spent a few months ploughing for Sigvart at Gore Farm. This was with horses.[1] Since tractors could not produce their kind and horses could, he considered the latter to be the most economical. Here was my opportunity, and I ploughed a long field on the left of the high road leading to Shaftesbury. I have described elsewhere the pleasures of ploughing. Apart from everything else there is this great fact: since it is an individual job, no one interferes with you, you have the field to yourself, and nature to yourself – could anyone in his senses call that loneliness? You have escaped from the whole roaring wrack of the world, and your escape is not into dreaming, not into idleness, but into work... It was with great regret that I had to abandon agriculture... This field, this place was all that I could desire: the view of a green hill far away; a near grassy slope scraping the sky, one square copse emphasizing the severity of its lonely bareness; a vale plunging steeply below into what glittering promised land?; above, those countries of the sky that change even as you gaze upon them, or perish before they are observed at all – all this to be seen from my station. I did not see it. I could only see my horses and my plough in perspiring concentration, but I knew that those things were there and that I was in the midst of them.

The years pass. I visit Dorset from time to time. I go through Tarrant Hinton, and gaze into 'E's farmyard looking exactly the same with its array of gear, with some degree of crisis still in the air though the man is dead; I go past fields in all of which I have had business; I go through Tarrant Gunville and up to my wood to see how it is going on, and it always has gone on; and then up to the high road towards Shaftesbury till I come opposite Gore Farm and see my long field. There I stop – amazed that I can say, 'I have ploughed that field'. To a countryman my mood of pride would seem strange or strained, and to some townsmen though not to all of them. But if these pages are autobiographical and if I am to make a confession here and there, I am obliged to admit that having been able to go over the fence, away from the road, and onto the field as a workman, gave me a feeling of belonging to the world which I was never able to have in the past.

Not very long ago – perhaps eight years – I was in the district again. I had gone up a steep hill past a landmark known as Wingreen, over a crossroads, till I came to a place on the road where I always stop. At a certain point on this road there is a very romantic view of the right; you do not look across the land but down into a steep narrow winding vale, its green rhythmic curves like poetry made visible. I always feel constrained to stop when I am passing here and gaze at this bleak, lonely and lovely way. It was about 6.00 p.m. on the day I speak of, and I noticed that a wheat field on my left was being carried (no combine harvester). It was quite a large field, perhaps thirty acres. I saw the rick and the rick builders in the distance, but only one man was left over to pitch and load a wagon: he had to pitch up the sheaves, then climb onto the tractor, go forward, stop, get down, and pitch up again. He was working near where I had stopped. I left my car, got over the fence, walked up to him and asked if he would like me to give him a hand. Much to my surprise (for I had expected a polite refusal of assistance) he said Yes. By good chance I happened to have a pair of boots in the car and a mackintosh jacket. I went and put them on and joined him. I climbed onto the wagon with a prong and said I would load. The loader receives sheaves pitched up to him and arranges them on the wagon. If he doesn't do his part of the job properly and *build* his wagon-load almost as carefully as if he were building a rick, there will soon be an inextricable mess of sheaves on the wagon ready to fall off and with no room for any more. I have no natural aptitude for seizing the best way of doing a thing, but once it is pointed out to me (nearly always just common sense), I am included to do it rather better than the professionals – being more fresh and keen. I like loading a wagon

154

and, quick with my prong work in dealing with sheaves, can build a load that will not topple over as the tractor draws it along over uneven ground. In a minute of so the labourer saw that I knew my business, all was easy between us, and together we erected a high wagon-load of wheat sheaves. I overdid it though, and as we approached the rick over some bad ruts, the pile swayed and trembled – but did not actually fall over. So I didn't lose face. We now pitched up to the rick, everyone in a good mood, even the boss who appeared. He could not make me out, and no doubt wondered if he would have to pay me. It was an exceptionally lovely summer evening; the clouds that gathered round the setting sun turned to rose, the white road grew whiter and the dark copse darker. We finished the rick before it became too dark, and shaking friendly hands all round I went away. It was good therapy for me. It put me in harmless conceit with myself, too private a conceit to bother anyone; or, for that matter, to bother myself; for it was natural in me to welcome a sense of relief at being able to change from being a spectator of 'the rural scene', or scenery-gazer, and to leave the road, climb over the fence, and become part of that scene.

5

Any reader of Thomas Hardy's novels, who had been working in his Wessex till about 1944-45 would not have found any colossal difference between Hardy's scene and our own up till 1944: some different things of course, such as the tractor instead of the horse, and a large amount of machine milking. Yet the agricultural scene would not have differed enormously from the old days. Possibly my account in *While Following the Plough* bears this out.

But the revolution which took place roughly in 1944 to the present day has altered the character of the scene more than between the days of Chaucer and 1944.

I refer to the coming of the combine harvester. When I was on the land there were only a few of them. Then swiftly, as with TV sets, they began to be used everywhere. These combines, remember, cut the corn and thresh it at the same time. That is to say there is no need for a binder to make sheaves, which are gathered into stooks, then made into ricks, and subsequently threshed. In addition, haymaking is now done by a machine which dispenses with the necessity of carrying the hay or making a hayrick, because while the machine moves across the field it cuts and parcels the grass into heavy oblong blocks thrown out onto the ground – (and often left there for a long time looking most untidy and unsightly).

These are admirable devices, it is said, making harvesting and haymaking easy work. That is true. But in order to enjoy them you must *remain on the field.*

There is the difficulty. The labourers do not remain on the field. They have been exchanged for metal. They have been sent into the towns – perhaps to make the metal instruments for which they have been exchanged. Anyway they are no longer there. The fields are empty. There is a harvest, and there is hay; but there is no harvesting, and no haymaking; and as for a 'harvest supper' amidst general gaiety and songs, even if such an idea occurred to a modern farmer there would be no one to attend such a celebration.[2]

I am sticking closely to the facts. I exaggerate only in saying 'no one' to celebrate. There is the farmer and one or two others, and sometimes quite a few more. But at a pinch *one man alone* could manage a combine and also a hay-machine. At a pinch the same man could do most of the winter and spring ploughing, harrowing, and drilling. That is an extreme, of course, there must be a man for the stock, and for the sheep – if there are any! But the little community bound together by work which made a large farm is gone; and as for the haymaking and harvesting in which a portion of the whole village joined, that is now only a memory.

I pay attention to this situation more as an historian and a sentimentalist than as a romanticist. A romanticist is a person who expects things to happen which will not happen – such as the restoration of the rural community. An historian sets down the facts. A sentimentalist laments the situation: and I think he has his place; it is legitimate to lament certain things. And I take the liberty of lamenting the fact that in the rural scene while 'labour is saved' the labourers are sacked. Only a select few remain.

It happens that here, from this angle, from the field – the only angle from which I am competent to speak – we see in clearest outline, in dire extremity, what the triumph of the machine actually means at the present time.

It means that without being able to introduce a Philosophy of Leisure (all talk about this is hot air) we have totally abandoned any Philosophy of Work.

I often think of Lethaby, the nineteenth-century architect and thinker who dropped pregnant remarks from time to time. 'If any man would be a saint, let him clean drains and dig the earth.' That is a metaphysical as well as a physical exhortation, and far from superficial. 'If we are ever to remake civilisation, we shall have to begin by recognising that it is founded first of all on labour, without which it cannot last for a day. We must understand, and as it is so mighty a necessity, we must even learn to worship work... human work, I say, not machine-grinding.' And there is his fable of the monk of the sixth century who having laboured in the fields all day found that a little bird had built its nest in his mantle he had laid on the ground. '*Understanding what labour meant*, he lent his cloak to the bird for the rest of the season.'

We are bound to qualify some of that today, and we certainly have to qualify Carlyle who went to a dangerous extreme in his fanatical philosophy of work. We need not qualify, or try to rule as right or wrong, a remark made by Goethe (for it is simply a statement of feeling), namely, Faust's discovery that the perfect moment – the moment when he would command all the clocks in the world to stop – was not when he was with Gretchen or Helen, but when he was organizing the draining of the marshlands, and establishing a new community where men could lead the good life.

We need not quarrel with the words of William Morris through John Ball speaking to the peasants: 'Fellowship is life and lack of fellowship is death; fellowship is heaven and lack of fellowship is hell; and the deeds that ye do upon the earth, it is for fellowship's sake that ye do them.'[3] Nor with T S Eliot in *The Rock*:

> 'What life have you if you have not life together?
> There is no life that is not in community
> And no community not lived in praise of God.'

In the context of both the fellowship was to be achieved by labouring together. I have always been very fond of a certain scene in Tolstoy's *Anna Karenina*. In that book there are two passages on the same theme; one is a famous piece about mowing which gave Levin such satisfaction and such a sense of brotherhood and *belonging*, which much appeals to me. The other is less well known, when again he comes out into the field of hay. He had expected to find the men in a bad mood, for there had been a row of some sort the day before. But he found them all singing and in the highest state of merriment. He was enveloped in it, and the wrangling of the previous day was forgotten. 'And that was drowned in a sea of merry common labour. God gave the day. God gave the strength. And the day and the strength were consecrated to labour, and that labour was its own reward. For whom the labour? What would be its fruits? These were idle questions – beside the point.' Wonderful lines: as audacious as they are simple; illuminating with a genius ray the main aspect.

There are other aspects. They have been amply attended to in modern times – at the expense of that spirit which Levin experienced. In life there can be no absolutes. My sense of this is so strong that it rules me out as a preacher of complete principles or final rostrums. I cannot lay down the law. I react without being a reactionary. Even if it were not entirely futile to do so, I could never take up an absolute stand against so wonderful and indeed so obvious, a tool as the combine harvester. But I do take up a stand against a current absolutely calmly assumed on every hand – namely, that *any* invention which saves labour is, *ipso facto*, a good thing. It is absurd to accept an invention as good simply because it is an invention. Yet this acceptance is just what we see the whole time. We have on TV programmes such as 'Things To Come' or 'Tomorrow's World' when an extremely cheerful and smug commentator, or 'scientist' in white coat and scarcely literate speech, will *assume* that the tawdry and ugly and horribly roboty gadgets which he displays are not only things which we need and want but are going to have. He will show us things which are to save us (*save*, mind you!) from doing things which it is really good for us to do ourselves. It is thought proper in responsible places to assume this as an absolute and to cast abroad the idea that no philosophy of work should be entertained by anyone at any time in any place. Yet in a sane society a person who brought forward a seemingly useful but silly or ugly invention would be ridiculed in public, and any man who suggested that 'raising the standard of life' is a necessary result of a 'labour-saving device' would be treated as if he were an infant.

The fact is, and the pundits in other fields have made it abundantly clear even if it were not obvious, that modern man is appallingly complicated in his psychological needs. He needs, and especially the young need, comfort, love, good meals, helping hands, smiling faces, security: they also need discomfort, scarcity, enemies, excitement, hardship, danger, resistance, and terror. In these last requirements British youth is grossly underprivileged. Instead they are offered sugar-plums in the form of pop music from morning to night by excessively friendly and jolly disc jockeys. No wonder many of them resent any mention of either of the wars, and resent also the novels of Dickens and Hardy and Tolstoy in which there is a kind of poetry in the poverty and in the struggle and in the hardship which belongs to a reality we covet, and which makes for fellowship. In the course of my life no remark has struck me so much as that made (and repeated) both by Siegfried Sassoon and Robert Graves and by several others less well known, to the effect that when they were on leave they could not wait to *get back to the front*! Life at home in the cities seemed to them so insincere and so lacking in brotherhood that they longed to get back to the trenches again. The significance of that is beyond description. What has happened to mankind that such a thing could be said? How deep must be the desire for fellowship! How great the betrayal of a *need*. Apparently no amount of sport or organized idleness will ever be able to take the place of overcoming resistant reality.

All this applies to men rather than to women. Women are not faced with the same problem. For them nothing very fundamental has changed since the days of Adam and Eve, seeing that their primary product is the production of mankind – which cannot be carried out by machinery of any sort – and they will always have their hand full in establishing domestic order. What must terrify them is the prospect of men in the future relying upon leisure to satisfy their mental, bodily, and spiritual needs. Women will always have plenty to do, but to have men hanging around trying to face the horror and tedium of leisure or contrived occupation, must be a daunting vista.

If these observations only applied to a few people there would not be the present widespread unrest. We used to be told about 'angry' young men, and their chief annoyance was supposed to have been about 'class distinction'. It is difficult enough at the best of times to get a word of sense or lucidity out of Mr John Osborne, and to have taken his lead about this is the limit. The class problem is more than half solved, and is in any case out of the realm of economics where the shoe pinched. No one can get really worked up about that any more. I think that what we see around us now is not so much anger as a deep unease regarding the way civilization itself is going. They wonder into what channel their Energy is expected to flow. The sporadic gestures of violence, and the demonstrations against teachers, and the turning away from science courses, are not just meaningless rowdyism. It is a *malaise* and a reaction against the present drift. It is a not very clear intellectual fury at the assumption that soon it will be quite all right for them to be called commuters going into town to deal with computers, and that somehow 'leisure' is going to make up for this.[4] The fact that they are extremely inarticulate when asked what is bothering them *au fond*, makes the matter worse. In the past it was so easy. You had a definite target. You assaulted the Bastille and brought about a Revolution. How do you assault the Evolution of a system of valuations in which Being counts for nothing and Production for everything?

One thing does surprise me, though. I do not understand why they are not angry about the spoliation of England. Since 1900 two million acres have been cut away, and it is expected that another two million will go before the end of the century. Anyone who has in his mind's eye how much a hundred acre field is, will be shocked at such a thought. No mandate is taken from the people concerning a decision of this kind in our undemocratic democracy. The government claims the right, for the sake of travel and Big

Business interests, to knock away when it chooses huge slices of land, to advance with bulldozers, just like a military operation, upon ancient houses, villages, households, and acres of farms in this small and beautiful country, and destroy them all. Voices are raised against this in the name of tradition, in the name of beauty, in the name of justice for those who will immediately suffer, in the name of silence and peace and religion, they may be listened to or they may be ignored. If they are ignored they are powerless to do anything.

But need they be powerless? Could not the youth of England protest against *this*? It would be no vague cause for the youth of England to stand up angrily against the destruction of England. They could do more than just protest and march. They could refuse to allow such proceedings to go forward in the name of democracy. They could point out that it is no good having an affluent society if you destroy your country. They could remind the so-called powers that be, that it is also *their* country and that *they* will be living in it when the people who perpetrate these things are dead. They could oppose such actions with force – yes, with arms. They could throw bombs at the bulldozers. There would be a battle each time they appeared. It would be war. But it would be a worthwhile one. Those who fought in it would indeed, if ever the words were absolutely true, be 'fighting for their *country*'.

6

I mentioned near the beginning of this chapter how my wife, Eirene, went to America with our daughters in 1940. Just as going onto the land led me to discover my literary line, so going to America led my wife to find hers. In America she met Dr Phelps who was a pioneer in the study of Cerebral Palsy (now often referred to as Spastics). She had always had a flair for medicine, and if circumstances had made it possible in the past she would have become a doctor. Through association with Phelps she discovered in herself gifts of which she had been unaware. Returning to England while I was on the land, it was not long before she started a Unit at Queen Mary's Hospital for Children at Carshalton, called the Cerebral Palsy Research Unit, and there justified her claim that the infantile cerebral palsies warranted special study and the development of special therapeutic techniques. She worked there for twenty years and her influence on the medical world in this field became very great. It was notable how doctors, with theory, but lacking the intuitional flair which Eirene possessed, would turn to her for a ruling. Thus, if they were confronted with a child about whom they were dubious as to whether he or she was Mentally Deficient or a victim of Cerebral Palsy though perfectly intelligent, they would not always be able to decide. But Eirene could decide at a glance and give an instant ruling, greatly to the relief of everyone. At Queen Mary's she made short work of the notion that separate parts of the child were the concern of separate therapists. Thus one therapist 'treated' his legs, another his arms, a third his speech, a fourth 'taught' his brain, while his trunk remained something of a battle gound.[5] It may seem obvious now that this was an imperfect approach, but she had to fight to abolish it in favour of treating the whole person. But she did succeed and her methods spread abroad, especially to Scandinavia and to Italy where she received a decoration from the state.[6]

Whenever she undertook to treat any child she never for one moment regarded it as 'a case' or withheld from the parents her full attention – and for this she received their lasting gratitude. It used to amuse me how people who had not yet met her, but had just heard of Mrs Eirene Collis, Head of the Cerebral Palsy Unit at Queen Mary's Hospital, were taken aback by her appearance. They expected to see a business-like, possibly squat, certainly tough looking person, and instead of this they found themselves confronted with a pretty, delicate-featured, young-looking woman who was able to speak to foreign parents or nurses, whether German, French, or Italian in their own language!

After the war I would have remained on the land combining the security of farm work with my literary endeavours, but I abandoned this idea so that we might all live together near Carshalton. By selling the house in Kent I was able to mortgage one in Ewell, and I took up again the Adult Education work. In the fifties my wife was suddenly struck down by a cerebral thrombosis which caused her to become completely paralysed on her left side – a brain damage not dissimilar from the palsy she had for so long striven to alleviate in others. She had always been very delicate and could not cope with motherhood or domesticity without much assistance. When the time came for her to turn to Cerebral Palsy she never rested, never relaxed, she became interested in one thing only and pursued it regardless of health or anything else. I doubt whether any lazy person is in much danger of a cerebral thrombosis. Laziness was unknown to Eirene, nor had she the ability to relax, and she was suddenly struck down. She never recovered. No movement ever returned to her left leg or her left arm. At first it was possible for her to sit in a wheelchair, but it was terribly difficult to dress and undress her. I looked after her for six years, day and night, though I never really mastered the art of lifting her without strain. Her ordeal lasted for twelve years, the last six in a Nursing Home where I could visit her with regularity. She died while I was writing this book.

Here I must say frankly that had she died a few years previously, and had I been able to get everything into perspective I would have tried to write more fully; but as it is I find it too difficult.

She had been dying slowly before my eyes for years, yet her death came suddenly. One day she had another stroke. When I reached her she was unconscious and though it seemed that she recognized me and our daughters, I am not certain. In the evening the doctor said that until the morning it would be impossible to know what the effects of this second thrombosis would be, and I was advised to go home. But instead of my telephoning early next morning, the matron rang to say that she had died in the night. I went to the nursing home, as I had gone for so many years to see the living person. I can never take reality for *less* than it is; and I have often wished that at funerals, not a closed coffin but an open one were brought into the church, the dead face visible to all. That would make people sit up and wake from the dream! At the nursing home the night before there had been the living, warm, breathing creature, and here she was now, a horizontal statue, severe, alien, unseeing and unbreathing, as cold as marble, and totally uninterested in communicating a single word. Anything – anything but this! I felt. I do not know if time will ever soften this harsh scene for me, but I doubt it. Of course it was a release for her, and I had been horrified by the thought that she might still have to suffer more and worse hardship. My friends thought that it would be a release for me as well as for her. But the heart of man is not only desperately wicked but desperately complicated. I *had* thought it would be a release for me. I had thought that it would be a relief not to have to walk through the dreary corridor to her room week after week, that I would be glad to be free. I never told her that I would miss her and choke with tears every time I *should* have been getting ready to go to her and bring her things. And she did not know this. She always managed to get me wrong, and I made no effort to make her get me right, for I did not know my own heart, I did not know that when the time came I would not be able to bear her *non*-existence. She read a lot of paper-backs. I decided to sort them out and put aside a number for the nursing home library. Shortly after the funeral I brought them in. This was a mistake. Going in and giving the books to a Sister, I found a terrible strain. As swiftly as could be I unpacked the books, unable to speak a word, and *fled* from the place with clenched fists. And it is because of this, and because of the words unspoken and the sorrow unknown, that time may not soften or heal the harshness of that final scene.

1 I did eventually plough at Hannan's farm, with a tractor.

2 In his *Welsh Country Upbringing*, D Parry Jones, while speaking of the modern total undermining of the solidarity of the rural community, says 'Haymaking was the happiest and gayest of all seasonal activities, by reason of the big, merry, and animate company that came together'. Can anyone answer what can make up for the loss of this?

3 'Morris said that for him "human happiness consists in the pleasurable exercise of our energies". Better this than the cynical hopeless insistence on the everlastingness of our imperfection, justifying grab while we can.' 'On Still Being a Socialist' by Geoffrey Grigson in *The Listener*, 23 October 1969.

4 In Tokyo nothing less than a yell of agony regularly goes up from the young before they are subdued.

5 See Obituary in *Occupational Therapy* by Mrs Jane Bradby, May 1970, and an Appreciation in *The Lancet* by Dr William Durham, August 1970.

6 *Il Problema dei Bambini Discinetici*, pp. 28-34. Publicazione a cura del Patronato Bambini Discinetici, Crema 1969.

FIFTH MOVEMENT...

... FINDING

1

These five to six years working at agriculture not only filled a psychological and physical need of mine but made a literary turning point for me. Here was material upon which I could impose form; and for the first time I could regard my books without dissatisfaction – a state one should arrive at by the age of forty-six or not at all. I had never really thought it possible to get on by 'lunching with everyone'. Talking with the Master of Balliol (A D Lindsay) some time in the forties I told him that I could only get on in the literary world after I had my lunches with agricultural labourers. He was quick to take the point. I said this to him because I knew he would like it, he was that sort of man.

This farm work brought me properly in touch with *facts*, and I am as fond of facts as I am of ideas. I never like to use an idea without linking it with a fact, nor use a fact without linking it with an idea; I like to use both to promote a vision of the whole. As I went ever further into the processes of Nature[1] I always sought to connect the part with the whole.

From a visionary point of view my approach and my timing were fortunate. The Reading Room days had not been entirely barren. There also I had sown; there also I had reaped to some extent; on a very humble scale, but a genuine one, and I did in the end come to a vision of the whole. *Then* I could really wake up to the thrill of the part. I went from the whole to the part, and ever since each new discovery of a particular has enriched my vision of the whole.

The approach from the other end is not always advantageous, and can be disastrous. If, as schoolboys, we start with the particular, if we have parts dinned into us and taken out of us in exams, then not only may we *never* come to see the whole, but we will also detest the parts!

As a schoolboy I was lucky because science was made so distasteful to me that I was never submerged under bits and pieces of knowledge, for I turned my back on it all, leaving my mind in this direction empty. Quite recently I got a letter from that brilliant poet, Martyn Skinner, who had just read my *Paths of Light*. In the course of his letter he said, 'Ah, I thought, if only there had been a science master with this sort of insight and outlook, one's whole life might have been different. And Keats' too – instead of "Philosophy will clip an angel's wings", he would have quoted:

> "How charming is divine philosophy,
> Not harsh nor crabbed as dull fools suppose
> But musical as in Apollo's lute." '

Had anyone at Rugby prophesied that such a thing would eventually be written to me, not only would I have been bewildered, but I would not even have been pleased, so great was my dislike of science at that time, as presented before my infant eyes.

But of course again I am grateful that I was kept off certain things so that later I could come fresh and strong to them. It was far better so. Far better, for example, that I should have been prevented from looking seriously at the moon until I had developed the adult's sense of wonder. I had been told, I 'knew', that the moon 'reflects the sun's light'. That meant nothing to me, it was just a school fact stuffed into Floor II of my head where the brain has no connection with the eye. It was not till I was fifty-six that I could take in that fact, and realize that the dark sky at night is really blazing with sunshine which we cannot see until the waves of light hit something, and a barren, lightless rock becomes a lamp. Until I was fifty-six, I didn't know that I didn't know this.

It by no means follows that everyone is qualified by the age of fifty-six to look at the moon. It may take longer. I could do so because I was writing on Light. It is clear that few of us are bright enough to know what we don't know, just as few of us can face what we don't feel, or what we don't believe. In my case there is the stimulus of my art to look at things as for the first time and start my readers from square one. This makes straight reading for them (and ensures accuracy, for no error can be afforded) since initially I write not out of my knowledge but out of my ignorance, not out of my strength but out of my weakness – so that in the end people may come to me for learning and for strength.

168

I would like them to come to me for synthesis. If I look up these books of mine in the London Library I find them listed under various heads: Agriculture; Forestry; Physics; Botany; Chemistry; and Water. Thus I am neatly tucked away in separate corners, though the aim of the books is to show that these things make a unity, that all things are all things. There is no Synthesis compartment in a library any more than in schools. A President of the Royal Academy once made a plea in *The Times* that my books should be used in the schools. He was beating the air. 'Sorry, Collis', said a headmaster to me (some of my best friends are schoolmasters), 'but we don't like synthesis. We cannot expect, for example, the botany master to teach physics as well, and that is the sort of thing you are suggesting. It would lead to inaccuracy in instruction and chaos in the curriculum.' 'I find that some boys go for it', I said, 'if they come across my stuff.' 'Perhaps they do', was the reply, 'but they also go for all sorts of things which should not be encouraged at an early age.' I tend to think he was right. But I fail to see why the existence of the books should be withheld from students who could make use of them. People tell me that sooner or later there will be a revolt against the parcel business: a revulsion (even in America!) against thesis; and a belief in the necessity of synthesis – and that then 'your time will come'. Let it come soon rather than late, is all I can say. Meanwhile it is assumed, even by those who complain in a loose phrase about there being two separate cultures, that one cannot do what actually I do do, and that therefore I cannot have done what I have done.

It is supposed, for example, that one cannot make perfectly clear what frost is, how molecules have got to work and formed the crystals, and so forth; and having laid that foundation of fact, then take the thing into the realm of truth: 'All things are transfigured, even barbed wire and iron railings. Nor does it matter how tender or small or intricate the object is; without smudging and without weighing down or breaking, the white print is cast. The spider's web hangs on the gate. Yesterday we might not have noticed it. Today it has caught and fixed the freezing vapour in its net – a photograph developed from the negative. We behold a double miracle: the weaving of the web by the living crawling creature, and the weaving of the filaments of frost by the molecules that in another mode tread another loom.[2]

Now, no scientist, *per se*, can, or indeed should, write in that manner; and no poet, *per se*, should do so, for the moment he says, in effect, now I am going to be poetical about frost (or fire, or water...), it is fatal, for immediately a barrier, a film is put between him and the reader. But if the style is raised unexpectedly while dove-tailed with sober statement, then the reader, taken by surprise and not by storm, can shift his vision without effort from the particular to the whole, from the fact to the truth of beauty.

It is not as if people failed to respond to a combination of the scientific and poetic approach to reality. In the same book I explain what snow is. I think I must have made about five hundred pounds from reprints of that in Digests in America and in England, and in various publications in Europe, and it still goes on. Simply because I took the trouble to be completely accurate scientifically about snow and yet bring it into the realm of the imagination, I received that response. Indeed, I have little to complain about personally. I have not been neglected. I have not been misunderstood, and this is surprising: in no preface, in no sentence did I ever mention the word poetry or make any claims in that direction; but never have I been taken as anything other than a poet – my approach is evidently so obvious that I have not even been called a 'popularizer of science'. Even the financial aspect of my endeavour has not been totally disastrous, for on behalf of my efforts, 'the Queen and Prime Minister were pleased to confer' (as the happy terms state it) a Civil List pension of three hundred a year – which, to your author, always expecting to die in a ditch, means as much as millions to your tycoon. And the way I put it financially to myself is that they said, in effect, 'Here, Collis, you can have £800,000, not to be spent in a lump sum, but invested at four per cent in cast-iron security'. Indeed, should I live for twenty years from the time of receiving it, I will have received £6,000. Thus, though living at a time when the word synthetic only means inferior food or shoddy material, my plea for synthesis in knowledge has not entirely ruined me. In any case the whole drift of my life has been such that I could never be deflected by specialists from trying to connect things. I am not afraid of being overpowered by these enemies. 'Meet them undaunted, and they shall have no power to daunt thee', is a fine saying which has always inspired me.

I form the impression that the public is no longer happy with information given only by scientists. People feel that there is something lacking, though they may not be sure what it is. The element that is absent is the faculty of imagination. And because it is not there the people *cannot* attend to what is being said. Sometimes when I listen to a scientist on TV, I think: 'This man has been injured, he has been maimed! He does have two arms and two legs and a face of sorts, but a bit of personal property has been stolen from him – he has no imagination, no spiritual faculty of apprehension.' So we are left cold and cowed, not mentally advanced or enriched by what he has said. His spoonfuls of information are about as digestible as a box of nails.

Think of the Astronauts. That was something, wasn't it? Some men got up and left this earth for the first time in the history of this solar system, and

170

sailed away, sometimes getting out of their vehicle to take a walk upon nothing, and finally printed their steps upon the moon. A footprint in a lonely place is always a pathetic and a tragic sight. Think of these now upon those barren sands, that for measureless centuries had remained unprinted by the trampling of any feet, and unechoed by the singing of any bird. Never had there been such an adventure, nor such adventures. I followed them day and night without any desire to go to bed. And I followed it the second time also. Yet in the main people began to express themselves as 'getting bored'. And why was that? For a good enough reason, I think. They craved for the Word – and they were given only words. Chiefly jargon of the feeblest sort. The astronauts themselves could not be expected to help. Just when the supremest powers of expression were called for, they were in command of scarcely more than baby language. True, one lot quoted the Bible, though they dared not quote the passage which says that in the beginning was the Word, and the Word was with God, nay the Word was God. One of them said that there was a good view to be had. And one said, looking back on the earth, that it looked a nice place, and that it was strange that its inhabitants spent so much time fighting each other, or any time at all doing it – strange too, he might have added, that one should have to go to the moon before properly realizing this.

Since Youth is concerned about the future, I would say – Beware of letting scientists assume so much power in every direction. They are deprived and handicapped men lacking a full awareness of human needs. Any paltry invention is to their minds a need. Let us beware of them! It is *their* attitude of thoughtlessness, plus their expertise which while it has given us so many marvellous things, recklessly causes the pollution of the waters, the erosion of the soil, the destruction by insecticides of the organisms which minister to the equilibrium of nature, the torture of countless thousands of animals for experiment, and the wiping out of any creature that gets in their way. Neither the artists of the world nor the ordinary people of the world are responsible for the attitude or for the means which make these things possible – it is the scientists. So I would say to Youth – Attack *them*, when it is called for. Laugh them out of court with vicious mockery when their values are obviously against humanity; if and when their gadgets are ludicrous, hurl them into the sea with savage contempt!

That is my advice. But, people may say, You are old, they are young, so why should they listen to you across the generation gap? Of that gap! Who invented it? The Press? or Television? Youth does not exist: nor Old Age: there are only young people and older people living in the same generation (to a person living in the next century, who is weak on dates, we will be

171

mostly contemporaries). Is it really held now that the views of a young person, *per se*, are of more importance than that of an older person, *per se*? Just consider: two men are walking along a road, they are bound upon a journey, there is no escape. One of them has gone further along the pilgrimage. He has observed many things. He has suffered many things. He has got stuck in the mud. He has taken wrong turnings. He has fallen among thieves. He has seen the celestial city fade into a mirage, and nothing but a misty horizon lead into promising lands. He has seen the savages and he has seen the saviours. Don't you think that what he has to say regarding the perils and the possibilities of the Journey is as important as that of the man who has not gone so far along the road?

In attempting to make the Synthesis which I have so much at heart I have continually been baulked by my own slowness, not to mention inertia and laziness. Slowness in developing, in writing, and in reading. Especially in reading. Not only do I read slowly but I often find it necessary to read the same book over and over again until I am sure of the upshot. If only I could read, and take in, as some people can, a page in half a minute, life would be easier. That would be a gift from the gods indeed. Yet I know that if a fairy could grant me that gift, I would be chary of accepting it. Too good a memory and a quick mind might possibly detract from imagination, and what I can make out of a combination of slowness and ignorance. It might rob me of any gifts which I may possess. I like to pursue a thing painfully to its conclusion; to ask myself what is actually being *said*; to satisfy myself that the author is saying what I think he is, and then take an audacious literary leap – which generally takes a lyrical or paradoxical form.

Thus with coal. It amuses me to logically pursue what it actually is. Having first made clear just how the Carboniferous Forests sank, often one on top of another, I could conclude: 'We take a piece of coal in our hands, a black stone. It is carbon, it is sunshine shaped into a solid. It is a piece of the sun itself we hold, the blazing ball itself turned into the dirty darkness of that rock. It may be very cold, freezing to the touch on a winter's day; yet still it is the ancient furnace that we finger, it is heat made cold, a frozen burning beam. We do not doubt this for a minute. We know how to change it back again. We put a piece of its own element in touch with it – its own essence, flame – and in a few minutes the box flies open and the trebly millioned years imprisoned sun streams out, and the ransomed rays that fell upon the ferns fall on us today.[3]

Having put it that way I was at liberty later to make another flight when coming to that era in the history of mankind when coal-mining became such an exciting thing, in the days of George Stephenson, and I could sing of the miner whose job is really a branch of agriculture and forestry, though he digs deeper, cuts without planting, and reaps where he has not sown:

'We must allow a certain epic grandeur in their theme. The power was divined. The wealth was realized. The possibilities seemed boundless. Naturally there was a coal rush. Claims were staked out by the enterprizing and adventurous, and messengers were sent down into the primitive forests. A strange journey indeed! Strange wanderings in those sunken lands! Pioneering down into the darkness, they explored the green old world of long ago. They made perpendicular roads and descended as far as three miles into the buried woods. They carved out galleries within them. They ran trucks through tunnels chiselled from the petrified leavings of the rotten reeds. And as they passed along the corridors encased by the corrupted ferns and penetrated ever further into the lost regions of the sunlit lands, the danger from gases obliged them to go in darkness with nothing to lighten their way save the phosphorescent gleam from dried fish.'

I wondered on publication whether I would be faulted in some degree as to the accuracy of what we have in a piece of coal, but no fault was found with it, though when my brother, Dr Robert Collis, gave a copy of the Arabic edition of The *Triumph of the Tree* to the Prime Minister of Nigeria, Abubakar Tafawa Balewa (who was very friendly with my brother before he was murdered), he said that the phrase 'frozen burning beam' had defeated the translator.

I have not been faulted by the specialists on any of my factual statements, least of all by the professors of physics and astro-physics, and this has encouraged me, for I am a great believer in sold foundations supporting a lyric element. The heavier the bricks the better; weigh it down, I say to myself, weigh it down well, and the thing will rise of its own accord. This applies just as well to nuclear physics as to easier themes, for when we grasp that the formula $E=mc^2$ means that we can now pass through the final fortress and behold the last links of the mighty locks which stabilize the earth, we have already entered the field of poetry and metaphysics.

It is the same with photosynthesis. The reader will perhaps be ready to agree with me that it is fair to say:

'In summary: the plants, whose unbloodied kingdom stretches across the whole world, alone of all living things flourish without hunting and feed without slaughter, simply turning the sky into the tissues of their temples. The sheep consumes grass, the man consumes mutton; neither has yet made any contribution as primary creators; such elaboration is confined to the soundless mills of the green cell in combination with the inexhaustible floods of light poured ceaselessly upon the earth. It is the vegetable cell which creates the substances, it is the animal which consumes and destroys them. But now a circular movement has been attained which is helpful to plants. The animals pass into the air the acids which the plants need: what the one gives the other takes. Thus the Circle, thus the Wheel turns for ever at its task; the vegetables perpetually decompose the carbonic acid, fixing the carbon and setting free the oxygen, while the animals take the food prepared and perpetually breathe out the gas. The plants, feasting upon the fumes of putrefaction and turning the relics of death into meadows of life, lead us into green pastures; so that even in our age, riddled as it is with scientific terminology, we can still pay tribute to the simplicity and grandeur of the theme with the rooted ancient words – *All flesh is grass.*'[4]

Recently I came upon what I now learn is a well known evocation of Flaubert, 'the style that somebody will invent some day, ten years or ten centuries from now. A style rhythmic as verse, precise as the language of science.' I admit to raising an eyebrow when reading that. Though perhaps the word 'invent' is a little curious, for style should arise naturally out of the author's approach and faculty, almost as a matter of course. As for rhythm, I have long held the view that when prose is at all raised it should scan even more imperatively than verse; otherwise the reader, having been given a lift, will be let down. And it is important that he should not be put down when on the level of imagination. An agricultural labourer once said to me when an aeroplane had crashed nearby and made a grim spectacle, 'It don't do for anyone with too much imagination to look at this; for he'd be seeing things as aren't there.' Now, that is a wrong conception of imagination. Fancy is the power to see what is not there. Imagination is the power to see what is there. Invention can use the facts of science to great advantage; but Imagination, defined by Wordsworth as 'Reason in her most exalted mood', concentrating upon the full reality of the situation, lifts us into the realm of truth, and when it is combined with art we may enter the field of beauty and of love.

2

I think I was able to make this synthesis in a happy frame of mind because by the time I came to do it I was at least at ease with my approach to Religion.

174

For a long time, like a good many people, I had made do with one or other theory of Creative Evolution. Our craving for a rational scheme of order and purpose and progress is really very great. The mind craves order. We respond, more eagerly than we might be ready to acknowledge, to anyone who can give us a satisfactory evolutionary scheme. Certainly I did. I began with Bergson, Samuel Butler, and Shaw; I suppose that they had established Purpose, and I felt a proper disapproval of the Darwinians for having 'banished mind from the universe'. Then came Teilhard de Chardin with his famous *Phenomenon of Man* which gave a fresh stimulus to the religion of creative evolution. He is more elaborate than any of the others, even tying it up somehow with Christian doctrine, to the delight of the weaker brethren. Furthermore, being a great palaeontologist, he supports his scheme with a formidable edifice of biology and physics. In fact he unfolds an evolutionary process based on physics and astrophysics. One of the things which depresses us most, in terms of our own dubious importance, is the immensity of the universe. Never mind, says Teilhard de Chardin, the stars cannot carry the evolution of matter beyond the atomic series. It is only on the planets, though so small, that the mysterious ascent into the sphere of high molecular complexity has a chance to happen. It is upon them that an evolution principally concerned with the building of large molecules is concentrated. They are the keystone of the universe. On our planet, the Earth, the construction of molecules has ensued apace through the mystery of atomic affinity. This increased until the most elaborate molecular construction, Man, was pressed into consciousness: the first Being not only to know, but to know that he knows.

If there is no hole in this argument then Teilhard de Chardin has restored Man to the centre of the universe. The cold hostility of the alien vast; the extravagant and erring galaxies, themselves uncountable, expanding in ceaseless chase through the unboundaried void, need not discourage us too much, for it is all lifeless, while we alone are the consciousness of the Force of Life.

Even if this is not true of all the rest of the universe – and I don't see how Teilhard de Chardin can be sure of this – we do know now that it is true of our Solar system. We do know that not Venus, Mars, nor Mercury; not the enormous Uranus, not Neptune, Saturn, or Jupiter, are able to promote life. In this Solar System our Earth is capable of it alone.

Is there any fact more important to grasp? I think we should pay enough attention to it to pin a map of the Solar System on a wall in our houses, look at it and say, 'Here alone in this comparatively small place, the incredible variety and abundance and beauty of life exists.' If we were really to grasp this, *could* we continue to pollute, to erode, and to despoil it? *Could* we possibly go on fighting each other for possession of it when in any case we do possess it? Can we not hope for enough Imagination all round to make a more sensible approach?

But this is sociology and politics, not religion. Nor is a scientific evolutionary theory a religious matter – it is simply a scientific theory. And a theory is always vulnerable to qualification or disproof. A theory was not good enough for me. I did not want my religion to be in vassalage to any intellectual postulate or parasitic upon any scientific scheme. As an ordinary man I knew I could never be learned enough to grasp all the pros and cons concerning Natural Selection, the Survival of the Fittest, and the like, and be able to accept a theory with joy or to reject it with derision.

I needed a firmer base. What was I to do? Where could I look for further proof?

As far as I could see there was nowhere to look. I had consulted the scientists: they described the world but they did not explain it. I had consulted the philosophers: they reasoned about the world but they did not explain it. I had consulted the priests: they made affirmations but I could not follow them.

Then I consulted the artists – the poets, the painters, the musicians. They remained silent, preaching nothing, arguing nothing, affirming nothing explicitly. They kept pointing at something, though I could not make out what it was. One of them, a sculptor, displayed a thing of his called The Thinker. A little light broke on me. Manifestly the Thinker was *not thinking*. Thoughts had come or would come to him, he was *taking* thought – by virtue of receptivity.

And I remembered the words of a great seer:

'...These things I say not in order to excite thought in you – rather to destroy it –

Or if to excite thought, then to excite that which destroys itself;

For what I say is not born of thought and does not demand thought either for comprehension or proof;

And whoever dwells among thoughts dwells in the region of delusion and disease – and though he may appear wise and learned yet his wisdom and learning are as hollow as a piece of timber eaten out by white ants.

Therefore though thought should gird you about, remember and forget not to disendue it, as a man takes off his coat when hot; and as a skilful workman lays down his tool when done with, so shall you use thought and lay it quietly aside again when it has served your purpose.'[5]

I also remembered the words of Jesus, Seek and ye shall find – and I continued my search. But now with far greater receptivity, never disputing, never asserting, letting my mind 'become a highroad for all thoughts, not a select party', even though I should appear characterless to people of strong character. Jesus said: Seek and ye shall find. He did not say that we would find that for which we sought. We find something else. In the end I found Beauty. As I pursued my way it kept coming before me, shining and glittering in my path. I began to pause. Then I stopped altogether. Was not this what the artists were pointing to? I had searched for Truth: I had come upon Beauty. This was my answer. It is a good thing for us to undertake these journeys, for we are likely to be rewarded with something more than we had hoped. Saul, the son of Kish, went out to look for his father's asses – and found a kingdom. I did not find the asses of truth but I discovered beauty, and was ready to affirm with Keats that beauty is truth and truth is beauty, and that that is all we really need to know.

That is not really a very difficult dictum, and perhaps we need not make heavy weather over it. It is just a question of being sure what is meant by beauty in this context. There are pleasing objects which we label as beautiful (though the fashion may change), and there is scenery which we may call picturesque if we choose. But this is not what is meant. It would be senseless to speak of beauty being truth in this connection, we couldn't squeeze any meaning out of such a statement. Rather we are referring to a quality of experience whose sign is joy, not pleasure. It is an experience; beauty is an experience, and a highly religious one at that. It is a way of knowing: a non-rational way – not irrational, which is a very different thing. It is not just a sense-impression giving pleasure. The impression is merely the occasion responsible for the 'knowledge'. It will be remembered that Kant opened his *Critique of Pure Reason* with the words, 'That all our knowledge begins with experience there can be no doubt. For how is it possible that the faculty of cognition should be awakened into exercise otherwise than by means of objects which affect our senses.' And he was careful to add 'But, though all our knowledge begins *with* experience, it by no means follows that all arises *out* of experience.' By which he meant that apart from ordinary empirical knowledge there is that which our own faculty of cognition *supplies from itself* while the sense-impression merely allows the occasion. 'we receive but what we give',[6] said Coleridge in his marvellous ode. And we need not ask, he added, 'What this strange music in the soul may be', what the sign is of this 'beauty-making power'. It is *joy*, 'We in ourselves rejoice!' So, we repeat, beauty is an experience of joy as qualitatively different from pleasure as non-rational divination is from irrational assertion. These are nice distinctions, but nonetheless important for that. The speciality of the experience can be dismissed of course by rationalists as delusion or self-deception. But joy of this quality is its own justification, its own argument – which is perhaps what Blake meant by saying that Exuberance is Beauty. The claim is that here we have a 'knowing' though it cannot be expressed in concepts, it is felt as a presage, a soul-knowledge of Something beyond, Something 'wholly other' which brings assurance. It might even be called a surmise or intimation of ultimate love. Or a code which we strive to divine. There is nothing in the nature of proof about anything; rather an intuition that the final truth about things is beautiful and good. 'Beauty', said Havelock Ellis, 'when the vision is purged to see through the outer vesture, is Truth, and when we have pierced to the deepest core of it is found to be Love.' And in saying that he was well content to worship consciously at that shrine, he added: 'This is a goddess whom I have worshipped sometimes in the unlikeliest places, perhaps even where none else saw her, and she has given wine to my brain, and oil to my heart, and wings to my feet over the stoniest path.'[7] Need one ask more than that from any religion?

It is only important that we should not neglect to cultivate our faculty of *wonder*. It is there in all of us. It started as Fear in early days. In the Middle Ages three monks came to Father Sisoes and complained that they were continually pursued by the terror of three things: fear of the river of fire, of the worm which dies not, and of the outer darkness. When the saint made no reply they were greatly distressed. Finally, he said, 'My brothers, I envy you. As long as such thought live in your souls, it will be impossible for you to commit a sin.' For he knew that from that primitive Dread could grow the positive Awe which is essential. 'Awe is the highest thing in man,' said Goethe in an utterance which has always struck me as the most splendid thing he ever said. 'Awe is the highest thing in man, and if the pure phenomenon awakens awe in him he should be content; he can be aware of nothing higher and he should seek nothing beyond: here is the limit. But for most men the vision of the pure phenomena is not enough, they insist upon going further like children who peep in a mirror and then turn it round to see what is on the other side.' Certainly, as far as I am concerned, the passages in literature which make most appeal in a religious way are when the awe and ecstasy of the poet combine to bear witness to the *numinous*. Thus Wordsworth when speaking of the Simplon Pass:

> 'The immeasurable height
> Of woods decaying, never to be decayed,
> The stationary blasts of waterfalls,

> *And the narrow rent at every turn*
> *Winds thwarting winds, bewildered and forlorn,*
> *The torrents shooting from the clear blue sky,*
> *The rocks that muttered close upon our ears,*
> *Black drizzling crags that spake by the wayside*
> *As if a voice were in them, the sick sight*
> *And giddy prospect of the raving stream,*
> *The unfettered clouds and region of the Heavens,*
> *Tumult and peace, the darkness and the light –*
> *Were all like workings of one mind, the features*
> *Of the same face, blossoms upon one tree;*
> *Characters of the great Apocalypse,*
> *The types and symbols of Eternity,*
> *Of first, and last, and midst, and without end.'*

The faculty of awe is not different in kind from that of wonder but it is more developed, and in my own case is not developed enough. My advance was a slow grind without any particular dramatic moment of enlightenment. Still, as described, I got out of the wood, and the sense of wonder does work wonders. I found myself freed from caring a rap about the great scientific controversies. I became too enchanted with the finished article to be concerned with which theory was right. I did not mind *how* the Fittest survived: it was the fact that they had actually *arrived* at all that amazed me. I ceased to desire an explanation of the universe, and could say with Keyserling, 'I love the miracle, I will have it so.' Problems were not solved – they were dissolved. Behaviourism and determinism and the like seemed to me only clever ways of being stupid and learned ways of being ignorant. I saw that no 'materialistic explanation' of life could deprive it of its glory, since the material is as immaterial as the immaterial, the ordinary as extraordinary as the extraordinary, the natural as supernatural as the supernatural, while the miracle of water is as great as any turning of water into wine. It occurred to me that the answer to the riddle of the world is to be able to *see* the world; and that instead of worrying about salvation we should recognize that vision *is* salvation.

In making this approach I am anxious not to draw a ring round it, as it were, and not to suggest that it is in a department of its own, cut off from others. I would like to break down all the unreal barriers that come between people who advance to the same centre from different angles. I felt really elated a few years ago when a celebrated Irish Catholic priest, Father John

179

Hayes, having read a thing of mine called 'The Books of Stone', wrote to me saying,

> 'I felt as if I had made a week's Retreat in a few minutes. Somehow it seemed years as I read it in minutes. I had to stop reading, just overwhelmed. I stood before God and felt as if nothing.'

This piece is about fossils and has not one word of theology in it. But this made no barrier between us, and that greatly relieved and encouraged me. For there should be no categories in this matter – Catholic, poet, mystic, and so on. Least of all should words like 'change' and 'conversion' be imprisoned in inverted commas, labelled off, limited, and narrowed down. I have indicated one way where there can be advance and change, and it might be called the Way of Joy; but there is also the Way of Suffering, there is the 'Dark Night of the Soul' – which most people experience in one way or another, whether they come out of it well or not. Those who do come out of it in a dramatic way (and it often is swift and dramatic) and too easily labelled as religious freaks, though the change and conversion to a new attitude differs only in degree from the more homely experience of others who have made an advance in this matter. In all cases it really boils down to the achievement of harmony out of the disunity of conflicting ideas, and, allied to this, conflicting selves. The number of circumstances in which this can happen, and the expressions given to it, have been brought together in William James' remarkable *Varieties of Religious Experience*. It happens more often than is generally realized, there is nothing esoteric about it, and it is not reserved for people who are particularly holy or cut off from the hurly-burly of the world. A friend of mine, Bronwen Astor, who achieved harmony from total disunity, is as anxious as I am to break down the sectarian barriers erected between various experiences of religion. At a certain time in her life she felt more consciously than most people the many selves conflicting within her, and this was brought to a head when she fell into despair on account of a particular emotional ordeal before marriage. One day this came to a climax. 'All at once', she tells me, 'I felt myself falling and falling into a total pit of darkness and nothingness, and at the same time a terrible pain passed right through my body from my head downwards as if a knife were cutting me in two, and I felt certain that I was about to die. Suddenly it passed. I was bathed in *light*. And when it had passed I felt a completely whole person, the many sides and selves no longer caused me a moment's trouble, and that particular emotional trial simply dissolved. When I read the supposedly difficult accounts by the mystics of their experiences I instantly understood what they were saying. This came as a great surprise to me, for I had never taken any interest in them or bothered to think about religion at all.'

Some people associate conversion with conviction of sin. It is generally the opposite, an experience of non-sin, of non-separation (the very word sin means separation), a sense of harmony, and a sense of direction. 'Wherever we have understood', Keyserling believes, 'we change from passive objects of fate into its active agents, be it to ever so slight a degree.' Lady Astor had the same sense of passing from passive object to active agent, and this agency has proved particularly fruitful in one direction. After her experience she found herself responding keenly to the affirmations of Teilhard de Chardin, and already her work with the Teilhard de Chardin Societies no less than her own talks on the subject have proved as productive as her Oecumenical activities. But with Bronwen Astor it is much more than a question of these insights and activities; it is now a trust in life's twistings, *and* in death's dealings, which is entirely unacademic and unspeculative and magnetic. In seeking to make Teilhard's message known there is nothing sectarian in her approach, and it is the attitude of love and worship (best exemplified perhaps in his *Le Milieu Divin*) which draws men together, that she would emphasize rather than the more rarefied concepts which can keep them apart.

3

It may be charged against my own avenue to religion that it leaves out of consideration morality, the question of life after death, and the problem of evil.

These are permanent questionings, and I can merely record a strictly personal reaction to them – for what it may be worth. As for morality, I need not say anything about that, since ethics is not the same thing as religion; though of course when the non-rational element in our Being which gives rise to Religion can be attached to a worthy scheme of morality, then both behaviour and religion gain a great deal. But everyone is not religious just as everyone is not responsive to art. As far as I can see they get on perfectly well without these things, as philistines have always done, and it would be an arrogant person indeed who would claim that non-religious people behave less morally than the religious, while it is very probable that the most ethically admirable of all are the humanists.

The problem of a future life is hopelessly speculative and anyone's 'belief' about it is not worth the breath with which it is spoken. There are those who *experience* reincarnation, and they hold one's attention. Anyhow they hold

181

mine, for they speak from an experience of some kind – which alarms me. For I do not wish it to be true, not at all relishing the idea of coming back, since there is no knowing where one might land up. It is a scheme they feel which makes sense of life; and no doubt it does theoretically; but when I contemplate any large crowd, say at the Wembley Stadium, it seems to me far too much of a scheme itself to make sense. Still, these are mere thoughts springing from a wish-unfulfilment. With regard to spiritualism my wish-unfulfilment is very strong indeed. For me the idea adds a new terror to life and a new terror to death. To life, because if someone known or dear to you could 'watch over you' after death it would be intolerable. It would be unpleasant at the best of times, but it is also only reasonable to suppose that the departed spirit would be watching over you at private or unseemly occasions – a daunting thought. A new terror to death, for the idea really horrifies me that I personally could become some kind of ghost who could be consulted by mediums and required to give information and messages, and even take notice of people sitting in a circle rapping a table – what a prospect!

Death has never been far from my thoughts, and I am never able to take lightly the death of people I know, their utter disappearance from the face of the earth, and either a slow rotting of the body in a coffin (why in a coffin instead of straight into the soil?) or becoming a little box of ashes after cremation, which shatters me. I do not feel so strongly with regard to my own death since there will then be no physical aftermath for me, and I think I could take it in my stride seeing that what was good enough for Socrates or Columbus, say, and for all the other billions, is good enough for me. In any case I am quite prepared to get the surprise of my life on dying – and discover a new mode of existence. At the worst, a real adventure. Yet, silence, that is what is called for on this subject, and attention paid only to the faint whisperings or tiny lights we may glean at odd moments when we are not setting out to think at all. 'As I was entering the Deep Cut, the wind, which was conveying a message to me from heaven, dropped it on the wire of the telegraph which it vibrated as it passed', wrote Thoreau, who of all men knew how to listen to the voice of the silence, and who fled far from the streets where it cannot be heard. 'It merely said: "Bear in mind, Child, and never for an instant forget, that there are higher planes, infinitely higher planes, of life than this thou art now travelling on. Know that the goal is distant, and is upwards, and is worthy of all your life's efforts to attain to." And then it ceased, and though I sat some minutes longer I heard no more.'

Finally, I hold it downright despicable for anyone to say that there is no sense in this life if there is not another one to follow. What greed! What ingratitude! This earth is a heavenly place, we could ask for nothing better in heaven. 'Paradise is here', said the great mystic Jacob Boehme, 'but Man is not yet in Paradise.' He can look in at the gate once in a while. Should that not be enough for us? True, we seek, and largely succeed, in making the place a hell, and in mean cities and unworthy works blinding the possibility of Vision. We can destroy our paradise. But that does not entitle us to claim another after death.

The 'problem of evil' is not so difficult. Nature 'red in tooth and claw' does not bother people overmuch as far as I can see. It is accepted quite cheerfully, for we are profounder than we think. 'We are cheered when we observe the vulture feeding on the carrion which disgusts and disheartens us, and deriving health and strength from the repast', said Thoreau. 'There was a dead horse in the hollow by the path to my house, which compelled me sometimes to go out of my way, but the assurance it gave me of the strong appetite and inviolable health of Nature was my compensation for this. I love to see that Nature is so rife with life that myriads can be afforded to be sacrificed and suffered to prey upon one another; that tender organizations can be so serenely squashed out of existence like pulp – tadpoles which herons gobble up, and tortoises and toads run over in the road; and that sometimes it has rained flesh and blood.' The impression made on a wise man, he held, was that of 'universal innocence'. Few of us face the facts as consciously as that, nor formulate our dim acceptance as metaphysically as Emerson who held that 'If the red slayer thinks he slays, or the slain thinks he is slain', both are wrong, but we do accept the fact that Nature exists by eating itself and taking in its own washing. To me this is a very real thing, no theory. I never tire of watching it, especially amongst the sea animals, so terrible yet fascinating and pure. The other day I watched a big fish with another fish half in and half out of its mouth. I felt sorry for the fish being eaten in this way. Then I saw that the fish which was being eaten (tail first) also had another smaller fish in *its* mouth – and I ceased to be very sorry for any of them. After all, in their own way they were expressing their membership with one another, even a primitive sort of love. It is a pity that learned men write such big books on subjects on this kind. There is generally only about one simple thing to be said, and it cannot float to the top of three hundred pages. In any case our minds are much more likely to take in a single remark made in passing without literary assault. 'So long as a man likes the splashing of a fish, he is a poet', wrote Anton Chekhov in a tiny little Notebook almost totally unprocurable, 'but when he knows that the splashing is nothing but the chase of the weak by the strong, he is a thinker; but when he does not understand what sense there is in the chase, or what use in the equilibrium which results from destruction, he is becoming silly and dull as he was when a child. And the more he knows and thinks the sillier he becomes.'

This has always been the common sense view of all who recognize the Order of Nature. We will find it in *The City of God* if we choose to go back as far as Saint Augustine who stressed what he called 'the universal peace' that guaranteed the Unity and the Order. Hang a person upside-down, he said, and watch what happens. It is a position contrary to the order, the natural law, the peace of that body. This confusion will disturb the flesh and be troublesome to it, and the soul may well leave the body owing to these troubles. Then what results? The body presses towards the earth: 'the very weight seems to demand a place of rest'. Imagine the body left alone day after day, either hanging in the air or buried in the earth. Order, natural law, peace, all return. The body dissolves into the earth and into the air. 'It is assimilated into the elements of the Universe; moment by moment, particle by particle, it passes into their peace; but nothing is in any wise derogated thereby from the laws of that Highest and Ordaining Creator by whom the peace of the world is administered.' Such a passage from *The City of God* draws the centuries together, combining as it does the scientist's conception of the indestructibility of matter and the rule of return with Wordsworth's sense of the transcendent Power that 'keeps the stars from wrong', and through whom 'the most ancient heavens are fresh and strong'.

Of course the problem of Nature red in tooth and claw is easier than the problem of suffering and misfortune as experienced by mankind. It cannot be solved. It can be dissolved as a metaphysical problem, while we deal with it as best we can on the physical plane. The best example I know of it is in the Fable of Job, which has been an inspiration to me personally.

The Book of Job is a remarkable drama. The technique is somewhat Shavian, though the conception of the play is foreign to the Shavian mind. We find in it a great deal of the usual discussion of the problem of evil – for in all ages it is generally discussed in much the same way, and if it has yielded to solution it has always been the same solution (there cannot be two).

You remember the story. Job was a man of substance with large estates and a happy family. All went well with him, and he himself did nothing wrong. Suddenly his good fortune came to an end. One day when at dinner, four messengers in succession arrived to tell him that his oxen, his asses, and his servants in one place; his sheep and servants in another place; his camels and his servants in another place; his sons and his daughters in another place, had all been destroyed.

Job was overcome and rent his mantle and threw himself on the ground. Yet still he worshipped God, crying out immortally 'The Lord gave and the Lord hath taken away; blessed be the name of the Lord.'

But there was more to come. Satan, from going to and fro on the earth, and from walking up and down in it, had observed while a good man will bear the loss of property and children with fortitude and piety, he will not, however good he is, submit without protest to a disfigured body and ill health. 'Touch his bone and flesh', Satan says to god, 'and he will curse thee to thy face.' And God decided to test him in this also.

In consequence Job finds himself covered with boils from head to foot. He takes a trowel to try and scrape them off, and sits down among the ashes. This is too much for his wife who says to him, 'Curse God and die.' But Job still stands firm. 'What?' he asks, 'shall we receive good at the hands of God, and shall we not receive evil?'

Hearing of his calamities his friends come to see him. At first they are so shattered at the sight of him that they are dumb and sit down with him on the ground without speaking for seven days and seven nights.

Then they make up for this silence. Job himself leads off by breaking into imprecations and cursing the day he was born in an almost Celtic stream of poetic fury: 'Let them curse it that curse the day, who are ready to raise up their mourning. Let the stars of the twilight thereof be dark; let it look for light, but have none; neither let it see the dawning of the day!'

At the spectacle of his casting down, Job's friends are alarmed and they try to find reasons to justify the situation. Eliphaz the Temanite, Bildad the Shuhite, and Zophar the Naamathite are intellectuals and moralists. At not inconsiderable length they make out a case for God, and by insisting that Job has been guilty of sins and hypocrisies, endeavour to show how his sufferings at the hands of God may be reasonably accounted for. But they fail to convince even themselves. The sincerity of Job's replies disarms them: for not only does he maintain his innocence but even in his pain and complexity he refuses to deny his feeling of the Divine Wisdom. Though he has said to corruption, 'Thou art my father', and to the worm, 'Thou art my mother and my sister', though all have turned away from him with abhorrence, he nevertheless suddenly bursts out 'Oh that my words were now written! Oh that they were printed in a book! That they were graven with an iron pen and lead in the rock for ever! For I *know* that my Redeemer liveth, and that he shall stand at the latter day upon the earth.' And to his tormenting friends he turns and says: 'But ye should say, "Why persecute we him, seeing that the root of the matter is found in him".'

185

When Job and his friends have exhausted themselves with argument, a young knowledgeable fellow called Elihu, the son of Barachel the Buzite, bursts out and is under the impression that his special pleading for God is highly effective. But suddenly God himself appears in person and punctures him by saying: 'Who is this that darkeneth counsel by words without knowledge?' And at this point the drama reaches the high point we have been waiting for, when a solution to the mystery will be offered.

We know what to expect. We are prepared for an authoritative statement from God reproving Job for complaining and pointing out that He has ends in view not to be comprehended by mortals, or that He has been testing the good and pure man, or other plausible and rationable explanations (though always exposed to a further Why?). But God does not do this. He does not mention Job's situation at all! Instead he points to the magnificence of creation. He witnesses to the sublimity of His works. He rehearses the glory of life. 'Knowest thou the ordinances of heaven?' he cries to Job: 'Canst thou bind the sweet influences of Pleiades, or loose the bands of Orion? Canst thou bring forth Maxxaroth in his season? Or canst thou guide Arcturus with his sons? Canst thou lift up thy voice to the clouds, that abundance of water may cover thee?' He shows the strength of His government and the domination of His command over all things as over the ocean to which He saith 'Hitherto shalt thou come, but no farther: and here shall thy proud waves be stayed.' In a series of flaming poetic images He summons up the incomprehensible miraculousness of creation before Job's inward eye, and then reminds him of the existence of the wild goats and hinds, of the wild ass, the unicorn, the peacock, the stork, the ostrich, the horse, the hawk, the eagle, the hippopotamus, and the crocodile.

Job is overcome. He does not submit; he *accepts*. Suddenly he accepts and cries out to God. 'I have heard of Thee by the hearing of the ear; but *now* mine eyes have seen Thee. Wherefore I abhor myself and repent in dust and ashes.' He has suddenly become a seer and his mind is set at rest.

But why? What revelation has he received that he has not had before? What new argument had he heard? Has he not reasoned along those lines himself, or tried to? Did not Elihu, the son of Barachel the Buzite, advance much the same view?

No. Not so. He has suddenly left Rationalism behind, and reached another viewpoint. God has not spoken to him rationally. He has not given him a new argument. He has given him a new perspective. He does not point to Purpose or Design. There is no teleological persuasiveness whatever in the Almighty's discourse. He mentions animals that offer the least support for that kind of approach. He speaks of the ostrich which leaves her eggs in the dust 'and forgetteth that the foot may crush them, or that the wild beast may break them. She is hardened against her young ones, as though they were not hers, her labour is in vain, without fear; because God hath deprived her of wisdom, neither hath he imparted to her understanding.' Nor does the hippopotamus with its unseemly gait and its bones that 'are as strong as brass' provide in its person the best possible example of a perfectly designed universe – yet the Lord is careful to say that this creature no less than the monstrous crocodile and the eagle whose young suck up blood, is "the chief of the ways of God". His method is not to convince by reason but by the *power of mysteriousness*. The tormented soul of the sufferer is appeased, not by the sudden light of a good reason, but by a feeling of *an intrinsic value* in what appears to be the very negation of reasonableness; the incomprehensible becomes, in itself, fascinating, and more inspiring than the comprehensible: the thought descends, the thought occurs, that All is Well, not because there are reasons for that thought but because there are no reasons. And the passage put into the mouth of God by the great dramatist does indeed 'express in masterly fashion the downright stupendousness, the well-nigh daemonic and wholly incomprehensible character of the eternal creative power; how incalculable and "wholly other" it mocks at all conceiving, but can yet stir the mind to its depths, fascinate and overbrim the heart.'

The profound German scholar, Rudolf Otto, from whose *Idea of the Holy* I have just quoted, mentions the story called 'Berufs-Tragik' by Max Eyth in which the Job theme finds a modern setting. It tells of the building of the mighty bridge over the estuary of the Ennobucht. 'The most profound and thorough labour of the intellect, the most assiduous and devoted professional toil, had gone to the construction of the great edifice, making it in all its significance and purposefulness a marvel of human achievement. In spite of endless difficulties and gigantic obstacles, the bridge is at length finished, and stands defying wind and waves. Then there comes a raging cyclone, and building and builder are swept into the deep. Utter meaninglessness seems to triumph over richest significance, blind destiny seems to stride on its way over prostrate virtue and merit. The narrator tells how he visits the scene of the tragedy.

"When we got to the end of the bridge, there was hardly a breath of wind; high above, the sky showed blue-green, and with an eerie brightness. Behind us, like a great open grave, lay the Ennobucht. The Lord of life and death hovered over the waters in silent majesty. The Lord of life and death hovered over the waters in silent majesty. We felt His presence, as one feels one's own hand. And the old man and I knelt down before the open grave and before Him."

'Why did they kneel? Why did they feel constrained to do so? One does not kneel before a cyclone or the blind forces of Nature, nor even before Omnipotence merely as such. But one does kneel before the wholly uncomprehended Mystery, revealed yet unrevealed, and one's soul is stilled by feeling the way of its working, and therein its justification.'

4

The sense of Something 'wholly other' is part of the experience of beauty. It is true that those who have know this most intensely have not always been the most balanced of men. The great and damaged Ruskin wrote in *Modern Painters*,

> '...There was a continual perception of Sanctity in the whole of nature, from the slightest thing to the vastest; an instinctive awe, mixed with delight; an indefinable thrill, such as we sometimes imagine to indicate the presence of a disembodied spirit. I could only feel this perfectly when I was alone; and then it would often make me shiver from head to foot with the joy and fear of it, when after being some time away from hills I first got to the shore of a mountain river, where the brown water circled among the pebbles, or when I first saw the swell of distant land against the sunset, or the first low broken wall, covered with mountain moss.'

He could not describe the feeling, he says, any more than explain a sense of hunger to anyone who had not experienced it; this 'joy in nature seemed to me to come of a sort of heart-hunger, satisfied with the presence of a Great and Holy Spirit.' But he was unable to hold to this vision. It passed from him, 'as from Wordsworth' he said. In his early life Carlyle also read the code in much the same way. 'What is Nature? Ha! Why do I not name thee God? Art thou not the Living Garment of God? O Heavens, is it, in very deed, HE, then, that ever speaks through thee; that lives and loves in thee, that lives and loves in me?' He too did not retain the vision.

These men were so intellectual that they did not make sufficient allowance for their unintellectual knowledge, or way of knowing. They were both very far from being whole men. But there are some men who become whole, and remain whole or holy, all their lives, quietly holding onto their soul-knowledge, retaining it with the same ease as they attained it – Walt

Whitman, for instance. I know nothing more helpful or to the point than a remark he made off the cuff in a prose piece called *Specimen Days and Collect*:

'There is, apart from mere intellect, in the make-up of every superior identity, a wondrous something that realizes without argument, frequently without what is called education (though I think it the goal and apex of all education deserving the name) an intuition of the absolute balance, in time and space, of the whole of this multifariousness, this revel of fools, and incredible make-belief and general unsettledness, we call *the world*; a soul-sight of the divine clue and unseen thread which holds the whole congeries, all history and time, and all events, however trivial, however momentous, like a leashed dog in the hand of the hunter. Of such soul-sight and root-centre for the mind mere optimism explains only the surface.'

These are the experiences out of which ultimate faith is built, and they make the core of religion, and are responsible for all religions worthy of the name. Out of these all sorts of conceptions regarding gods, and heavens and hells, and redemption from sin, and rebirth, and so forth arise, rational attempts, ideograms, pictured flights, to give non-rational experiences a habitation and a name.

That this should be lost sight of and the expressions confused with the experiences, is a sad state of affairs.

Whenever religion is discussed in public – and it often is – there is a bland assumption that all that is needed is to have a doctrinaire on one side and an agnostic on the other, while perhaps a humanist takes the Chair as a kind of referee (not much loved by either side). Hardly ever is the core of religion spoken of at all, or any suggestions advanced as to how we might *awaken* the capacity to experience religion – which in so many people is there to be awakened and cultivated and understood as such. These intimations, said Wordsword, which though as difficult to nail down as a bit of smoke, these 'fallings from us, vanishings', are yet 'the fountain-light of all our day', and the 'master-light of all our seeing'.

This *ground* upon which the soul stands is not a rational base, it is beyond the understanding, yet can give us a little peace sometimes, which passes that understanding.

But some of our clergy do not like this at all. The Bishop of Woolwich, in making a bid for being Honest about God, gives the approved view. He acknowledges the experience but says, 'To make the knowledge of God depend upon such experiences is like making it depend upon an ear for music', and preceeds that remark with a passage in which he confuses piousness with mysticism, and follows it with a chapter on Jesus ten times more difficult to follow than any of the sayings of the mystics – who may be defined as men who are no longer mystified and with no motive for mystifying others. One is constrained to reply that just as those who have no ear for music must do without music, so those with no slight degree of religious experience must do without religion and make do with conceptions, as they have always done. This attempt to limit our human capacity for knowledge can fairly be described as highly irreligious. Indeed, 'this proceeding of constructing a "humanity" ', says Rudolf Otto[8], 'prior to and apart from the most central and potent human capacities is like nothing so much as the attempt to frame a standard idea of the human body after having previously cut off its head.'

The worst of approaching the divine in this conceptual manner is that it leads to the assumption of an intimacy with God which is as offensive as it is unwarranted. It is an attitude which has been met with disfavour by the profoundest spirits throughout the ages. 'But that is an impertinence to say that He who is beyond the apprehension of even the higher Powers can be comprehended by us earthworms, or compressed and comprised by the weak forces of our understanding!' That exclamation came from a great Father of the Church, Chrysostom, against those who claimed to 'know God as He is known to Himself'. The Father was also a lord of language and frequently let himself go against 'Conceiving' and 'Comprehension' and the idea that God could be defined by 'Notions'. 'We should call Him', he declared, 'the inexpressible, the unthinkable God, the invisible, the inapprehensible; who quells the power of human speech and transcends the grasp of mortal thought; inaccessible to the angels, unbeheld of the Seraphim, unimagined of the Cherubim, invisible to rules and authorities and powers, and, in a word, to all creation.' I cannot help thinking that such words must make more appeal than the current way of talking about God and *to* God. To take an extreme example, I will never forget how during the flying-bomb period of the war which was devastating and frightening in England, a very well known bishop prayed over the radio to the Almighty for protection, adding, '*especially at Southern England*', asking God, in fact, to be so kind as to keep an eye on things between, say, Middlesex and Bournemouth. If that kind of god existed such a ludicrous request should have been enough to make him die laughing. Again one is reminded of Chrysostom crying out 'Dost thou, a man, presume to busy thyself with God? Nay, the mere properties of man suffice to show the extent of this folly; man that is *earth* and *dust, flesh* and *blood, dung* and the *flower of dung, shadow* and *smoke* and *vanity*!' If some exception might be taken there to an outmoded idea of matter itself, we can turn to many other great men who have expressed the same distaste for imprisoning deity in a personal image. When Eckermann sounded Goethe on his idea of the divine he replied, 'Dear boy, what do we know of the idea of the divine, and what can our narrow conceptions presume to tell of the Supreme Being? If I called him by a hundred names, like a Turk, I should yet fall short and have said nothing in comparison to the boundlessness of his attributes.'

Nevertheless, we are bound to recognize that it is natural that man should rationalize and conceptualize his religions feelings into Doctrine, Scheme, and Organization. It must be natural or it would not always have been done. It is natural also that Doctrine should favour an Ethic and preach it. But we have reached a stage now when the majority of people have grown utterly indifferent to the concepts – without understanding the reality behind them, they confuse the expression for the experience, and are encouraged to do this by the clergy, even told by an honest bishop not to bother about their intimations of the divine but to stick to the very conceptions which have ceased to attract them. The result is that the Ethic is eroded as much as Religion, and the churches become still more empty.

It seems a pity. A great many people are naturally religious, but they need help in the cultivation of receptivity, in the awakening and developing of that 'knowledge' which bypasses understanding and brings peace. What better than a priesthood to help them, and an organization, a Church, to contain them? They could be taught to realize the significance of their moments of vision, however humble they may consider such moments. There are so many approaches. The experience of the beauty of the visible world is one, but only one. They can get it through music, never better than when that music is allied to the ritual of the Mass, which can be for anyone, quite irrespective of any concepts, an *awe*-inspiring experience. They can get it through prayer, especially when it is corporate (since it is so difficult in isolation) if we define prayer, as Keyserling does, as 'the opening of the consciousness to the influences which are awaiting liberation in the innermost depths of the soul, which when liberated connect the spirit directly with God.' They can get it through literature, especially through that branch of literature we call Scripture: think of the sheer *movement* in the Words, transcending immediate sense and nourishing the *open* mind as surely as a sunrise – 'Eye hath not seen, nor ear heard, neither have entered into the heart of man, the things which God hath prepared for them that love him'. They can get it through Jesus Christ.

191

The Christian Church has the great initial advantage over others in possessing the extraordinary fact of Jesus. Even if he never existed he would still be a great fact – the repository in which is held, the image in which is enshrined, the highest ideals of Man. But we do not have to take that view. 'And Jesus went before them: and they were amazed; and as they followed, they were afraid.' Obviously that was not invented; it was a simple report of an experience of awe of a phenomenon which was amazing, and which was so powerful in effect that Christianity could grow from it. We today can still open ourselves to a contemplation of that phenomenon or numen or whatever term we need, and enrich our spiritual awareness. It is not too difficult to do this since the New Testament is such a striking achievement and so soaked in numinous feeling – that is, so long as we do not use modernized versions which, evidently composed by unreligious clerics and unliterary scholars, eliminate the most important elements.

I love churches. I hate to see them empty. I wonder whether there is any real reason why the Church might not now make way for a religious approach, so that the services and rituals could again be full of meaning, the emphasis gradually shifted from the strictly ethical and conceptual, that we may come to grasp what Jesus meant by saying that the kingdom of heaven is within us; how that mustard seed can grow into a tree; and how the command to Judge Not postulates a lever with which we may open ourselves to the possibility of vision. We could be given the end of the thread of that Golden Ball of which Blake spoke, which unwinds and leads us in at Heaven's door.

1 Thus, after *While Following the Plough*, I wrote: *Down to Earth*; *The Triumph of the Tree*; *The Moving Waters*; *Paths of Light*.
2 *The Moving Waters*
3 *The Triumph of the Tree*
4 *Paths of Light*
5 'Have Faith' in Edward Carpenter's *Towards Democracy*.
6 i.e.: we can only receive if we have the faculty to Respond.
7 For an appreciation of Havelock Ellis' approach to religion see my book on him, *An Artist of Life*.
8 The one-timer Professor of Theology in the University of Marburg, whose *Idea of the Holy* (the first of many editions was in 1923), has put so many of us in lasting debt.

John Stewart Collis

Farewell to Argument

In this intriguing glimpse at East and West, John Stewart Collis sets out his case that the West should lead the world into a new spiritual age by moving beyond the bounds of industrialisation. In putting forward this argument he compares the contribution of Gandhi and D H Lawrence and finds Lawrence's thinking on the new spirituality to be more compelling. *Farewell to Argument* outlines the philosophy that led John Stewart Collis to be labelled a pioneer of the ecological movement.

An Irishman's England

As an Irishman educated in England, John Stewart Collis had a unique perspective on his adopted country. Sufficiently distanced, he could observe and record without bias or malice. Here he portrays the extravagance and the apparent contradictions of the English. After a rapid discussion of London and the provinces, he then examines English political and cultural life. In so doing, Collis holds up a sympathetic mirror and makes some perceptive and enlightening revelations about England and the English.

JOHN STEWART COLLIS

MARRIAGE AND GENIUS

'Few of us know much about the married life of even our closest friends. Nothing is so secretly guarded as this matter.' With this thought, John Stewart Collis sets out to examine the specific roles played by the wives of Strindberg and Tolstoy.

For Strindberg, three times married, the failure of his principal relationships was a source of guilt and suffering. For Tolstoy, marriage to Sonya Behrs eventually brought disillusionment and conflict. Using his rare literary skill, John Stewart Collis interweaves intimate details and public facts of both men with compassion and insight.

SHAW

In this acclaimed study of fellow Irishman, George Bernard Shaw, Collis writes with characteristic subtlety and perception. He portrays this immensely important freethinker, playwright, campaigner and journalist whilst debunking the myth that Shaw was a shameless self-publicist. Collis does not shy away from less palatable aspects of Shaw's personality. In this short, critical account he paints a vivid picture of a man who fought valiantly for Humanity while often forgetting the human beings around him.

JOHN STEWART COLLIS

THE VISION OF GLORY

The Vision of Glory is a highly original examination of natural phenomena and of how all things are interconnected. Combining scientific accuracy with beautiful prose, it is also a splendid poetic study of man's relationship with his environment.

'John Stewart Collis' divine gift is to explain the extraordinary nature of the ordinary' – *The Sunday Times*

THE WORM FORGIVES THE PLOUGH

The Worm Forgives the Plough combines two works of John Stewart Collis. The first, *While Following the Plough*, is a highly personal account of his experience as a labourer on the land during the Second World War. Written with intense personal feeling, this book defines John Stewart Collis' philosophy on nature and man's relationship to the land. The second, *Down to Earth,* is an extraordinary series of meditations on remarkably prosaic things, such as the potato, the plough, the ant and the dunghill. Collis is a unique combination of scientist and poet and in this remarkable book he shows his rare love and understanding of the world around him.

'He is the poet among modern ecologists' – *The Times*

OTHER TITLES BY JOHN STEWART COLLIS AVAILABLE DIRECT FROM HOUSE OF STRATUS

Quantity		£	$(US)	$(CAN)	€
	AN ARTIST OF LIFE: HAVELOCK ELLIS	8.99	14.99	22.50	15.00
	THE CARLYLES	8.99	14.99	22.50	15.00
	CHRISTOPHER COLUMBUS	8.99	14.99	22.50	15.00
	FAREWELL TO ARGUMENT	8.99	14.99	22.50	15.00
	AN IRISHMAN'S ENGLAND	8.99	14.99	22.50	15.00
	LEO TOLSTOY	8.99	14.99	22.50	15.00
	LIVING WITH A STRANGER	8.99	14.99	22.50	15.00
	MARRIAGE AND GENIUS	8.99	14.99	22.50	15.00
	SHAW	8.99	14.99	22.50	15.00
	THE SOUNDING CATARACT	6.99	12.95	19.95	13.50
	THE VISION OF GLORY	8.99	14.99	22.50	15.00
	THE WORM FORGIVES THE PLOUGH	8.99	14.99	22.50	15.00

ALL HOUSE OF STRATUS BOOKS ARE AVAILABLE FROM GOOD BOOKSHOPS OR DIRECT FROM THE PUBLISHER:

Internet: www.houseofstratus.com including synopses and features.

Email: sales@houseofstratus.com please quote author, title and credit card details.

Order Line: UK: 0800 169 1780,
USA: 1 800 509 9942
INTERNATIONAL: +44 (0) 20 7494 6400 (UK)
or +01 212 218 7649
(please quote author, title, and credit card details.)

Send to: House of Stratus Sales Department
24c Old Burlington Street
London
W1X 1RL
UK

House of Stratus Inc.
Suite 210
1270 Avenue of the Americas
New York • NY 10020
USA

PAYMENT

Please tick currency you wish to use:

☐ £ (Sterling)   ☐ $ (US)   ☐ $ (CAN)   ☐ € (Euros)

Allow for shipping costs charged per order plus an amount per book as set out in the tables below:

CURRENCY/DESTINATION

	£(Sterling)	$(US)	$(CAN)	€(Euros)
Cost per order				
UK	1.50	2.25	3.50	2.50
Europe	3.00	4.50	6.75	5.00
North America	3.00	3.50	5.25	5.00
Rest of World	3.00	4.50	6.75	5.00
Additional cost per book				
UK	0.50	0.75	1.15	0.85
Europe	1.00	1.50	2.25	1.70
North America	1.00	1.00	1.50	1.70
Rest of World	1.50	2.25	3.50	3.00

PLEASE SEND CHEQUE OR INTERNATIONAL MONEY ORDER.
payable to: STRATUS HOLDINGS plc or HOUSE OF STRATUS INC. or card payment as indicated

STERLING EXAMPLE

Cost of book(s):. . . . . Example: 3 x books at £6.99 each: £20.97
Cost of order:. . . . . Example: £1.50 (Delivery to UK address)
Additional cost per book:. . . . . Example: 3 x £0.50: £1.50
Order total including shipping:. Example: £23.97

VISA, MASTERCARD, SWITCH, AMEX:

☐ ☐ ☐ ☐ ☐ ☐ ☐ ☐ ☐ ☐ ☐ ☐ ☐ ☐ ☐ ☐ ☐ ☐ ☐ ☐

Issue number (Switch only):

☐ ☐ ☐

Start Date: Expiry Date:

☐ ☐ / ☐ ☐   ☐ ☐ / ☐ ☐

Signature: _____

NAME: _____

ADDRESS: _____

COUNTRY: _____

ZIP/POSTCODE: _____

Please allow 28 days for delivery. Despatch normally within 48 hours.

Prices subject to change without notice.
Please tick box if you do not wish to receive any additional information. ☐

House of Stratus publishes many other titles in this genre; please check our website
(**www.houseofstratus.com**) for more details.